The Spirit of Vanderlaan

by

Susan Harris Howell

The Samantha Hayes Series

Cover Art by *Teddi Black*

The Wild Rose Press, Inc.
PO Box 708
Adams Basin, NY 14410-0708
Visit us at www.thewildrosepress.com

Publishing History
First Edition, 2024
Trade Paperback ISBN 978-1-5092-5888-8
Digital ISBN 978-1-5092-5889-5

The Samantha Hayes Series
Published in the United States of America

Dedication

To the many students who served as the inspiration for
Allie, Levi, Jeff, Sydnee, and Chess.

Acknowledgements

Thank you, Isaac Marvel, for suggesting I write this novel. I couldn't be more grateful for your challenge and your insightful comments on the manuscript. Dr. Deepika Suri and Alice Steele, thank you doesn't begin to cover my appreciation for the countless drafts you critiqued and your confidence in me. Natalie Hanemann, thank you for your straightforward critiques and encouragement. To beta readers, Erin Steele, Ruby Colvin, Anna Marie Laffoon, and Mary Gaskins, thank you for your input and for being a part of this journey. I am forever grateful to my editor, Dianne Rich, and The Wild Rose Press for giving this new author a chance.

Much gratitude goes to Katelyn Howell for getting my work into the public eye. Many thanks go to two university colleagues: Dr. Tammy Harris, APRN, walked me through medical information on allergic reactions; and former chief of police, Bill Cassell, filled me in on police procedure. Mackenzie Whaley and Deja Thompson Fair, thank you for your good-natured humor and insight on names and accessories for Levi and Chess. As always, Melissa, you kept me grounded and confident. Thank you so much for enjoying this process with me. To my husband, Dwayne, thank you for your confidence in me, respect for my work, and patience in the time I have given this book. And thanks to all the students who made my office their home over the past thirty plus years. First, you gave me a meaningful teaching career; then you inspired a writing career. If I gave extra credit, I'd surely give it to each one of you.

Chapter 1

Monday, August 20

A latte in one hand and class material in the other, Dr. Samantha Hayes closed her office door with her foot and stumbled into the hallway of Prescott Hall. She quickly assessed her attire: white slacks with an orange, tailored, sleeveless blouse, and sandal pumps that would take her through a busy day. She reached for the gold scarab charm on the chain hanging loosely outside her blouse. *Good—it's there. I don't have time to go back.* Her first day of a new semester at Vanderlaan University and she was already behind.

As she reached the door of her classroom, her hurried pace gave way to a slower, measured step. Levi Corliss, one of her research assistants, stood in her place behind the podium at the front of the room. He stood tall, with dark skin and tight black curls. That he was still a student himself hadn't deterred this senior from regaling her first-year students with what promised to be an entertaining lecture on psychology as a major.

"We all know psychology is a fascinating discipline. But keep in mind, you won't be able to actually read minds until you're—" Levi simulated a stern expression as she walked through the door. "Dr. Hayes, you're late and you know how I feel about tardiness. See me after class."

Samantha put her books on the table next to the podium, held out her hand for the marker he was holding, and stepped aside so he could make his way around her desk. She bowed slightly in mock deference to Levi. "My apologies for the interruption."

"No worries. I was just leaving." He turned with a smile and a wave at the students he left to her charge. "But I'll be back." Several laughed and called out their good-byes. His one-man-show, like an opening act before a concert, had her students in a great mood for this first day of the semester.

Her classroom was just big enough for the thirty students seated before her in university-issue tables and chairs. A markerboard lined the front wall of the room, with her desk, podium, and computer to the side. Small windows along the outside wall let in enough natural light to make the room inviting. Unfortunately, the same windows offered a scenic view of the university courtyard and, on occasion, gave Samantha competition for her students' attention.

After introducing herself, Samantha reviewed the course syllabus and assignments for the semester. She kept it brief, however, since her primary goal for day one was to get acquainted with her students. Today, as she had done on each first day since she began teaching at her alma mater, she asked a question for her students to consider: "If your life were made into a movie, what genre would it be?"

While most claimed that comedy or drama would best depict their lives, a few leaned toward the ever-popular mystery, and one insisted that science fiction best captured the spirit of his eighteen-year-old life thus far. Several students laughed congenially, the stiff awkwardness of the first meeting behind them.

"All right, now that you've picked your genre, who will play *you* in this movie?" After a few minutes, most had identified the actor who could do their part justice. The undecided students were given suggestions by the more vocal of the class, with everyone chiming in before the activity came to a close. As the atmosphere reached the level of camaraderie Samantha strove to create, she caught a glimpse of Levi's face smashed against the window of her classroom door. Shaking her head and chuckling, she opened the door and motioned him in, along with four others who lined up across the front of the room.

Wait. Samantha did a quick recount. Someone unfamiliar had slipped in with the rest. Samantha couldn't see the young woman's face as she crept to the back of the room and quietly found a seat behind another student. *Ah, a latecomer to class.* Samantha would need her name for the class roster, but she hated to call out someone who was obviously taking such care not to disrupt. She'd get her name after class.

"Before we dismiss, I want you to meet my student assistants." Samantha motioned to the entourage at the front. "One option you have this semester is to participate in research we conduct here at Vanderlaan. If you choose to do this, they will help you through the process and will be a resource for writing your papers. I'll let them give you their names—"

"And whether their life is one of science fiction or horror," said one brave first-year student.

"And who will play them in the movie of their life," added another, amid the laughter of the now relaxed body of students.

Samantha chuckled. "Why not? Start us off, Levi."

"That's me," he said with the contorted face they had just seen at the window. "First of all, my life is a comedy, and my part would be played by someone tall, dark, and handsome." His outstretched arms called for agreement which readily came from his now adoring fans. "I bring life to Samantha's—Dr. Hayes's—research team. Oh," he added casually, "and I'm her favorite." He tried to sell it with a smile and tilt of the head, which brought laughter from all but his research peers who gave him good-natured eyerolls.

The bright-eyed student immediately to Levi's right saluted as she announced, "I'm Sydnee." Her dark hair was pulled back into a ponytail and looped through the back of a ball cap. While her distressed jeans happened to be stylish, they resulted from the regular wear and tear of a student on a tight budget. "And make no mistake"—she punched Levi's shoulder—"*he* is not her favorite. I am." She flashed a smile. "And my life movie? Adventure! With the part of Sydnee going to anyone mouthy enough to pull it off." With a confirming nod, she motioned to her right for the next introduction.

With his shoulder-length hair and sandaled feet, Jeff brought to mind images of the 1960s and civil rights protests. Samantha suspected that if he would grow a beard and learn to play "California Dreamin'" on the guitar, the image would be complete.

"I'm not as flashy as these two," Jeff said. Amid protests from his peers, he insisted, "No, no, I'm not. But I *am* a good writer and work in the writing lab if you need help."

"And your life is a…"

Jeff squinted and quietly added, "A documentary on the life of a writer. My part could be played by that guy...you know..." He looked to his peers. "The one who was in that movie with that girl?" Laughter from everyone. Jeff's smile was easy and good-natured as he shook his head. "We'll hold auditions and see who turns up."

Samantha added, "Trust me. If you need writing help, Jeff is the one to ask. You're up, Allie."

"That's me." Allie waved, her smile self-assured and friendly. Short, blonde locks fell casually across her forehead. In a crisp, floral dress and sandals, Allie carried herself with unassuming confidence. "I'll be tutoring for this class." She then looked around furtively and lowered her voice to add, "My life story will be a mystery, played by someone with just the *right amount* of reserve."

"And somebody beautiful. She'd *have* to be beautiful!" added the last of the five. Jumping forward with arms and legs outstretched, Chess balanced a newsboy hat on her black curls while her hoop earrings jangled against her black skin. "I'm Chess and my movie is a fast-paced, quirky, feel-good comedy. I'm the newest member of this group and can't wait to get started!"

Samantha glanced at her watch. "Okay, we're almost out of time for today, but—"

"Wait! Wait!" students protested. "Who will play you, Chess?"

"I shall play myself." Chess bowed while more laughter ensued, and students applauded.

"Now—" Samantha began again.

"No! Wait!" Her students again objected with good

humor. "You haven't told us about *your* life movie, Dr. Hayes."

"Ah! Well, my life is a dramedy. And I'd be played by—"

"Somebody really old," Levi mused. "And bossy."

"Levi," Chess scolded. "Don't listen to him, Dr. Hayes." While Levi pretended to be hurt at Chess's response, a few students freely called out names of blonde, energetic comedians who should audition.

"Okay, so you now have the challenge to live your life as you'd like to see it on the big screen." Samantha paused to give a knowing look and allow for the laughter that always came. "You also know whom to ask if you need a tutor, writing help, or want to take part in our research. And my office is always open if you need me. See you next class."

Chairs scraped against the floor and chattering began. Students smiled as they tentatively approached classmates, no longer strangers.

And speaking of strangers, Samantha needed to catch the latecomer, get her name, and add it to the class roster. She swiveled her neck and scanned the now shifting crowd. Had the young woman left already? How was that possible? She'd been on the opposite side of the room, away from the door.

Oh, well. Samantha shook it off. *It can wait. It's not like I won't see her again.*

****

Samantha's crew scattered in different directions to get to their next classes. Each promised to come by later to fill her in on the jobs and fun that had kept them busy over the summer. Samantha would be excited to hear it all, along with their latest angst regarding

6

relationships, career decisions, and families back home.

Samantha's office afforded a good place for these conversations. Immediately inside the door sat a small furniture grouping, two chairs and a sofa surrounding a coffee table where countless personal problems and professional decisions had been discussed. A dish filled with candy sat in the center of the table, recently stocked with her students' favorites. With the department's storage room on one side and a conference room on the other, voices in her office were muffled from other students or colleagues who worked on the floor. On the other side of the room, several chairs surrounded a cafeteria-length table where she and her students could spread out their research material. Her small workstation consisted of bookshelves lining the wall and an L-shaped desk extending out and around, creating a cubby of sorts where she could work, resources within arm's reach.

On her desk, three brass frames held pictures of Samantha's family. In one, she and her husband, Rob, laughed into the camera while on vacation this past summer. She didn't remember what they had both found so funny. A joke maybe. More likely just the easy laughter that arises when having fun with someone you love. Either way, the picture was one of her favorites.

The other two frames sported pictures of their daughter and son, Elyse and Lucas, in academic regalia from each of their last graduations. Elyse was now a public relations specialist working for a social media site outside of Los Angeles. Since she was in a committed relationship with the sun and surf, she had declared California her permanent home. Lucas was just as happy with Midwestern climes and had put down roots in Indiana where he taught high school music. His passion for building a successful marching band meant long hours of disciplined work for himself and his students. While the physical distance made frequent visits with their grown children impossible, texting and social media kept them close emotionally.

As Samantha arrived at her office, several new students were outside her door needing her signature for schedule changes. Colleagues greeted her in the hall, asking about her summer and relaying stories of their own. She loved the excitement and promise of a new semester. If the only thing accomplished today was to soak in the positive energy around her, it would be enough.

Still, if she could cross a few things off her list, so much the better. She promptly answered several emails before tweaking her first lecture for one of her classes. Before long the first two of her crew arrived with stories to tell and problems to be resolved. Jeff plopped onto the sofa and Levi onto one of the chairs. Each helped himself to candy from the dish.

"Sam," Levi said. "I know I talk a good talk, but I've got issues."

"Say it isn't so." Samantha barely suppressed a grin as she looked up from her work. While she wasn't sure to which issue Levi was referring, she agreed that he did indeed "talk a good talk." His confidence and the easy banter they enjoyed brought energy to this office, just as it had done this morning in her first class.

Levi waved his candy wrapper as he chewed. "I have no idea what I want to do, and I gotta figure this out soon. I'm graduating this year. I need to get accepted into grad school and I don't know where to even apply."

She peered over her reading glasses. "You do know that most seniors are in the same boat, right? Most students have no idea what they'll be doing after graduation."

"But who am I kidding?" Levi blew out a long breath. "I won't get into graduate school with my grades. That first year of college—" Levi gave a thumbs down and blew a raspberry.

"But your grades got better. And other experiences weigh in, too, like the research we're doing. Don't worry. We'll get you in."

"*We* will? Hmm." He flopped his head back on the sofa.

Allie entered the office. "Hey, everybody."

Levi's head popped up. "Al! I heard you got a fabulous new car over summer."

"I did," Allie said. "And I'll take you all for a ride if you want. But first I need a water. Samantha?" She motioned to the fridge.

Samantha nodded. "I stocked up. Help yourself then tell me about your car."

Allie twisted the cap off her water as she sat on the end of the sofa. She gave a modest account of her summer travels with her parents and the purchase of a car for her senior year. Samantha guessed that Allie was downplaying her own excitement out of respect for the others' monetary constraints. Nevertheless, her news was met with warm enthusiasm from each along with requests for rides. Jeff's plea rang out the loudest though when he announced that his laptop wasn't in his backpack where he'd put it.

"I know I brought it with me." Jeff stared into his backpack then around the office as if it might have walked off on its own. "I remember putting it in here. I need it for class. What did I do with it?"

"Probably in your room." Allie motioned Jeff to his feet. "Let's go. I can get you to Braddock Hall and back faster than the speed of sound."

"You live in Braddock?" Samantha asked. "I did too for a while. What floor are you on?"

"Second."

"Seriously?"

"Yeah, last room on the left, overlooking the baseball field. Why?"

She laughed. "I lived there—*in that room*—one summer."

"No kidding? They let you live in a guy's dorm?" Jeff slung his backpack over a shoulder.

"They used it for women back then. Funny I've never heard any of you talk about where you live." Samantha chuckled. "I guess because most of the time you all live in this office."

Levi begged to be included in their mini road trip as they hurried from the office. Allie agreed but motioned for him to pick up speed.

"Can I drive?" Levi sprang from the sofa. "I've never driven the speed of sound, but I think I'd like it."

Chapter 2

Wednesday, August 22
"Knock knock."

Samantha looked around the door of her closet where she had been searching for the jug of water she kept for watering plants. They would not last through the week if they didn't get a little attention. "Hey, Jeff. Make yourself useful." She handed him the water jug and pointed to the droopy philodendrons which lined her windowsill. "Water my plants."

"I think it'll take more than water at this point. Why don't you take better care of these?" he asked with an amused smile.

"Because I'm too busy taking care of students. Neglecting a plant is one thing. But not doing enough for students?" She shook her head. "Not okay."

"Fair enough," he conceded with a nod and watered each plant. "Poor little guy," he muttered at the sprout in direst need of life support. "At least you haven't killed one of us yet, Dr. H."

"What—" Samantha's head snapped to Jeff.

"I mean, with us students, it's not all on you." He returned the water jug to the closet. "But I would like your opinion on something if you have a minute."

"I do," she replied. She sat and motioned for him to do the same.

"Okay, so I like a girl in your Intro to Psych class."

Samantha nodded. "Maddie DuCharm."

"How do you *know* these things? I haven't told *anybody* I like her!"

"I see all and know all, Mister Hannan," she said with a trance-like tone while holding her fingertips to her forehead. "I saw you two talking in the cafeteria and connected the dots. But hey, congratulations on talking to her. I know it's not easy for you."

"Yeah, we've talked in the caf, but that's it. I can't ask her out. I just freeze up." Jeff paced. "How did your husband do it? I mean, the first time he talked to you, what did he say?"

Sydnee barged through the door. "What did who say about what?"

"Do you ever knock?" Jeff asked. "What if this had been a private conversation?"

"I don't knock on doors that are *open.*" Sydnee flopped on the nearest chair. "Besides, what wouldn't you want me to hear?"

When he didn't respond, Sydnee followed Jeff's gaze toward the research table. "Hey, is that your laptop—the one you lost?"

"Where did you find it, Dr. Hayes?" Jeff's eyes lit up. "I've looked *everywhere* for it. It wasn't in my room. I checked lost and found. Even had one of those emails sent out to everybody on campus in case someone found it." Jeff logged on. "Doesn't look like it's been damaged. Man, I'm relieved!"

Samantha looked over her reading glasses. "I didn't find anything, Jeff. That's the first I've seen of it. Did you bring it in, Sydnee?"

"I'd love to take credit, but nope."

"But—" Jeff shook his head, mouth open. "It

wasn't here Monday…" Jeff looked around the room as if it held secrets for him to uncover. "Before Allie took me to the dorm, I checked the table, chairs, even your desk, Dr. H. It wasn't here, I'm sure of it. And no one brought it to you since?"

Samantha pursed her lips and shook her head. "Not unless they're invisible or walk through doors. My office is locked unless I'm sitting right here."

Jeff shook it off. "Well, whatever. Glad to have it back. I'm heading to the library to tackle the stats homework. See you all later."

"Well, that was weird," Sydnee concluded. Her face lit up as she switched topics. "Allie told me you lived in Jeff's room."

"Well, not exactly *Jeff's* room. At the time it was *my* room."

"Yeah, but the *same* room." Sydnee glanced at the open door. "I need to talk if you have time. With the door closed? Sometimes it's hard to talk privately in here," she said as if she had just discovered an incredible truth.

"Sure thing. What's up?" Samantha closed the door and sat on the sofa.

"I got in trouble yesterday at work. My boss was mad because…well…you know I'm direct."

Now there is an understatement. "You most certainly are."

"So when a customer complained that the university's recruiting so many students from other countries, naturally, I said something."

Samantha lifted her eyebrows to prompt Sydnee to continue. As if anything could have stopped her.

"I told him he didn't have all the facts and before

he criticized he should speak with someone from the university to make sure he wasn't spreading inaccurate information and—"

Samantha narrowed her eyes. "You said this to whom?"

"I told you. One of my customers. And—"

"I know." Samantha touched Sydnee on the arm. "But who was the customer?"

"He's the district manager of the store. He had come to check on—"

"Sydnee—" Samantha closed her eyes and scrunched up her face.

"But it shouldn't matter *who* he is."

"Yes, but you didn't need to say that to *any* of your customers. You need to think before you speak, Syd."

"I do think. But I can't just play nice while he says things that aren't true."

"I understand. But there's a time to speak, and a time to refrain."

"But I feel like I'm selling out if I just nod like I agree. Dr. Hayes, that just isn't right," Sydnee said through gritted teeth.

"It feels like that, I know. But, Syd, *no* one can speak the truth *all* the time. There's a place for tact and tolerance of others' views whether you agree with them or not. And it isn't selling out to allow others to speak their own mind. Especially when you aren't the one who will lose business if the customer gets mad. Your boss will. So what is said to customers is his call to make." When Sydnee tried to protest, she quickly added, "And one day, you'll be the boss and can take on the responsibility of what to say to whom."

Sydnee settled back and drummed her fingers on

the arm of her chair.

"Did you lose your job?" Samantha said softly.

"No, he didn't fire me. I need that job, Dr. Hayes. Between tuition and repairs on the clunker I drive…"

"I wish you didn't have to work so hard. Your parents couldn't help you out just a little?"

"Probably not, but I wouldn't ask anyway." She shook her head. "At least Ronald is old enough now to help at Mom and Dad's store. When I was his age, I was there before and after school every single weekday." Her palm tapped the chair, stressing her consistent commitment to her family's only source of income. "Before I left for school in August, I had a long talk with him about stepping up since I can't be around as much. If I were closer, I could help them on weekends."

"Then you would have one more job and you do too much as it is. But I get it. And one day your hard work will pay off. You'll be a forensic psychologist and can drop all the part-time work. But in the meantime"— she tapped Sydnee's arm—"you go in tomorrow and practice tolerance and celebrate freedom of speech."

"Freedom of customer's speech, not mine."

Samantha's head swayed to one side and then the other. "For now, yes. But your day will come. Promise." Sydnee's cell rang, and Samantha stood and moved to her desk.

"Hey, you still want to study?" Sydnee asked the caller. "I don't have my book. Let me run back to my room to get it and…you want to just study there? My roommate's out…okay. I live in Stratton, room 210."

Samantha was bent down at her computer to turn off the screen when Sydnee's words commanded her attention. *Stratton Hall, room 210.* She straightened up and looked at Sydnee who was putting her cell back in her book bag.

"You live in Stratton Hall? Room 210?" Samantha asked with bewildered amusement.

"Yeah, why? Did you live there too?" Sydnee laughed as she threw her book bag across her shoulder.

Samantha nodded, her forehead creased. "I did."

****

Clad in jeans and a T-shirt, Levi lounged on the sofa in Samantha's office, tossing a ball as he speculated on explanations for the room coincidence. "I'm just saying, you could be living out some unresolved dilemma from a former life or something. Like maybe Jeff, Syd, and Sam were business associates and one of you embezzled or ran off with the other's spouse or something and now you're put in this life to figure it out. Or"—he stopped tossing long enough to point for emphasis—"you were triplets who didn't get along and now you have to fix your relationship before you can move on." Levi continued the ball toss.

Samantha sat at her desk, halfway listening to their banter while entering attendance records for today's classes. "And what in the relationship needs to be fixed?" Samantha asked without taking her eyes away from her computer screen.

Levi propped himself up on an elbow. "Maybe your mom liked one of you best and the others were jealous." He nodded, winked, lay back down, and continued tossing.

"Go ahead. Make fun. But I'm not ruling anything out." Chess's large hoop earrings clanked as she paced the length of Samantha's office. "You'd be singing a different tune if you lived in one of Dr. H.'s old rooms."

"But I don't," Levi said. "I'm in an apartment off campus."

"I didn't know you have an apartment," Jeff said. He scrolled through surveys at the research table with Sydnee. "They're hard to come by. Where is it?"

"Valley Village over on Polk Street."

Samantha looked at Levi over her reading glasses.

"I know the place," Jeff said. "My roommate just moved from there. He couldn't take the noisy upstairs neighbors."

"He lived on the opposite end from me. I'm down next to the open lot. It's pretty quiet down there."

Samantha removed her glasses and leaned her arms onto her desk.

"Too bad you didn't live off campus when you were here, Dr. Hayes," Chess said. "You could have—"

"I did live off campus my last semester. In Valley Village."

As all activity ceased. Samantha had the level of attention she could only hope for during a lecture.

"In the apartment next to the open lot."

"Are you serious, Dr. Hayes!" Chess whirled around to face the others. "*Now* what do you all think?"

Sydnee offered a dry laugh under her breath. "It's just a coincidence, Chess. When you consider that we all go to school here and each of us lives *somewhere*, the fact that a couple of us—"

"Three of us," corrected Chess.

"—three of us," continued Syd, "live in rooms Dr. Hayes lived in, it's not that weird. Think about it. How

17

many rooms are there in the four dormitories on campus? Levi, you work in Student Services. How many are there?"

Levi sat up. "Braddock has 220 rooms. Stratton is about the same size. Of course, Wade and Ohtli are a little smaller, maybe 150 in each. So, what's that…about…?"

Sydnee had calculated on her cell as Levi spoke. "All right, that's a total of 740 rooms give or take, and Dr. H. lived in three of them. So the odds of three out of the five of us living in one of her rooms are…"

"Very small," Chess said. "So it can't just be a coincidence."

Jeff objected. "No, Chess, small odds don't eliminate the possibility of coincidence. In fact, that's what a coincidence is, two things happening even though the odds are very slim. And coincidences are *going* to happen. Statistically, it's a given."

"Exactly." Sydnee held up her hand to Jeff for a high-five he obligingly gave.

Allie and Levi smiled at each other.

"You think it's a coincidence?" Allie asked Jeff.

"I didn't say that."

"Oh, come on, Jeff!" Sydnee said.

"I'm not saying I believe anything supernatural is going on here. I'm not saying I don't. There just isn't any way for us to know." Jeff shrugged. "Besides the odds are only slim if we're sure it happened by chance. Is there any way this was done on purpose, Dr. H.?"

"I don't see how. Why would anyone orchestrate such a thing?"

"No reason I can think of," Allie said as she curled her feet underneath her. "Samantha, did you ever live in

18

377 of Stratton?"

Samantha took only a moment to consider. "Nope."

Levi went back to tossing the ball. "Sorry, Al."

"Actually," Samantha said, "I did live in one other room though." All eyes turned to her. "Stratton 331."

"Woulda been nice for that to be *my* room," Chess said. "But that's okay. I still have plenty to work with. It just means that whatever the connection is between you, Jeff, Sydnee, and Levi, does not include Allie or me."

Chapter 3

Friday, August 24

As she walked to her first class of the day,
Samantha congratulated herself that for the first time
this semester she would arrive at her own class on time.
A glance at her watch revealed she even had five
minutes to spare. With Douglas Hall in sight and her
classroom on its main floor, she was sure to make it on
time—

"Samantha!"

Grrr! So close. Although showing up late for class
frustrated her, she was mostly annoyed by the person
who was about to detain her. *If I ignore him, maybe
he'll go away.*

"Samantha!" This time he was more insistent.

Samantha released a breath of resignation. She
should have known better. He wasn't the kind to be
ignored. Samantha turned to face him as she reached
the door of the building. She hadn't been at Vanderlaan
long enough to flout someone who carried the weight
around here that he did. "What can I do for you, Len?"

Dr. Len Titus stood before her, dressed as always,
in a suit with a starched white shirt and tie which he
would loosen by afternoon. His graying hair with a
precise part on the side had become his hallmark, along
with his hands-on-hips pose and gravelly voice. Levi's
imitation of each was spot on, although professional

decorum required that Samantha refrain from the encouragement her laughter would ensure. Since Len Titus was of slight frame, someone unfamiliar with this man might assume passivity or weakness. Not Samantha.

"I see we're both teaching in Douglas Hall this semester," he said. "Hope I won't be in your way." He peered over his wire-rimmed glasses. "Or you in mine."

Samantha took a breath, gritted her teeth, and walked through the door. She would use the back entrance next time.

****

Samantha was barely in the classroom when the questions began.

"Dr. Hayes," one student's voice rose above the others, "I hear you lived in Levi's, Syd's, and Jeff's dorm rooms."

"Ooh, gross. Don't they have rules against that?" asked one student in the back of the class.

Even an early morning encounter with Len couldn't diminish her enjoyment of student banter. "Not in the same rooms at the same *time*," Samantha answered. "But yes, several of my students live in rooms I lived in while I was a student here."

"That's freaky," another said.

"No, it isn't," Levi said. "*Everybody* lives *somewhere,* and the same dorms are still here from back in the stone ages when Dr. H. was a student. So obviously current students live in each of her old rooms." He shrugged. "What's so freaky about that?"

"It's freaky," Chess said, "because of all the students who are in campus housing right now, the three who live in her rooms are students she advises and mentors and who hang out in her office." She sat back and crossed her arms. "*That's* what's freaky about it."

One student joked, "I think you're all part of some social psych experiment to see how you react." The others chuckled.

"Yeah, has anybody checked to see if Dr. Whitmer had anything to do with housing assignments these past few years?" said another.

"If this is like an experiment, we're not all participants. I don't live in one of her rooms and neither does Allie," Chess said. "And *none* of us live in the other room she had, 331 Stratton."

"Room 331…" one of the students said, her eyes closed. "That's…where?"

"I'm on third floor of Stratton," answered another. "Isn't that close to your room, Allie?"

"Uh uh." Allie shook her head. "Must be on the other side."

"No," another insisted. "I'm on the other side and room numbers there are higher."

Allie shrugged. "It's not mine. I don't know who lives there now."

"Enough already about rooms." Levi changed the subject. "Dr. H., are you going to Psych Club's ice-skating party this weekend?"

A dozen or more voices chimed in with pleas for her to join them at the local rink. Anything to delay the lecture a few more minutes.

"No way," Samantha said. "I have work to do, papers to grade, and a lot of class prep for next week. Besides, the last time I was on skates, it was not a pretty sight." From what she could gather very few of her students could skate either, but that was the difference in being their age and hers: they believed they could do anything; she gladly embraced the fact that she could not.

Amidst the easy conversation of the others, one of the older but less vocal students, Rochelle, rolled her eyes and tapped her pencil on her desk.

Well, it is *past time to begin.* "As much as I hate to interrupt, I hope you'll pardon the intrusion of my lecture," Samantha said with mock deference.

While students shifted in their seats, a few who always waited until the last moment pulled note-taking paraphernalia from their backpacks. Ms. Pencil-Tapper muttered just loud enough for Samantha to hear, "Finally."

****

Samantha was headed toward her office when Sydnee and Jeff caught up with her. The usual flurry of students scurrying from one class to the next was sparse today. In fact, judging by the sunshine and the frisbees flying around Stratton lawn, several classroom seats would remain empty over the next hour.

"Will you be in your office later? I'd like to enter survey data if you're around," Syd asked. "I have work right now, but my only other class today was cancelled. Dr. Caldwell's at a conference. So, I have time this afternoon. Jeff, if you're there too we could make a lot of progress."

Samantha grinned, happy that Sydnee still had a job to go to.

"But wait'll you hear." Sydnee grabbed Jeff's arm. "Guess who I saw today in the cafeteria and guess what I said to her?" Sydnee's eyes danced with excitement.

"Who?" Jeff asked with caution. "And what?"

"I saw your Maddie—"

"She's not *my* Maddie, Syd—"

"Well, whoever's Maddie she is, I let her know *someone* might be interested, and—"

"You did what!" Jeff jerked his arm from Sydnee's grasp. "What were you thinking? I didn't ask you to do that!"

"I know, but I wanted to—"

"But *I didn't* want you to. I told you I liked her in confidence. Man, Syd! I can't believe you did that." He stopped walking; Samantha and Sydnee followed suit.

Sydnee pulled back and, for only a moment, was speechless. "I'm sorry, Jeff. I was trying to help. I know you like her and have trouble with this sort of thing."

"Yeah! And now I have more trouble. Sheesh, Sydnee, what's wrong with you?"

Samantha caught her breath. Her chest tightened. Jeff was cautious, proceeding slowly with forethought. Sydnee was impetuous, rushing in to make things happen. Put it all together and there would be enough tension to destroy the atmosphere in her office for the rest of the school year. With Levi and Allie both graduating in May, this school year could be the last for both her research team and her office as she knew it. And it wouldn't even last *that* long if Sydnee and Jeff were at odds with each other.

"Let's talk about this calmly. Jeff, Sydnee was trying to help. I'm sure she didn't mean to upset you or to break a confidence, or—"

"Jeff, it wasn't like you think," Sydnee explained. "It wasn't weird. The only reason I said anything at all was because—"

"It doesn't matter." Jeff's breath shook. "I know you want to help. But please don't, okay? Let me do this my way."

"Okay," Sydnee agreed softly.

In silence, they all resumed their walk toward Prescott as Samantha offered a quick prayer of gratitude that a blow-up had been averted. She then took a deep breath to steady herself because problem averted was not the same as problem resolved.

As they reached a fork in the path, Sydnee paused before heading toward her car. "So, I'll see you later this afternoon. Jeff, you'll be there, too?" She spoke with caution.

He nodded.

****

Samantha and Jeff continued their walk to Prescott in silence. The building which housed Samantha's office and other social science faculty was not a long walk from her classroom. In fact, a person could get from any point A to any point B on campus in just a few minutes on foot. But today's sunshine and light breeze slowed their walk as they approached their destination.

Prescott Hall was one of the older buildings on campus. The two-story, red brick structure was lined with windows on both floors and featured a broad, arched entryway. A few steps spanned the archway and led to a covered porch and a stately door that was the building's main entrance. The walkway leading to Prescott was lined with several benches and as many light posts for illumination after dark.

Samantha moved toward one of the benches and asked, "Are you okay? I mean with Syd. She meant well."

He shrugged. Picked up a twig from the bench before they sat.

"Oh, I know. I'm not as mad as I let on." He played with the twig and offered a subtle grin. "It's a little hard to be mad and, you know, grateful at the same time."

At Samantha's quiet chuckle, Jeff waved the twig. "But she does need to learn that she can't do things like this."

"And you're the one to teach her?"

Jeff grinned slightly. "If no one else will."

Samantha shook her head and smiled. She leaned in his direction and in a lowered voice asked, "You want to tell me what *is* bothering you then if it isn't Sydnee?"

"This room thing." He rolled the twig between his hands. "What does it mean? I keep trying to make sense of it, but—" He tossed the twig to the side. "I got nothing."

"Hmm. You got nothing," repeated Samantha. Jeff didn't always share them, but he was never short on ideas. He would examine them for inconsistencies and flaws before discussing them with anyone. It was part of his process when assimilating new information. "Does it have to be *about* something?" she asked.

"I think it does." He leaned over, elbows to knees, fingertips together steeple-like. This position, also part of his process. "But what? I can't see how it could have a rational explanation. Maybe something spiritual?" He turned to meet her gaze.

She shrugged. "I can't imagine how. But I do have confidence that at some point, Mr. Philosopher, you'll put together a theory to explain everything."

"You think so?" He laughed.

"I do." She nodded. "But for now, go enjoy this beautiful afternoon. Do you have any more classes today?"

"Just the one Caldwell cancelled."

"Good. Then do something outdoors for a few. Come to my office later and I'll get you and Syd started on data entry. It'll take your mind off of the unexplained."

Jeff nodded in agreement as his cell buzzed. With one glance his eyes popped then quickly shifted to Samantha as he mouthed, *Maddie!*

Samantha gave him a pointed look. "Complain if you must, but Sydnee gets results."

As she rose from the bench, Jeff's whispered, "Psst...Dr. Hayes. Don't tell Syd, okay?"

Samantha mimed that her lips were sealed.

****

Samantha barely reached the steps to Prescott when stopped by her pencil-tapping, eye-rolling student. "Dr. Hayes," she said. "We have an exam next week and you spent ten minutes today talking about where people live! I'm a non-traditional student and don't have time for this. If you'll tell me how long you usually shoot the breeze before you begin class, I'll just come in later. Now I know you don't like people being late but if you haven't started yet, technically it's not late." The last part of her soliloquy she said with the fervor of an attorney about to prove the defendant guilty as charged.

"Well—"

"Also"—she held out a notebook which she evidently expected Samantha to take—"I had planned to ask you questions about the highlighted portion of my notes. But since there wasn't time in class, I'll just let you read these at your leisure and write in some clarification in the margins. Then I'll be back to pick it up later today."

"Wait," Samantha said. Rochelle was still holding out her notebook. "I am more than happy to answer any questions you have during class or in my office. But I don't work on assignment. Come by my office later today and I'll be happy to clarify anything you don't understand."

When Rochelle opened her mouth to speak, Samantha stopped her with the palm of her hand. "As an older student you likely have a good bit of work experience, so let me say that your professors here are comparable to an employer anywhere else, and as such are to be treated with the same level of respect. That means you *request* help, but never *demand* it on *your* schedule. Now, I have somewhere to be, but I do hope you'll come by later for help with your notes."

And with that, Samantha walked to her office. Without Rochelle's notebook.

Chapter 4

Saturday, August 25
Samantha Hayes and her husband, Rob Donovan, lived in a two-story house on Carlyle Court in the subdivision of Hamlin Path. While they didn't know their neighbors well, they were pleasant enough when Samantha happened to pass them on her morning walk through the neighborhood. The yards were small and well-tended, although most of the backyards were shielded from view by shrubs, trees, and the occasional fence.

Their home was a modern craftsman-style, stone house that sat beyond a circular drive. Large windows on either side of a columned porch framed the front door. Barely visible from the street was a brass door knocker featuring the letters *D* and *H* in calligraphy. Given to them by their teenage children for their twenty-fifth wedding anniversary, they had brought this family keepsake with them from their prior residence. Along with muted exterior lighting which surrounded the entrance, their home exuded a warmth Samantha treasured.

An inviting home was important to Samantha. She enjoyed coming in each evening to her soft-yellow-trimmed house with her husband's chrysanthemums that lined the front drive. She always smiled on those evenings when, circling around to the side drive which led to their garage, light shone from the window of their den and kitchen—a signal that Rob was back from his travels.

She also enjoyed that her students came around occasionally when they needed time away from campus. Since they were used to cafeteria fare, they appreciated home-cooked meals. She was happy to provide a home-away-from-home for her troop.

But more than that, Samantha and Rob's move to Vanderlaan meant selling the only home they had shared with their children, Lucas and Elyse. It was a bittersweet decision. And although their grown children would never say so, not having their childhood home to visit over holidays was an adjustment. So Samantha and Rob created a warm, inviting place where their son and daughter could visit and feel they had come home.

But today, Lucas and Elyse were miles away and her students were otherwise occupied at a Psychology Club event they had begged her to attend. And just as she predicted, today held no time for ice-skating. Rob would leave this morning for a five-week book tour to promote his latest whodunit, *Murder in the Suburbs*.

Although she was thrilled by his success, she dreaded his being away for such a long stretch. In the past, when a tour coincided with her summer or winter break, she would pack a bag and go along. But no way could she leave for a month with school in session. So this time, she resigned herself to staying home.

Their shih tzu, Millie, scampered from room to room as Rob brought the last of his luggage into the foyer. He lifted her to say goodbye and receive a few dog kisses before putting her down. Samantha followed with his briefcase and put it with the rest of his cargo.

Rob gave Samantha last-minute instructions on the care of his sunflowers and mums while he was away.

She shook her head. "The flowers are doomed. Have you ever considered planting the fake kind? No water or sunshine needed," she said with an enticing lilt to her voice.

He grinned. "Humor me?" He grabbed an umbrella from the closet, stuffed it in the side pocket of his suitcase, then checked to see that his laptop was indeed in the case where he had packed it only five minutes prior.

Samantha smiled. "It's there." She put her arms around his shoulders and rubbed the back of his neck. His hair was cut closer than usual, probably so it wouldn't need another cut until he came home.

"I just wish you could go, too."

"Nah, you'll be so busy, you won't even notice I'm not there."

"Bet I will." He wrapped her in a hug and kissed her. "Love you, Sammy."

"Love you, too."

"And try to remember the sunflowers?"

She held up her right hand as if taking an oath. "I promise to take care of them as if they were my own office plants."

He grimaced. "Maybe I should cancel the tour."

"Leave." She pointed to the door. "And don't give away the ending to your fans. They hate that, you know."

He picked up his bags. "Funsucker," he muttered as he left.

****

With Rob gone, she set about her day's work. Her

first task was to read through her tenure application packet one more time before sending it to the chair of her department. The process wasn't new to her. Almost twenty years ago she had successfully achieved tenure status while teaching at Hayward College. And four years ago, as she accepted the position at Vanderlaan, she knew she would have to prove herself at this institution before acquiring the job security tenure provided.

Of course, it wasn't without risk. Anyone denied tenure at Vanderlaan was as good as fired. That professor would have one academic year in which to find another place of employment; they were rarely encouraged to apply again. The process was intense, but Samantha wasn't worried. She had come to Vanderlaan aware of their expectations and eager to prove herself. From her first semester, she set out to give the university no reason to doubt her value to the institution and their students. So while she did her share of complaining, the challenge of it—having her accomplishments validated in this way—appealed to her.

Then over the past summer, as she approached her fifth year, she completed the application, compiled her course evaluations, listed her service to the campus and community, collected letters of recommendation from colleagues, and detailed her research and the publications which had emerged from it. Today she read through the entire packet one last time. Satisfied that it accurately reflected her professional accomplishments, she clicked *send*. While it would be months before her application made it up the ladder of committees and finally to the trustees who would make the final decision, today she crossed *tenure* off her list of things to do.

Next, she graded a stack of papers, tweaked lectures for the following week, and previewed a video clip she would show on Monday. She didn't mind working from home; good thing, since that was where most of her class prep took place. Ideally, she preferred to leave office hours free for research and her students who stopped by to talk. At the pace she was moving today, she would achieve this goal for the coming week.

By mid-afternoon, however, Samantha had made a respectable amount of progress and decided to stop in to watch a few minutes of the ice-skating fun. She drove out to the rink vowing not to spend more than one hour away from her desk. If she kept to her plan, she could grab a salad on her way home and eat while grading one more set of papers.

****

A blast of cold air hit Samantha as she walked inside the rink, making her grateful she had changed from shorts and a T-shirt into tights and an oversized, long-sleeved blouse. The mingled sound of young voices, music, and the crunch of skates on ice brought a smile to her face. The new rink gleamed with white, from the outside walls to the ice itself. The short wall that separated the skating area from the sidelines showed only slight scuff marks. While most of the patrons were on the ice, a dozen or so sat around tables close to the concession stand drinking hot chocolate, talking, and laughing.

Making her way to the periphery of the ice, Samantha spotted several familiar faces. First-timer

Sydnee and a boy Samantha didn't know showed a respectable amount of persistence, if not agility, on the ice. Veteran skater Allie guided Chess slowly around the edge of the rink, stepping out occasionally to glide solo. Levi sat on the sidelines removing his skates while others laughed at the tale he was spinning. And Jeff was talking to Maddie! *Good for you, Jeff.*

"Hey, Dr. Hayes! Over here!" Two first-year students glided toward her.

"You're both pretty good at this."

"You skating? C'mon, we'll help."

She declined, pleading the importance of life and limb. Within a few seconds, Samantha caught sight of Allie and Chess working their way toward her. Chess had now ventured a few feet from the edge and proudly gave Samantha two thumbs-up. Despite her lack of progress, Chess's eyes were bright, and her laughter echoed in the rink. Did anything ever get her down?

At that very moment, however, something did get her down. Without preamble and within a split second, Chess went from upright to flat on her back. And while her fall was cushioned somewhat by her backside, which had the grace to hit first, her head took the brunt of the impact with a *crack* that claimed everyone's attention. Allie was first to Chess's side, followed closely by those skating nearby and just as quickly by Levi and Jeff who had been watching from the sidelines.

"Are you all right?" "What happened?" "Can you get up?" rang out from the vicinity as Chess assured everyone she was fine. As Allie helped her up, however, evidence to the contrary appeared on Chess's jacket and on the ice where she had hit. Smears of blood moved from her head to her hand as Chess touched the place of impact. Allie immediately asked Levi and Jeff to help her get Chess to the first aid station. Together they led her off the ice to a small room to the side of the rink.

Samantha caught her breath and hesitated briefly before walking with deliberate steps toward the first aid station. She came to a complete stop at the door when she saw Chess on a cot with a blood-soaked cloth to her head. Allie took off Chess's skates while a woman wearing a smock and name tag put on rubber gloves. Levi and Jeff backed away from the increasingly crowded room to let Samantha through. Lightheaded, Samantha pushed herself through the door, made her way to Chess, and sat down before her knees gave way.

The nurse proceeded to ask Chess various questions to determine the extent of her head injury. *What day is it? Do you know where you are? Who is the president of the United States?* Chess answered all to the satisfaction of the health care professional who told Chess they would clean her wound before sending her to the local emergency room for stitches. Chess endured with only an occasional gasp of pain.

Samantha reached out to hold Chess's shaking hand only to immediately regret it. The stickiness of dried blood would have made her recoil, but she refused to desert Chess, who squeezed her hand like a frightened child. So while Allie returned Chess's skates and answered the questions of concerned friends, Samantha stayed put. She only hoped the pounding of her own heart would not attract attention and require an explanation.

After Chess's wound was cleaned and bandaged,

Allie stated that she would drive Chess to the ER. "I can't ride in your new car. My clothes are all—" She grimaced at her blood-stained shirt.

"The blood's dry. It'll be fine. Besides, think how fast my car will get us there." She directed Chess's attention away from the injury.

Samantha pointed to Allie. "Keep it under the limit, missy." Samantha disliked conceding the role of caregiver to someone else, but Allie had things under control. Besides, it couldn't be helped.

Samantha quickly walked toward the women's restroom, which, thankfully, was empty, went in, and locked the door. With deep, shaky breaths, and no longer fighting the tears, Samantha moved immediately to the sink where she scrubbed her hands vigorously, several times. She reached into her purse for her cell phone, scrolled quickly through her contacts, and tapped her thumb on the one she sought.

She took a deep breath when instructed to leave a message. "Debra, this is Samantha Hayes. Could you give me a call please? I need to talk to you." She waited a moment, decided she had said all she needed to for now, then added, "Thanks," before ending the call.

She continued to hold her cell, however, as she paced, all the while trying her best to take even, measured breaths. *Think of something else. You've washed your hands. You're safe. You'll talk to Debra when she calls back. Breathe.* She was surprised that her reaction was this intense. The sight of blood had not frightened her this much in a long time.

As she debated whether to stay or go home to await Debra's call, her cell rang, making her jump. With another shaky breath and a sigh of relief, she answered.

"Debra? Thanks for calling...Okay...actually, no I'm not okay. I hate to bother you, but something just happened."

Chapter 5

Her talk with Debra calmed her down, but the return of this fear made her uneasy. *What is this? Why now?* So, when her therapist suggested they meet first thing Monday, she agreed. Samantha was nothing if not a first-rate client.

Dr. Debra Joren's office was conveniently located between Samantha's home and her own office on the Vanderlaan campus. A variety of professionals practiced in the surrounding offices. A person could be treated for everything from acne to cataracts without leaving the Office Park Plaza. In fact, if so inclined, Samantha could have strolled a bit farther and stopped in to donate blood. But considering her meltdown Saturday after Chess's injury, that seemed ill-advised.

As Samantha stepped into Debra's waiting room, she was greeted by a chatty receptionist who always seemed one step away from a meltdown herself. In contrast, the room itself was conducive to relaxation. The office was decorated in muted shades of olive and beige with a large clock on one wall that ticked off the passing of time. Samantha found the setup comforting. She sat down in one of the four chairs and debated thumbing through one of the issues of *Time* or *People*, neatly placed on each of two end tables. It was then, however, that Debra appeared at the door which led to her private office and motioned for her to come on back.

Samantha had walked through this door once a month for the past four years. She initially sought a therapist after she came to Vanderlaan and found herself uncharacteristically anxious. Whether it stemmed from the move, a new job, the fact that she wasn't needed as much by her now grown children—Samantha didn't know. But by the time she got the anxiety under control, Samantha found that time with Debra helped her maintain balance in a busy life. This was priceless and she didn't plan to quit anytime soon.

Debra followed Samantha into the office which matched the waiting room's clean lines and soft colors. A small sofa and several chairs in a partial circle made up the furniture grouping in Debra's office. Shelves lined one wall with books on grief, trauma, the power of intuition, and holistic therapies. A large picture window opened to a cluster of trees, which must have been restricted from public access. In the four years her gaze had wandered there, Samantha had never seen a person or animal amble by.

As they each took their respective seats, Debra wasted no time asking Samantha how she felt since they spoke on Saturday. Debra's style as a therapist was both casual and direct and carried over to her physical appearance. Her blonde hair was pulled back on both sides and gathered in a messy bun with strands on both sides of her face. Glasses framed eyes that conveyed thoughtful intelligence. Debra's warmth and authenticity made it easy for Samantha to open up, and, as a rule, Samantha had more to say than their fifty-minute hour would allow.

But today was different. Samantha sat in silence. Debra waited.

Samantha finally spoke. "I don't know what happened. Chess fell on the ice, and I freaked out. I haven't felt this way in a long time—this complete panic over nothing."

"I doubt that it was over nothing, Samantha."

"It was, Debra. Chess was hurt but not in immediate danger. You'd have thought she was at death's door the way I reacted."

"Anxiety is a type of warning system, Samantha." A partial smile tugged at the corner of Debra's lips. "I don't have to tell you this."

"But warning me about what? I haven't felt this way since I first came to Vanderlaan. That's why I came to you initially, remember?"

Debra nodded. "But we never did figure out what was behind the anxiety back then. I'm wondering if Saturday's incident was related somehow." Debra settled in. "What triggered it this time?"

Samantha closed her eyes. "I don't know. I had a good week. Students are back. My classes are going well. I've submitted my application for tenure." Samantha opened her eyes. "I've been there long enough now to apply."

Debra smiled and nodded her congratulations.

"My research team is back and at work. Except one day Syd and Jeff argued. Stressed me out." Samantha dismissed this with a wave of her hand. "But they're fine now. Then each of them trooped in to tell me about trouble at work, with their families back home, stress about applying to grad school. I pulled each back from the proverbial cliff. Oh! And I have a new student who acts like she's *my* boss." Samantha huffed and rolled her eyes. "Then Rob left Saturday for several weeks. But so far—"

"*So far?*" Debra smiled. "You're one week in, overrun with student problems while your husband is away for an extended period of time as you prepare for the biggest promotion an academic receives and you wonder what triggered your anxiety this past weekend."

Samantha chuckled.

Debra turned her head slightly in question. "Did I leave anything out?"

"Only the bossy student." Samantha shrugged. "But I need to solve problems when I can. If this student is more capable than he thinks or that student needs to rein in the brutal honesty, I can't just *not* say something. And I need to apply for tenure this year— it's time." She chewed on her lip and shook her head slowly. "But...something about Chess falling. It was too familiar."

"How so?"

Samantha shifted positions. "When I saw Chess fall...knowing something terrible was happening that I couldn't prevent." Samantha closed her eyes. "It's the same feeling I have when they consider a career possibility that will never work or apply for a job I know they won't get, or they fight over *everything* and *nothing* in my office." She clenched her fist, opened her eyes. "That sick feeling that they'll be hurt, and I won't be able to prevent it. Or worse, I do prevent it and shouldn't."

"Because...?"

"Because it's bad advice but they take it anyway and it messes up their lives."

"What do you do when I give you advice?"

"You don't advise a lot."

"But I do occasionally. Then what do you do?"

"I listen. I respect your opinion."

"And then you do what I advise?"

"Not always. If I don't believe it's right for m—" Samantha smiled despite herself.

Debra laughed. "Exactly. So, what makes your advice more powerful than mine that it can't be ignored if necessary?"

Samantha sat up straighter to excitedly make what she knew would be an irrefutable point. "Because they're younger and more impressionable. That's why."

"I'll give you that. But they *are* still adults and ultimately responsible for what they do with your advice. You know"—Debra shifted in her chair—"your students aren't the only ones you advise, Samantha. You have a grown son and daughter and you advise them when it's called for. But I've never once seen you overly anxious about what they'll do with it. How is that different?"

Samantha gazed out the window as she considered Debra's question. "I suppose because Rob and I raised Lucas and Elyse to be independent thinkers. As they were growing up, we allowed them to make more and more of their own decisions. And when they made mistakes"—she shrugged—"we know we'd be there to help if needed." Samantha sat back, bit her lip. "But with my students, this time—right now—is all the influence I'll have with them. I only have a short time to get it right."

"That makes sense," Debra said. "Still, it's hard to

make relationships work that way."

Samantha's stomach tensed. *It's the only way I* can *make it work.*

Chapter 6

Monday, August 27

Samantha was grateful she had completed so much work before visiting the rink on Saturday. Chess's ice-skating injury had marked her weekend, and Samantha was hoping for a less eventful and more productive week. Toward that end, Samantha drove to campus immediately after leaving Debra's office and found a parking place close to Prescott Hall. When she walked into her office, Samantha immediately realized something was off. It was quiet. The chairs were empty. The only light came in through the slats of partially closed blinds. The place had a weird vibe.

Ah! I'm alone in my office.

"This calls for action," she said aloud to no one but herself. Not that she didn't love the usual office traffic, but if she hurried, she could do some of the work she hadn't done over the weekend. What to do first? She needed to return a call to the university counseling center with her assessment of a student she had referred for depression. She needed to look through a couple of reports for a committee she chaired. A former student had requested a letter of recommendation which she needed to send out soon.

But before she could decide which of these tasks had a rightful claim to the top of her list, a knock on the door let her know deliberation was unnecessary.

"Hey, Allie. Chess, how's your ice-skating injury?"

"Not bad. Want to see?" Chess sprinted toward Samantha's desk.

No! A thousand times NO! But before she could think of a plausible excuse for not looking, Chess parted her hair and turned so Samantha could take a peek. While she was pleased to know Chess was on the mend, Samantha was even more grateful there was no blood to send her shrieking in terror to the Prescott restroom.

As Chess ran on to her class, Allie asked if Samantha was busy. "I just need to talk to you about my practicum."

Since Allie's goal was to be a therapist, Samantha had introduced her to one of her own graduate school friends, Bill Gordon, who directed the local community mental health center. As a senior, Allie was eligible for a practicum placement at the center. After meeting Dr. Gordon, and with Samantha's hearty recommendation, Allie applied for the ten hour a week position which would run throughout the semester.

"Yeah, how is it going?" Samantha sat at her desk and shuffled through her mail, while Allie took a seat on the sofa.

"Okay. Dr. Gordon let me sit in on group therapy"—she blew out a sigh—"and it was hard for me."

"Hard? How so?"

"The clients. They have a lot, and I mean a *lot*, of problems. Dr. Gordon takes it all in stride, but I don't know how."

"You don't know how because you're still a student. That's why you're doing a practicum—to learn

45

more about what it's like." Samantha threw away several pieces of junk mail from textbook publishers.

"Yeah, I'm learning all right. Learning I don't have a clue what I'm doing. I would be at a complete loss with clients like his."

"You're at a complete loss *now*. But, Allie, you can't expect to know how to treat clients at this point. You'll get all that in graduate school. Don't be so hard on yourself. It's too early to assume you're clueless." Samantha sorted her opened mail into stacks.

Before Allie could raise another objection, the department secretary walked in with a note for Samantha. "From Dr. Gordon, at the clinic. He wants you to call him back today. Hi Allie."

"Hi Christine. Is the message about me, Sam?"

"Hmm? Oh, I don't know," Samantha said absently as she put the note in her pile of messages to return.

"And these—hot off the press." Christine placed a stack of exams on Samantha's desk.

"Thanks. There's another exam to be copied on my keyboard, please."

"When will you call him back?" Allie persisted.

Samantha stared at Allie. "Who?"

"Dr. Gordon. Are you going to call him right away? Do you think he wants to talk to you about me?"

"I'll call later today. But no, it's probably about an article I proofed for him."

Allie nodded and took a deep breath.

Samantha sat on the sofa to look over an updated class roster when Allie continued. "Oh, I almost forgot. I checked and there is no room 331 in Stratton. And you know what's odd? None of the rooms on that side of the dorm match the pattern for all the other floors of

Stratton. Rooms on first, second, and fourth floors go from numbers one to fifty. Like 101 to 150, 201 to 250 and so on. But on the third floor it's different. Those run from 351 to 399. Weird, huh?"

Christine had finished gathering the items to be copied and was almost out the door when she stopped. "It's because they changed numbers on that floor after that girl died in one of the rooms about...I don't know...maybe twenty years ago?"

"Died! Are you serious?" Allie's eyes widened.

"Sure am." Christine leaned against the door casing. "Her name was Annika something or other. I hadn't been here long myself. But I remember they found her dead one morning. I don't know if they ever decided what happened." She shrugged. "An accident of some sort. But you know what? Nothing much was said about it after that first day or so. Kind of like they didn't want to call attention to it. I always figured her parents wanted it kept hush-hush."

"Still. A *death*. Did her parents have that kind of pull?" asked Samantha.

"Oh yeah. Big Vanderlaan donors. If they'd have wanted it swept under the rug"—Christine gave a pointed look—"then swept it woulda been. It would have been nice for people around here though to know for sure." Christine added, "You should team your psych students up with the criminal justice kids and get them to figure this one out, Sam."

"Ha! Sure. And they changed the room numbers?"

"Yeah, no one lived there the rest of the semester. Soon after they took out several rooms to add a kitchen and renumbered the rooms. I think no one wanted a room where someone had met their end, and this way

47

folks wouldn't know which one it was. Just my opinion." Christine shrugged. "So all numbers on third floor are off."

Allie asked, "You don't think she died in 377, do you?"

"Don't know. Like I said, I was new here and have never been in the dorm myself. Well, I'll go make your copies."

"Thanks, Christine," Samantha said absently. Allie and Samantha sat there, neither of them saying a thing.

When Samantha got up, Allie immediately followed. "We going over there to check it out?"

"Oh, yeah," Samantha replied.

****

Samantha and Allie walked in silence onto the third floor of Stratton Hall. What could either of them say that would make sense of what they both instinctively knew? As Allie walked to her room and Samantha walked to what had once been her own, they each knew that those rooms would be one and the same.

And they were.

Chapter 7

Monday, August 27

As Samantha came through the doors of Prescott Hall, Sydnee and Jeff were outside her office. "Hey, you two. Come on in." Samantha unlocked her office door. They deposited their things and grabbed drinks from her fridge. She motioned them away from the research table, however, and toward the sofa and chairs where she headed herself. "No, let's talk first."

"Yeah, I don't want to work right now anyway." Sydnee popped open a juice and reached for the candy jar. "You're almost out of these, Dr. Hayes. Can you get the strawberry kind next time? They're a little better. Not so..." she made a startled face, communicating the strong taste of the one she now chewed.

Jeff stared at Sydnee with an expression of amused awe.

"What?" Sydnee looked from Samantha to Jeff and back again. "I like strawberry better."

"You just tell her to get the kind you like?" Jeff said. "I don't guess you could buy the candy yourself?"

"Want me to restock your candy bowl, Dr. H?" Sydnee asked through a juicy glob of taffy.

"No, sweetie, I got the candy covered. But thanks, Jeff, for the suggestion." She nodded in his direction. Samantha then filled them in on the discovery of Allie's room being one of her own. She had just finished when Chess danced into their midst.

"I just heard!" Chess exclaimed. "I saw Allie in the library, and she told me. And I just saw Levi and told him. He's on his way over."

"We're here," Levi announced as he and Allie entered the office. "Let the brainstorming begin. Seriously, we don't leave this room until we figure this thing out." Sydnee made room for Allie while Levi rolled Samantha's desk chair over to the group, swiveled it, and sat with his arms resting on its back.

Levi said, "Jeff, last week you asked if someone could be behind this. And, Sam, you didn't think so. But the way I see it, that's the only logical explanation."

"I agree," Sydnee said. "It's the only thing that makes sense."

"And I *dis*agree," Samantha said. "This someone would have to know where I lived back then *and* be capable of assigning rooms to each of you several decades later. There's no one who—" Samantha's lips parted. "No one except Kelly DeVore." She shot a glance at Levi.

"My boss? The one who assigns housing to students? *That* Ms. DeVore?" Levi said.

"And there you go." Sydnee laughed. "Case closed. See, Chess? Always a logical explanation."

"Not so fast, Syd," Allie said. "Samantha, would Ms. DeVore have any reason to do this?"

Samantha answered Allie by picking up her office phone and punching in the number of her colleague. "Kelly, hi. Samantha Hayes. Listen, something's come up that's, well…I can't imagine how it happened but since you're the housing director...Oh yes, I know we're at full capacity this time of year. I'm not asking for...No, no, students aren't complaining already. At least not to me." She offered a nervous chuckle.

Samantha explained the recent discovery that four of her five student assistants lived in her former rooms. She took a deep breath before plunging into the oddest question she had asked a colleague in a long time. "Since you're one of the few people here who knew me then and where I lived...and you assign rooms to students...No, I don't think you memorized anyone's living arrangements back then...I mean, why would you...? No, I don't think you're messing with *any*body, Kelly. It's just so odd that...how could a coincidence of this magnitude even...No, no, it was just a thought...Yes, I will. You too."

After hanging up, Samantha ran her hands down her face in mortified embarrassment. "She had nothing to do with your room assignments. And will probably have nothing to do with *me* from here on out."

"You believe her, Dr. H.?" asked Jeff.

"I do. There wouldn't be any reason for her to assign students to my rooms and then lie about it."

"Unless..." Allie tilted her head. "Unless she *had* to keep us in the dark. When Chess and I brought up the room thing in class last week, someone joked that maybe we were part of some social psych experiment. Like maybe Dr. Whitmer was in on it."

Sydnee said, "And then enlisted Student Services—or at least Ms. DeVore—to help pull it off."

"Ooh, I like that!" Chess's hooped earrings danced along with her nodding head. "And he's doing this to see how you all react? Can professors experiment on each other like that? Wouldn't they have to tell them first?"

"Not if telling them would compromise the study," explained Allie. "They'd have to keep everyone in the dark so participants would behave normally."

Levi looked at Samantha as if she had just grown an extra nose. "But that's only *if* the professor is a *participant*. If she were, say, one of the *experimenters* she'd know but wouldn't be able to spill the beans."

Samantha laughed and held up her hand as if being sworn in. "I know nothing about this, Levi. Whatever *this* is."

"So...are we back to explanations that aren't rational?" Chess looked hopeful.

"I think so," Jeff said. "Because even as an experiment, it just doesn't fit."

Sydnee groaned in mock agony.

"It doesn't." Jeff gained steam. "Neither Ms. DeVore nor Dr. Whitmer knew me before I came to Vanderlaan. And they certainly didn't ask me to hang out in this office. What about the rest of you?" He looked around at the others. They each responded with a shake of the head. "The only one who could've had a hand in that was Dr. Hayes. So, if you aren't in on it"—he motioned to Samantha—"then *something*—something extraordinary—is going on here."

Chapter 8

Monday, August 27

While Samantha agreed that no one on campus would have had the motive, much less ability, to pull off such a feat, the idea of a supernatural explanation made her uneasy. Where was this going? Were they talking God or ghosts?

Jeff asked, "But wouldn't there have to be a purpose for a coincidence of this magnitude? Like something we're supposed to learn."

Allie shrugged. "Only if you see it as part of a larger plan or a God-thing." She sped up and put out her hand toward Jeff. "And I know you do, Jeff. No offense."

"None taken." Jeff nodded.

As the self-appointed leader, Levi looked around as if he expected to take motions from the floor. On cue, a hand went up. Levi nodded in Chess's direction, and she began. "You four must have something in common that I don't share." She quickly continued, "And I'm okay with that, but maybe it's where we should begin to unravel this thing. What is different about me than the rest of you?"

Comments identifying Chess as the youngest, artsy, and excitable were offered before Sydnee abruptly concluded, "You talk a lot."

"I'm somewhat different too," Levi said, "since my

place isn't on campus."

"Right," Chess said. "So, what do we have in common that the rest don't?"

"You're both black," replied Sydnee.

Chess and Levi looked at each other as if checking the accuracy of Sydnee's observation.

Allie said, "But Levi does live in one of Samantha's residences. Chess doesn't. That's not the same at all. Levi is still one of us."

Jeff leaned forward and placed his fingertips together steeple-like. "One thing no one's considered. Even in the time Dr. Hayes has taught here, other have lived in these very rooms. Do we know who they are? Are they still around? Do they factor in?"

"Kasandra lived in my room before I came in," Allie said. "She and I were roommates before she transferred. But she isn't here anymore."

"I'm by myself," Levi said. "Looking for a roommate but no luck yet. Jeff, you have a roommate?"

"I did, but he moved out after a few days. Had family problems and decided to wait out a year. And I have no idea who lived in the room before I came."

"Well, I do," Sydnee said. "Have a roommate, I mean. Shayla Kanaan. But I don't see any significance there. Chess?"

"I'm still with Julianna, but don't know how that would tie in."

Jeff leaned back into his chair. "It probably doesn't. I'm just reaching."

"I don't think it does either," Levi said. "This isn't about who else lived in these rooms. Because we—all of us here—are the ones connected to Sam. We're the ones who occupy her office every day. The ones she mentors. What is it about *us*?"

Allie said, "Maybe we're supposed to learn from any mistakes Samantha's made so we won't make them ourselves."

"*Mistakes?*" Samantha feigned offense. "What you see here is state-of-the-art humanity."

"State-of-the-art?" Levi said. "Need I remind you of the lackluster persona of this office before I breezed in?"

Chess giggled. "I so wanna be you, Levi."

Allie continued, "I just mean if we're looking for similarities, the struggles we have now that you've already resolved might be a good place to start."

"But the struggles I had aren't unique to you four," Samantha said. "Most students go through the same. And helping students navigate them is what mentors do." She couldn't resist, however, a brief reminiscence. "Dr. Carns—Emma—was my favorite professor and the *best* mentor. Goodness, but I wanted to *be her.*" Samantha smiled at the memory. "Emma introduced me to the fight for gender equality. She wanted to change the world and I wanted to change it with her." Samantha chuckled. "Allie, you remind me of myself at your age. I mean in your desire to change the world. I only wish I'd have had your confidence at that age."

When she caught a look pass between Allie and Levi, Samantha asked, "You don't plan to let the world stay as is, do you?"

Allie glanced at Levi who nodded in what seemed to be encouragement.

There's more here that she isn't saying. At least not to me.

"No, of course not." Allie offered a shaky smile.

"I'm just not as confident as you seem to think."

Samantha dismissed Allie with a wave of her hand. "You're so much more together than I was at your age and don't need half the reassurance I—"

"But I do need it, Samantha!" Allie clenched her fist and sat up straighter. "That's just it. Everybody thinks I have it all together and I don't! I'm confused and I don't know any more about where I'll end up than everybody else. And my parents don't help any. They're so used to my 4.0." Allie's eyes squeezed closed. "*Stupid* GPA—it doesn't always mean you know what you're doing. I'm just better at faking it than everybody else." Allie pulled her knees to her chest as she settled back into her chair.

Silence enveloped the room. Levi sent a victory fist pump into the air.

"Wow," whispered Chess. "Allie's as messed up as we are."

"And you're happy about that?" Sydnee asked softly while keeping her eyes on Allie.

Chess leaned sideways toward Sydnee and continued her whisper, "Are you kidding me? She's Allie Donnel—the girl most likely to succeed at *everything*. If she's confused, there's hope for us all." With her eyes still on Allie, Chess went back to her original position, as if watching a movie she couldn't pull herself away from.

"Allie, I don't know what to say," Samantha said. "You appear so confident in your choices, in your plans. I had no idea you needed more from me."

"I would just like to be a mess sometimes and not feel like I'll let you or my parents down."

"Hey, no chance of that. With me or your parents."

"I told you Sam would get it." Levi popped a miniature candy bar in his mouth. "Your parents will too, Al. Trust me. I know things. I'm a psych major."

"Well, I like direct," Sydnee said. "No one wonders what you're thinking or what you need. They know."

"But being direct has consequences, Sydnee." Samantha gave her a pointed look. "That's why I avoid pushing too hard."

A brief silence preceded her students' unified yelps of dismay.

Samantha looked around the group. "What?"

Sydnee offered a furtive smile and raised eyebrows. "You are kind of strong-willed." Then with a two-handed stop sign, quickly added, "It's not an insult. I, myself, think strong-willed is a good thing."

Her peers agreed quickly, with Levi's voice carrying above the others. "It's just you feel strongly about what some of us—"

"*All* of us," Sydnee said.

"Thank you. *All* of us," Levi continued, "do in school, in our careers, in our *lives*."

"I've got *opinions* if that's what you mean. I'm your teacher and mentor. I'm paid to have opinions. You silly people." Samantha dismissed their comments with a wave of her hand as she got up and moved back to her desk.

"Silly? I don't think so." Levi swirled in his chair then rose to follow Samantha to her desk. "Who was it that barreled into the emergency room last semester demanding to speak to the doctor when my appendix burst?"

Samantha chuckled. "They let me in, didn't they?"

"Because you told them you're my *mother.*" Levi shook his head. "Not that I wasn't glad you were there, but, Sam, who *does* that?"

"Besides your mother? I do, that's who. And they took care of you right, didn't they?" She wagged her finger at him. "They needed to know you had a parent there."

"But when my real mom got there, they wouldn't let *her* in. She's still sore, you know."

"She is not. She sent me a thank-you note."

Sydnee spoke up. "Dr. H., what about the grad school application you sent in for Allie?"

"Now that was just a mix up. Allie left it on my desk and told me to hold it for her."

"And did you?" Sydnee teased.

"I mailed it for her."

"Exactly!" More laughter from each of them.

Levi picked up an envelope from Samantha's desk and held it to his chest with both hands. "You were supposed to *hold* it for her."

"But if I remember correctly, Allie wasn't sure about sending in her application." Sydnee checked with Allie who shrugged.

"But an application wouldn't commit her to anything, and she had a better shot getting in than she thought," Samantha said.

Sydnee and Levi exchanged skeptical looks.

Chess jumped in. "I can't believe you all. You're kind of hard on Dr. Hayes, aren't you?" She directed her attention to Samantha. "Are you okay with this?"

"She asked and we're just being honest." Levi plowed ahead. "And you're in this, too, Chess. Remember when Sam volunteered you to speak to the first-year psych majors? You were scared to death and wouldn't have done it if Sam hadn't already told the other psych faculty you were in."

"True. But when it was over, I was really glad I did it." Chess quickly nodded.

"It's not that we don't appreciate it." Levi tilted his head. "Sometimes it's great. But you do push just a bit."

Maybe, but Samantha wanted the opinion of someone less inclined toward the comedic. "Allie, what do you think? Is this a problem?"

"You are opinionated and pretty direct. But like I said"—Allie shrugged—"sometimes I need more input not less."

"So sometimes I need to back off. Sometimes I need to step up." Samantha looked to them for clarification and received a nod from each. While Samantha put on a good front, their comments about her strong-willed opinions did not exactly take her by surprise. If they only knew how many times she had wanted to flat out scream, *No! For the love of all that's holy don't do that!* they would appreciate the level of restraint of which she was capable.

But to hear that sometimes she needed to do more, gutted her. *Is there anything worse than not doing enough?*

No, there was not. And wherever this room connection led them, ghosts of her past seemed to be vying for her attention.

Chapter 9

Wednesday, September 5

As with the beginning of any semester, many things and people clamored for Samantha's attention. Between teaching, advising, mentoring, and the flow of students through her office, it was easy to focus on the present rather than the past. Today was such a day.

Levi came to her office asking for letters of recommendation to three graduate schools where he planned to apply. Each boasted programs for students undecided on a focus and would prepare them for a number of career paths.

"I just emailed you the links for the schools, so if you'll write a letter for me, I'd really appreciate it, Dr. Hayes."

"I will do that pronto. But, hey, I'm Dr. Hayes now? Why so formal?"

"I just figured I should show you a little respect," he said casually as he made his way over to the sofa.

"Ha! You always give me as little respect as possible," Samantha shot back as she sat.

A troubled expression was his only response. It was unlike Levi to not meet her banter with his own.

"Levi, I've never seen you like this. Are you okay?"

"Am I disrespectful to you?"

As Samantha offered a quick wave of dismissal,

Levi persisted. "No, really, am I disrespectful to you? I kid a lot and we banter back and forth all the time. I don't mean for it to be, but is it disrespectful?"

"You're serious."

Levi tilted his head and raised an eyebrow.

"Levi, you've known me for three years. Why ask me this now?"

"I just wonder sometimes about how it looks to others. Like, Chess—"

"Chess adores you. She wants to *be* you, Levi."

"And then there's Sydnee." He sped up to finish before Samantha could interrupt. "Who says everything she thinks and even *she* doesn't joke around like I do."

"She hasn't known me as long as you have."

"And Jeff, he doesn't clown around or call you Sam."

"You know I don't mind my research assistants calling me by my first name. In fact, every one of you called me Dr. Hayes until I suggested otherwise. Jeff, Sydnee, and Chess *don't* use my first name, but they could." Samantha paused. "Levi, we've had this discussion before. You know all this." Samantha sat back, amused.

"But it's not just the others in this office." Levi seemed to weigh his words carefully, then let out a burst of air. "This is awkward."

Samantha was no longer amused. The back of her neck tingled the way it did when the boss calls an unexpected meeting or when a spouse says *We need to talk*. She had the ominous sense that a storm cloud had moved in and at any moment would break.

"Levi, what's this about?"

He nodded slightly. "You know Dr. Titus is my

advisor for my math minor. He told me yesterday that the way I clown around with you—with everybody—is disrespectful. And I don't know, Sam—Dr. Hayes— maybe he's right. I try to keep it within bounds. I'm never like this with any other professor and you never act like you mind. And I kid around with other students, but no more than they do with me. But then when he asked me to stay after class and told me this..." Levi finished with a blank look and shake of his head.

Unbelievable. Of all the mean-spirited stunts. Samantha and Len had history. Years ago, before they came to Vanderlaan, they both taught at Hayward, where he was dismissed after only three years.

While the Hayward administration usually ignored run-of-the-mill student grumbling, consistent complaints levied against any faculty member they addressed. And complaints about Dr. Len Titus were nothing if not consistent. During each of the six semesters he taught there, a steady stream of students complained that he was rarely available for office hours and would not respond to their emails or calls. His rude demeanor in class prompted more than a few to change majors and file formal complaints with the dean.

His rapport with colleagues was no better. In addition to shirking his share of the academic load, he had little appreciation for the diversity of the Hayward community. Samantha served alongside Len on Hayward's admissions committee and had to call him out for several racist comments he made during their first meeting. Later when he directed sexist comments toward another math professor, Samantha encouraged the colleague to speak openly with the administration. When his contract at Hayward was not renewed at the end of the year, Len blamed Samantha for what he saw as her role in his termination.

After a few semesters, Len landed at Vanderlaan, although at a lower rank and salary than at Hayward. Samantha heard through the rumor mill that Len had gotten the position because he had attended sensitivity training, swore to mend his ways, and was a cousin to one of the more generous Vanderlaan donors. So when the psychology position opened at her alma mater, Samantha didn't hesitate to apply. Vanderlaan was big enough for both of them. It would be fine.

However, when she had been there about a year, the university hired Barb Skeen to teach in the Math Department. She was fresh out of graduate school and a friend of Samantha's daughter, Elyse. During Barb's first year at Vanderlaan, Len worked with her on a research project in which she did the lion's share of the work. But when the report came out in a prestigious academic journal, Barb was not listed as co-author. He pleaded oversight yet did nothing to correct the mistake. Not with the journal and not among their colleagues at the university. Shortly after its publication, he was awarded tenure.

Barb shared her anger and feelings of betrayal with Samantha, who encouraged her to blow the whistle on Len. But as a single mother, Barb was desperate for job security. Being a team player, she reasoned, would help gain her colleagues' support in a few short years when she would be up for tenure herself. So she kept quiet. Allowing injustice to go unanswered was almost impossible for Samantha. But out of respect for Barb's wishes, Samantha kept quiet, too. At least, formally.

The next year when Samantha chaired the

Academic Integrity Committee, she set up a series of speakers to provide faculty training in professional writing. In a calculated attempt to put Len on notice, Samantha asked him to lead the session entitled, "How to Avoid Plagiarism: Giving Credit Where Credit is Due."

Afterward, when he opened the floor to questions, Samantha asked Len to elaborate on the protocol in place for those rare instances when colleagues stole work from one another. She knew it was a cheeky move, but the stone-cold look in his eyes as he answered her question left her unsettled. Had she gone too far? Was it worth putting Len on notice when she, herself, did not yet have the job security tenure provided?

She had no doubt that Len's comments to Levi stemmed more from their history than from Levi's behavior. Would Len use Levi for payback to Samantha? Of course, he would. Would Samantha allow Levi to be a pawn in Len's game of revenge? No, she would not.

Samantha took a deep breath to steady her voice before speaking. She would not cast an unfavorable light on a colleague in front of a student—even when the colleague was Len Titus, and even when the student was Levi Corliss.

"So that's it. Based on what Dr. Titus said, you're worried about being disrespectful."

He nodded. His face solemn.

"Levi," she began calmly. "This situation is bigger than your behavior. It goes back farther and involves more than you joking around with me or anyone else." *Wow. I sound like I have this totally under control. I'll pick up my Emmy after work today.*

"I don't understand."

"You don't have to, Levi. I do. Just know this is not about you." She stopped short of saying she would handle it. That would be too much like telling your teenager you would speak with their teacher about an unreasonable assignment. At least, she would imagine, never having done such a thing herself.

Levi continued to watch Samantha as if awaiting an explanation.

It didn't come.

"Do you trust me to tell you the truth?"

Levi nodded. "Yeah, I do."

Samantha's words were steady. "I love our banter. I am glad you call me Sam."

"It's not disrespectful?"

"If I felt disrespected by you or any of my students, you wouldn't have to ask."

The creases across Levi's forehead disappeared as he chuckled. "Yeah, I can imagine."

"Trust me, Mr. Corliss," she bantered. "You *cannot.*"

Chapter 10

Wednesday, September 5

After Levi left her office, Samantha paced and weighed her options. She could just ignore Len's interference. Levi now knew that Dr. Titus had spoken out of turn. He obviously trusted her opinion over his math professor's. No harm, no foul.

Samantha stopped pacing, hands on hips. But then Len wouldn't have to answer for his behavior. Allowing injustice to go unchallenged was not Samantha's strong suit. It left her unsettled with too many unspoken responses ricocheting in her mind. Besides, she didn't believe for one minute he would cease and desist efforts to sabotage her relationships with other students. No—ignoring the injury was not an option. She shook her head and resumed pacing while clicking the retractable pen she held.

Samantha could speak with their dean, Monique Easton, about her history with Len and his most recent caper. The dean would say something to Len, and he would cut out the nonsense. Len would not fare well going toe-to-toe with Monique, and he knew it. The downside of this plan was Samantha's age: She was an adult, not a child who needed her mother to call out the neighborhood bully. No, she wouldn't hide behind Monique.

Of course, she *could* confront Len herself. She

paused her pacing and stopped clicking. Make it clear she would not tolerate his interference. A smile tugged at her mouth. Oh, the satisfaction—like jumping into a cool swimming pool on a sticky, August afternoon. The only problem was the last time she and Len talked face to face, it hadn't ended well. *Click, click.* More pacing. She had said things she later regretted and still felt the twinge of guilt that an annoyingly healthy conscience evokes. Did she have the financial resources for the number of sessions with Debra such an encounter would necessitate? She didn't know.

But confronting Len made more sense than ignoring him or calling in a third party. And if she planned her response and executed it carefully, regret wouldn't be necessary. Directness was one of Samantha's strengths; she would use it. She tossed her pen onto her desk and marched out of her office. Should she call ahead? Probably, but she wouldn't. Why give him the chance to avoid her? Inside the entrance of Shelley Hall, Samantha found Len's name and office number on a placard along with those of his colleagues. His office would be about halfway down the hall on the left. A beam of light on the floor outside his office indicated his door was open. This thing would be started and finished in the next few moments. Samantha put on her big girl face, walked to his open door, and knocked lightly to announce her presence. He looked up from his computer screen. In characteristic fashion, Len peered over his wire-rimmed glasses with his mouth slightly open, as if calculating the cost her presence would mean to his daily allotment of time and energy.

"Hello, Samantha. What can I do for you?"

"Len, I'd like a few minutes. Are you free?"

"Certainly." He turned from his computer and motioned for her to have a seat.

"One of my students tells me you've suggested that he's disrespectful to me and inappropriate with his peers. Your comments have caused him considerable turmoil. He's now second guessing the way he interacts with me and even his closest friends."

"If this is about Levi Corliss—"

"*If* this is about Levi? Are there others, Len?"

"Samantha, I'm Levi's advisor for his math minor and this doesn't concern you."

"If this were only directed at his work in your courses, his behavior with you, or even in your classes, I would agree. But that isn't the case. How many times have you even *seen* him interact with his friends or with me?"

"I watch Levi. I see him with his classmates. I attended the presentation you two gave on campus last semester. I'm within my bounds as his advisor to let him know when his behavior is out of line."

"So on the basis of a few classes and one presentation you decide he needs to interact with me and his friends differently? I'm sorry, Len, but that's just irresponsible. Not to mention we both know what this is about."

He shook his head and pushed himself back from his desk. "This has nothing to do with you, Samantha, or any differences you and I have had over the years."

"It does, and you know it!" Her neck and face were hot with anger. "Levi trusts you, Len, and for you to make him doubt himself purely out of spite for me is inexcusable!"

"You should talk. Look at your own inexcusable behavior, butting in with my colleagues at Hayward and here at Vanderlaan. Even if I were using Levi—which I am not—you are hardly in a position to accuse me."

"Do you ever think about the harm you can do? To students? To colleagues? When it's more about revenge than doing your job—"

"And what's this about some"—Len made air quotes—"room connection you have with your students? You should be setting an example for them of rational thought, not pandering to this…this…paranormal bunk."

"*Pandering*? Paranor—" Samantha gritted her teeth. *No. He won't distract me from the issue.*

He stood, hands on hips. "I do my job and mind my own business. I suggest you do the same."

Was his posture meant to intimidate? Samantha stood, hands on hips. She could take up space too. "Look, Len, this is the bottom line. You will not use a student to get back at me for whatever difficulty you had keeping a job at Hayward—"

"Samantha—"

"No." She held up her hand. "I'm still talking. You will cut out your antics with Levi and if you *ever* try to get at me through one of my students again, I promise you, Hayward will look like the highpoint of your career."

Samantha turned and walked out of his office, down the hall, and out of the building.

The day was still hot and sticky. But jumping into that pool had helped.

****

Len pushed himself out of the chair with force as

he rose to pace. *Just who does she think she is? Coming in here bossing me around.* His breath was shaky. He loosened his tie. Exactly why he preferred numbers over people. Numbers are certain, predictable. They give way to no one. You bring in the human element, mistakes happen.

If Len Titus had his way, his job would brook no interruptions from humans and their constant neediness. Colleagues—constant source of criticism. Not enough office time. Not doing his share of committee work. Not enough community service. Working against faculty morale—whatever that meant. Bah—who needed them.

But students! They're the worst. This one wants extra credit; that one needs help understanding. Continuous complaints that I'm rude and lack interest in student success. He kicked at his desk chair. If he didn't need better student evaluations to appease the administration, he would forget that students were on the other end of this teaching thing. Of course, there were a handful of students over the years who earned their keep. Those who glommed onto him for fear of not passing. Losers, sure; but valuable when it came to boosting his student evaluation averages.

And then there was the one who helped him get tenure back at Hayward. She'd come in looking for a mentor and research experience. As much as he loathed working with others, he recognized an opportunity when he saw one. The plan was for her to write the first draft and for him to edit it. He would then get it published which would satisfy colleagues who railed against his lack of student involvement.

As it turned out, she was a quick study, incredibly

bright, and an excellent writer. After meeting with her only a couple of times to discuss the project, she got to work and handed him an exemplary manuscript, better than he could have hoped for. The next day he called her to his office.

"It's good," he had said. "Very good. Did anyone help you with this?" He peered over his glasses.

"Of course not." She almost seemed offended. "I would never turn in someone else's work."

"No, of course not. I'm simply impressed. This is fine work."

Mercifully, his phone rang preventing his thoughts from travelling further down that road. It never helped to think too much about her anyway. Best the whole thing be forgotten.

****

Samantha called Rob as soon as she got out of voice-range of those entering or exiting Shelley Hall. She told him about her conversation with Levi then her confrontation with Len. "So, I marched in and told him to back off." She laughed. "It felt great. He's without a doubt the most cantankerous human being I've dealt with at Vanderlaan. Or at Hayward, either."

"Good for you. Did you slap him around or just pulverize him with your words?"

"Words, sweetheart. Always with words."

"Think he'll straighten up?"

"He better." She slowed as she approached Prescott. She wanted to talk freely and wouldn't be able to if surrounded by students and other faculty.

"I'm glad I caught you before you left for the afternoon. Will you have a busy evening?"

"Sure will. Plus, I'm working out a plot for my

next book. How would you feel about a murder on a college campus? Maybe the psychology professor could be guilty?"

"Hmm…Depends on whom she kills. And you wouldn't let her get caught, would you?"

"Meh. I'd have to. Good moral take-away."

"Killjoy. Hey, I need to get back to work. Call me tonight?"

"I will. Love you, Sammy."

"Love you, too."

Clarence Whitmer appeared next to her and held the door as she walked into Prescott.

"Well, you've certainly made Vanderlaan history, Dr. Hayes." Clarence's greeting was as relaxed and jovial as the man himself.

"What do you mean?" She followed him into his office and stepped around the journals stacked along the walls and desk. Chairs, however, remained free of clutter. Samantha sat in one.

He laughed as he threw his briefcase on the floor. "The little come-uppance you gave Len just now." He leaned back in his chair with his hands behind his head.

"You know about that! How?"

"His secretary." He shrugged. "She was outside the door."

Clarence regularly taught a class in Shelley Hall as it fulfilled a requirement for both science and psychology majors. "Granted, it's probably an overstatement to say you made Vanderlaan history, but you are so my hero." He chuckled again.

"I didn't know I had an audience, Clarence. Does Len know people overheard?"

"Nah." He waved his hand and sat upright again at

his desk. "Besides, Len needs to be taken down a peg on a fairly regular basis. Not that it does any good, but…"

"So you have trouble with him too?"

"Oh, Samantha, everybody has trouble with Len. Don't pay him any attention. He's not been right since…well, since before he came to Vanderlaan." Clarence leaned back in his chair again. "I was here when he got hired. He was fairly mild in those days, but still crotchety. Rumor has it, he and his wife had been living with his parents. I think he had lost his last job and was in debt to his eyeballs. Then his wife left him. Too much for her, I guess. So, by the time he got this job, he was pretty down and out." He leaned forward again.

"Down and out, huh?"

"Can't say he didn't bring it on himself." Clarence pointed and raised his eyebrows. "The man is a jerk, no doubt about it. He probably got fired for good reason. Heaven knows, I'd have kicked him off Vanderlaan's campus years ago if it were up to me. But you"—he shook a finger at Samantha, nodded and grinned—"you got moxie, Samantha."

"Yeah, I do." Samantha nodded. A knock at his door reminded Samantha that Clarence's students needed his time. She waved in a student who hesitated at the door. "No, come on in. I'm just leaving."

As she walked down the hall to her own office, she pulled out her cell, thumbed it on, and pressed Rob's name. With her office empty, she closed the door, left the light off, and sat in the chair that was out of view to anyone passing by.

When Rob picked up, she plunged in with a

whisper, "Len's wife left him after he left Hayward."

Rob whispered back, "Has anyone called the cops?"

She chuckled and spoke in a normal tone. "No, wise guy. But I feel bad. Clarence just told me Len and his wife had to move in with his folks after he got fired from Hayward and she ended up leaving him. Evidently, he went through a pretty rough time after that. Might be why he didn't have a job for a while."

"Do I have to tell you that you were not the reason his marriage failed? *or* that he and his parents didn't get along? *or* that it took him a while to land on his feet?"

"No. No, you don't." She stood up and flipped on the lights. "You're right. Len's problems were not of my making. Ever think about therapy as a career?"

"I don't fix people. I plot murders then leave enough clues for their killers to get caught." Rob reminded her, "And you—stop thinking about Len."

"Yeah, yeah. I will."

For the rest of the afternoon, Samantha answered emails, returned calls, and helped several students who needed to make last minute changes to their schedules. She also thought about Len, his broken marriage, and his trouble keeping a job.

Chapter 11

Monday, September 10

"Did you tell your sister you know?" Samantha asked.

"I couldn't," Christine said. "Not with her trying so hard to plan this party. Maybe I'll work on my look of surprise. How's this?" She raised her eyebrows and stretched her jaw into a tense contortion of a smile.

"Like you need to practice." They laughed as they began the day in Christine's office over caramel lattes. Her desk held a computer, stapler, and a caddie with paperclips and sticky notes—the usual office paraphernalia. A framed picture of Rex, her regal dachshund, stood sentinel next to a stack of trays each with its own label. One was marked, *Work for Today*, another tagged, *Work for Tomorrow*, and still another, *Not in This Lifetime*.

Before long the first floor of Prescott Hall would come to life. Students with questions for professors. Professors with questions for Christine. Christine with more to do than a workday would permit. In fact, Samantha expected her merry band any minute to work on research. But for now, these two friends took advantage of the quiet to catch up.

"So what about you?" Christine leaned back in her desk chair. "Has Dr. Titus said any more to upset Levi?"

"I don't think so. Levi's his old self."

"You mention it to him?"

Down the hall, the outside door of Prescott opened and closed. Samantha leaned sideways to see who was on the hall. Two students stood at Clarence Whitmer's office door. One pointed at the posted sheet of office hours and said something Samantha couldn't hear; the other checked her watch.

"Goodness, no." Although Samantha felt justified standing up to Len, Levi still didn't need to know. She wouldn't weaken the respect he held for another professor.

The door opened again. Samantha peered out of Christine's office long enough to see Chess, Sydnee, and Allie walk in. "Hello, ladies. My office is open. Go on in and get started. I'll be there in a minute." Samantha relaxed again in her chair and took another sip. More doors clanging down the hall signaled the official beginning of the workday.

"Darn that underhanded, vindictive Len Titus for putting me in this situation to begin with!" Samantha huffed. "I could just wring his scrawny little neck!"

"But really, Sam, how do you feel?" Christine raised an eyebrow and sipped. "If he upsets you this much, you should speak with Debra about it."

"Sure. What's a therapist for if not to talk you down from murdering a colleague?"

"Don't resort to anything so drastic yet. I'd prefer not to visit you in prison." Christine finished her last sip and turned her chair toward her desk.

Samantha looked at her cell. "Ooh, I need to scram. Thanks for the chat, friend." She tossed her cup into the recycle bin. As she headed out Christine's door, she all but ran into Levi who seemed to appear out of nowhere. Samantha's hand flew to her chest as she caught her breath.

"Sorry," Levi said. "Didn't mean to scare you. Jeff and I just got in and can't find the key to the research cabinet."

"Oh. I have it." Flustered, Samantha handed him a key ring from her jacket pocket. He took it and jogged off toward her office.

Samantha winced and whispered to Christine, "Did he hear me? What I said about Len?"

Christine offered a slow shake of her head and furrowed brow. "I don't think so. He couldn't have been here long. We would've seen him."

"How unprofessional!" Samantha said between clenched teeth. "Talking about a colleague in earshot of a student."

"But you didn't know he was there. And he probably didn't hear anything." She waved her hand. "You're fine, really. Don't worry."

Samantha took a deep breath, nodded, and walked to her office.

****

Levi dashed into Samantha's office. "Okay, we gotta think quick! She knows we know. Or at least that *I* know."

"About what?" Chess asked.

"That she's seeing a therapist. I just overheard her say something about it to Christine. I walked up and she saw me. So, she *knows I know!*"

"Levi, we've known for a while now that she's seeing a therapist," Allie said calmly. "We agreed not to tell her we know, but it's okay if *she* tells *us*. Why did you eavesdrop?"

"I didn't. Not intentionally. I just walked up, and she blurted out something about a therapist." He looked off to the side, crinkled his forehead. "And killing somebody, I think…"

"Dr. H isn't going to kill anybody," Jeff said. "Just play this cool, like nothing happened." Footsteps from Christine's office grew louder. Jeff's instructions accelerated. "She'll tell us what she wants us to know. Until then, we don't say anything."

Everyone darted to the research table. Jeff, Levi, and Chess plopped down as if music had stopped, and chairs were at a premium. Sydnee, elbow on Jeff's shoulder, feigned supervision. Allie scattered files.

Fake smiles.

Awkward poses.

Samantha reached the office door. Stopped. "You look like mannequins in a store window."

****

Had Levi heard what she said about Len? Had he shared it with them? She needed to clear the air. "Levi, I need to talk with you before we get started today."

"Sam, it's okay, you don't need to explain anything." Levi stood. "We already know and it's okay. We should have told you when we found out. But who you talk to is totally your business."

Quick nods from the others.

"Seriously?" Samantha sat on the arm of the sofa. "Everyone knows?"

"Well…not *everyone*. Just us," Levi clarified. "And we agreed not to share it with anybody."

More nods.

"I'm pleased you're okay with it, Levi. Frankly, I

didn't say anything because I didn't want to upset you."

"Why would I be upset? This is your business. We respect that."

"True, but I went because of you so—"

"You went because of me?"

"Sure, Levi, that was the whole point."

"The whole point?" Levi lowered himself onto a chair. "Are you serious?"

Allie stepped closer to Levi, put her hand on his shoulder.

Whatever Samantha had expected from Levi, this wasn't it. Was he okay that she spoke to Len or not? She lowered herself from the arm to the seat of the sofa and proceeded with care. "Sometimes when a professor has an issue with a student, it takes a third party to straighten things out."

"But when I left the other day…after you and I talked…you seemed okay."

"I was. But that didn't mean it was settled."

Levi stared into space, his mouth open. Allie sat down beside him, put her other hand on his arm.

"I…I could have gone with you," Levi said.

"Gone with me?" Samantha blinked. "No! I wanted to keep you out of this."

"Out of it?" He let out a brief humorless laugh. "I'm right in the middle of it."

"You're only in the middle because you were *put* in the middle." She sat up straighter. "Look, the bottom line: I need to apologize. You might have heard me say some unkind things. It was unprofessional to speak so freely where students could overhear. I'm sorry. And maybe underhanded and vindictive was a poor choice of words, but—"

"Wait. What? Who's underhanded and vindictive?" Levi bolted out of the chair, rubbed his hand through his hair.

"Dr. Titus!" Samantha gave way to annoyance.

A spark of light in Levi's eyes. The faintest glimpse of a smile. Was Levi okay? Did he not mind that she had intervened with Len?

"You spoke with *Dr. Titus* about the discussion *you and I* had the other day?"

"Of course."

"And *he* is the one with the issue?"

"Sure."

"And *you* are the third party who went to straighten it out."

"Yes."

Levi's smile turned to laughter. Allie's hands released Levi and flew to her face. Chess patted her chest as she gulped in air. Sydnee and Jeff sat back and chuckled quietly.

"What just happened here?" Samantha searched five faces.

Levi whispered, "You called Dr. Titus *underhanded* and *vindictive!*"

"Yeah, but..." A smile tugged at Samantha's lips. Her head turned slightly. She squinted. "What were *you* talking about?"

"Dr. Titus, obviously." Levi moved to the research table. "We ready to get to work?"

"No, no, no, Mr. Corliss." Samantha waggled a finger and shook her head. "Who did you think I called underhanded and vindictive?" She followed Levi to the table, leaned in. "What did you overhear just now in

Christine's office?"

Levi exaggerated a shrug.

Allie took the reins. "We know you're seeing a therapist. We should have said something earlier but didn't want to intrude."

"At least until now," Sydnee blurted, "when Levi told us you knew we knew because he overheard you and Christine." She walked past Levi, pushed her chin out. "She didn't know, Levi. This was all for nothing."

"I don't mind." Samantha laughed. "But how did you find out?"

Jeff put his fingertips to his forehead. "We see all and know all."

Everyone chuckled. Allie explained, "I found out last semester when Elyse called to ask me to measure that wall because she wanted to get you the movie poster for your birthday."

Samantha nodded. "The one over the sofa."

"And I told her you would be suspicious if one day I just pulled out a tape measure. She said to just sneak in when you were in class or at your therapist's."

"Then one day," Levi picked up the story, "Ms. Confidentiality here let it slip."

Jeff took his turn in the relay. "We were all at your house finals week, when Snoopy here"—Jeff motioned to Levi—"saw an appointment card on your fridge and asked, 'Who's this Debra Joren that Sam has an appointment with next Wednesday?' "

"And that's when I came in the room," Allie claimed back the story, "and said 'She's a psychologist. Why?' Remember my roommate last year used to see her?"

Samantha nodded and giggled.

"Then they were all like 'ooh, are we supposed to know Dr. H. sees a therapist?' " Levi said.

"Except for me." Sydnee put up an index finger. "I said maybe Dr. H. is consulting with her about something."

"And it would've worked too had Al not gotten flustered." Levi shook his head at Allie. "You're so transparent."

"We didn't mean to snoop, Dr. Hayes," Chess stated.

"I did," Levi admitted.

"Well, the rest of us didn't," Chess said. "And we didn't say anything outside our group. Honest."

"Thank you, Chess. All of you. But if I cared that people know, I wouldn't leave the information out where it could be seen." She moved to her desk. "But that you kept it to yourselves out of respect for my privacy is just the nicest thing."

"Yeah, we're outstanding young people. But let's not lose sight of the real issue," Levi said. "You don't like one of your colleagues and, for that, we are extremely disappointed in you."

Just because he found it humorous did not diminish her responsibility. Samantha rolled her chair up to her desk, placed folded arms on its top. "Levi, I'm sorry I said those things about Dr. Titus. He and I are not best of friends. But I hope that won't diminish your respect for him as your teacher."

"Maybe if you told me more." Levi leaned in and wiggled his eyebrows.

"Not a chance, Snoopy."

Chapter 12

Tuesday, September 11

Samantha opened her office door to grant entry to a book-laden someone. "Allie, is that you under there?"

"Thanks, Samantha," Allie said, textbooks in each arm and a pencil between her teeth. She carefully opened each text to the places marked with paper clips and removed the pencil. "Last night I did some research for my paper on Carl Jung. The one for senior seminar. I found some really cool things." Allie sat down at the research table and motioned for Samantha to join her. "Do you know about Jung's thoughts on synchronicity?"

"Sure, the idea that some things happen without any direct cause and effect relationship, yet still hold meaning."

"You mean like a coincidence?" asked Jeff.

"Sort of." Allie tilted her head slightly. "Only more relevant than a coincidence. See, Jung had a patient once who wouldn't consider anything which couldn't be explained rationally. He couldn't get through to her. Then one day she told him about her dream in which someone had given her a piece of jewelry—a golden scarab—"

Samantha's head snapped up.

"A scarab? What's that?" Chess asked.

"It's a bug, Chess. A beetle," Jeff replied.

"How do you all know this stuff?" Chess muttered while Allie continued.

"Then while she was talking about the scarab dream, Jung heard something hit the window. He looked out and saw—" Allie stopped for effect. "—a scarab beetle! He opened the window and picked it up and handed it to the patient!" Allie's eyes widened as she nodded.

Sydnee squinted. "And the point is…?"

"The *point* is that no way those two incidences could have been related in a cause-and-effect sort of way. The dream didn't cause the bug to fly into the window and the bug at the window certainly didn't cause the dream or for the patient to recount the dream. Those two things happened simultaneously and at the very moment our man Carl would notice it and could use it to help his patient."

"And it made you think of our room connection," Samantha said.

"Of course. This room connection can't be explained rationally either—there is no cause and effect. It's just an occurrence that, to us anyway, has meaning. Synchronicity."

Silence.

"Ooh, I like." Chess grinned and rubbed her hands together.

"Well, you would," Sydnee said.

"What's *that* supposed to mean?" asked Levi.

"Just that Chess likes anything that's paranormal. Out there. Unscientific."

"I don't either," Chess replied. "Well, maybe I do. But—"

"But that's what this situation *is*, Sydnee," Allie

said. "Something 'out there' which defies scientific, rational thought."

"Yeah, I guess." Sydnee continued her work.

"Are you like Jung's patient, Syd?" asked Chess. "Does it have to be rational for you to believe it?"

"No, not at all. I'm intrigued by the whole thing and, you're right, none of it can be explained scientifically. But just to call it 'synchronicity' doesn't give us an explanation."

Jeff said, "What I don't get, how is this any different than saying God planned it or put it into motion? Providence, they call it."

"Nothing I guess," Allie said. "Maybe just whether or not you believe in God. And I'm not saying I don't," she added quickly. "But you wouldn't have to believe in the traditional sense to allow for synchronicity."

"Ha! So synchronicity even works for heathens like me?" Sydnee said.

"I didn't say you're a heathen, Syd. Man, you're difficult." Allie tossed the book on the table and walked over to the couch where she plopped down next to Levi.

Samantha's chest tightened at the brewing conflict. She redirected. "Have I ever shown you the necklace I wear?" She held out the scarab charm and explained, "My grandfather wasn't a Carl Jung aficionado, but he did tell me that the scarab symbolizes transformation and rebirth. He gave me this pendant right before he passed away. I had just left Hayward and come to Vanderlaan. Said it would remind me to stay open to all the transformations a move would bring." She smiled, remembering.

"It means *transformation*?" Chess squealed, as her hands flew to her mouth. "And Jung's patient was *transformed* by the experience? How are you not loving this, Sydnee?"

"Don't waste your breath, Chess," Allie said as she took the chocolate mint Levi offered. "But I am intrigued that others have experiences like this and put thought to what it means. Take it or leave it, Syd."

"Well, *I'll take* it." Chess picked up the book Allie had discarded and thumbed to the paper-clipped sections.

"Pluth—" Allie held up an index finger.

"Pluth?" Levi slowly turned to Allie.

"I'm chewing." She swallowed and continued. "Plus—synchronicity and faith in a higher power aren't mutually exclusive. Who's to say it can't be both? But—" Allie sat up quickly and took one of the books back from Chess and turned to another page she had clipped. "This author says there's a lot more to it. He believes that when synchronistic events occur it might be that we have planned those events earlier—like in a previous life—"

"Oh brother." Sydnee rolled her eyes.

Allie held up her index finger toward Sydnee. "—to let us know we're in the right place at the right time."

"So I was right when I said it was about resolving some dilemma from a former life." Levi smiled at Allie and tilted his head. "You're welcome."

"I don't guess it would have to be about resolving dilemmas, but—"

"I can't believe you two." Sydnee's palms went up. "Dr. H., do you buy any of this? Former lives, leaving messages for our present lives crap?"

"I don't know that I do," Samantha said. "But I try to keep an open mind on things I don't understand.

"So do I," Chess quickly added. "And if this is a former life thing, then we—or you all anyway—planned the whole room connection back before this life so you would know, what…that you were on the right track or something?"

Allie nodded. "That's the idea."

"What do you think, Levi?" Chess asked.

Levi tilted his head and raised his eyebrows. "I reserve judgment."

"Chicken," Syd said as she continued her work.

"No, Syd. I'm open minded."

"Yeah, yeah, me too." Chess pulled her legs up under her in the chair she occupied. "So, if this is synchronicity, I want to know the whole story. Allie and Levi—you two must have been the first to meet Dr. Hayes since you've been here the longest, right?"

"That's right," Allie said. "We were in Intro to Psych our first semester."

"And you took her class right away because you were psych majors?"

"Oh no," Allie and Levi said simultaneously.

"I hadn't decided yet what I wanted to major in," Levi said. "I just signed up for psychology as a general education requirement. You did too, right, Al?"

"Yeah, I was an English major, wanted to be a lawyer. Then when I got into psychology, I loved it and came by several times to talk to Samantha about becoming a therapist."

"And I had no idea what kind of job I wanted. I just knew it would involve psych. Then I would come by to pester Sam about career options. And she just always begged me to hang around to cheer up this dreary hole of an office."

Allie hit Levi with a pillow. "Then we kept coming by and kind of made this place our home."

"She needed us, Al. Her life was pretty bleak before we sauntered in."

"You mean other students didn't hang out in here before you two?" Chess asked.

"No, they were the first," Samantha said. Whereas Hayward had paid for student research assistants, Vanderlaan did not. Unfortunately, without the help, Samantha found it difficult to accomplish all she had hoped that first year. The quality of Allie's and Levi's writing, however, impressed her and an idea formed. She asked them if they would serve informally as her research assistants in exchange for some experience that would build their graduate school applications. That is, she said, if they had the time. Goodness, but they had the time, and to her surprise wanted to spend it in her office. So they readily agreed to her offer and her research team was born.

"And when did you join the group, Jeff?" Chess asked.

Jeff looked up from his computer screen at the research table. "I came in a year after Allie and Levi. I was an English major, hadn't added psychology yet. And, as I recall"—Jeff smiled sheepishly at Samantha—"failed the first exam I had with you."

"No way," Chess said.

"You just had a difficult transition into college, but you came up to speed pretty quickly after that," Samantha said.

"Initially I came by for study tips. And, of course, Allie and Levi were here a lot." Jeff laughed as he moved over to the empty chair next to Chess. "You two acted like you owned this office. Allie, I remember you showed me where the candy was stashed and the sodas and juices in the fridge, like you wanted me to—" Jeff struggled for the right words.

"Move in?" Levi supplied the phrase.

"Yeah." Jeff laughed. "Honestly, it was the first time I felt like I had a group of friends who wanted me around."

"Really? Why, Jeff?" Chess asked. "You're so much fun."

"I don't know." Jeff shrugged. "In high school I was more serious than the other kids. They always said I thought too much, whatever *that* means. But in here, thinking about things that mattered was okay. I liked that."

"Then I realized what a gifted writer Jeff is and asked him to work with me on an article," Samantha said.

"I was so glad!" Jeff stretched his legs out. "I wanted to work with you like Levi and Allie but didn't know how to get there."

"See, I would just ask," Sydnee said.

"Ha! No, Syd." Levi pointed at her as he got up and headed for the fridge. "You would stomp in and just announce that you're working with us. Because that's exactly what you did." In an exaggerated impersonation of Sydnee, Levi clomped back toward the sofa, sat down, and announced, "Hi, I'm Sydnee Baldwin. I belong here and I will *not* go away." Then in his normal voice, Levi continued. "Then she reaches into my backpack—"

"I did not." Sydnee laughed and shook her head.

"—and I had to wrestle it from her." Levi sat

down. "It was quite the spectacle."

"You are strange, Levi." Sydnee chuckled.

Jeff laughed. "Well, I was here, Syd, and Levi nailed it. Because I wondered how anybody could just *do* that." Then before Sydnee could protest, Jeff added, "It's not a criticism. I was impressed."

Allie laughed. "Then Samantha handed Sydnee the candy dish, told her not to bother Levi's things, and voila, she was part of our merry band."

Sydnee stood up and took a slight bow. "I'm gratified you all remember my arrival so fondly."

"Then I came along in a pretty ordinary way," Chess said. "I wish I had a story for how I found this office. Maybe that's why I'm not part of this room connection."

Samantha smiled. "Chess, you are *anything* but ordinary."

"You entered talking and haven't stopped since," Sydnee said.

Levi winked. "And you're my prodigy. So by the time I graduate you'll be head of the Hayes Hecklers."

"But what does all this mean in terms of synchronicity?" Allie pulled the group back to the original question. "We all came here, individually, not knowing we were each—except for Chess—living in rooms where Samantha once lived. We have become closer to Samantha than any other professor. Then we learn we have this room connection."

"And it still doesn't explain anything," Sydnee said.

"But it does. Sort of." Allie got up and paced. "We have a connection with no scientific, cause and effect relationship, and yet, given our relationship to

Samantha and each other, this connection has meaning. Just like with Carl Jung and his patient, this will help us all move forward."

Allie held up a palm to preempt Sydnee's protest. "I don't know how, but we each have something to gain from this room connection."

Chapter 13

Tuesday, September 11

Samantha was intrigued with the idea of synchronicity and impressed, as always, with Allie's passion for learning everything she could about anything she didn't understand.

"I like the idea of synchronicity. But what if it's more supernatural than that?" Chess asked.

"What you mean is, you *want* it to be supernatural." Sydnee laughed and went back to her data entry.

"What do you mean, Chess?" asked Allie.

"I wonder…what if it has something to do with your room and the girl who died in it."

Samantha and Allie exchanged a glance.

"Something to *do* with it?" Levi laughed. "You think she died then set up our room assignments?"

"And knowing our aptitude for research," Sydnee said with mock eagerness, "wanted us to join forces with Dr. H. so we could investigate the reason for her death." Sydnee shook her head and resumed her work. "Honestly, Chess."

"Cut it out, you two," Allie said. "Chess, do you really believe people hang around after death to…*do* things?"

"Or *say* things," Sydnee said. "Like 'boo!' "

Chess gained momentum. "I've heard some pretty

convincing stories. People who actually see someone who has died. And some of those people used to not even believe in...well...*ghosts* or whatever, but then they feel different after it happens to themselves. This one book I read was based on a true story where this guy, every year on the anniversary of when he proposed to his girlfriend, would see her sitting outside in his car."

With all eyes on her, Chess raised her eyebrows. "And, *yes*, on the night he proposed, he and his girlfriend had a wreck and she *died in his car.*"

"Maybe he was hallucinating," said Sydnee. "Think how traumatic it would be if your girlfriend died right after you'd decided to get married. Trauma does things to people. Right, Dr. H.?"

"Sure, Syd. Hallucinations aren't common though."

"I bet they're more common than dead girlfriend sightings." Sydnee kept working.

Chess walked over to the research table and sat across from Sydnee. "And I saw another story about this high school boy who killed his parents before killing himself. I think they abused him as a kid. Then he appeared to his friend next door before leaving for good." Chess picked up a pen and pointed it at Sydnee. "And the friend hadn't even heard yet that he died. She didn't find out about it until later that evening after the bodies were found."

Allie asked, "Did he say anything to her? The friend next door, I mean?"

"No, she said he just stood there in his bloody sweats, looking sad, then he faded away."

"See that's proof right there." Sydnee grabbed the

pen back from Chess's hand. "Every ghost story includes what the dead person was wearing. Even if people do have spirits that saunter around after they leave the body, their *clothes* don't."

At this, Levi raised both arms in a V shape. "Yes!"

Allie tilted her head to the side as if pondering the possibility of spirited activewear.

"What do you think, Dr. Hayes?" Chess turned in her chair toward Samantha. "Don't you think it's at least possible that people stay around after death to take care of things, say good-bye, whatever?"

"I don't know, Chess." Samantha offered a skeptical smile.

"Jeff, what do you think?" Chess asked the only one who had yet to weigh in.

"I think we can't possibly know everything about life, much less what happens afterwards."

"See, Syd? Even Jeff, who is a very logical person, admits that some things we just don't know." Chess's exuberance gave way to calm reflection as she continued. "You know, Syd, you're a lot like Jung's patient. You need a scarab experience."

"Yeah, well, I'm not likely to have it. I'm not a fan of jewelry or bugs."

"No, but you need an experience that will convince you there's more to life and death than meets the eye."

"Ha! What do you mean—like a séance?" Sydnee replied.

At that, Allie bit her lip, Levi dropped his head on the back of his chair, Jeff's eyes darted to Chess, and Samantha winced—as they each awaited the inevitable.

"A séance!" Chess exclaimed.

****

"Chess, for the record, I am not taking part in a séance." Samantha spoke with a firmness usually reserved for students who begged extra credit during finals week.

"Dr. Hayes, it would be so easy. We have your office and the table. We can come in tonight after dark. No one will be around. I'll bring some candles for atmosphere—"

Jeff's eyes twinkled. "Why wait until tonight? Why not now?"

"Jeffrey!" Sydnee slammed her computer closed and moved toward her book bag. "Outside of me, you are the most logical human being in this *room*, probably on this *campus*, and you are encouraging Chess to converse with dead people! What's wrong with you?" She threw a pillow from the sofa to punctuate her last remark.

"I *am* logical, Syd, which is precisely why I think we need to explore all possibilities before we reject any. If Dr. H. gives the okay for the use of her office, Chess, I'm in."

"Well, I'm out. Out of the office, out of the discussion, out of my *mind* for hanging around this long." Sydnee reached the office door, turned around, and threw her book bag over her shoulder. "Dr. H, I'll come back tomorrow to finish up data entry. Houdini, here, will be too tired tomorrow after his heart-to-heart tonight with the ghost of students past."

"You spooked?" Levi asked.

"Nooo," Sydnee said as she left the office. "I'm a rational human being."

"That's actually for the best. You don't want non-believers in a séance." Chess's words came quickly and with confidence. "How about you, Levi?"

"No, I'm not spooked. But why candles?" Levi changed the subject. "Don't people have these things at night so it'll be dark?"

"Sure, but you want the atmosphere to be warm and inviting. I've read a lot about these things," Chess said. "So, Levi, you in?"

"As tempting as it sounds," Levi said, "I have a prior engagement with my cat—"

"No, Levi, you have to come!" Chess ran to the sofa and knelt down to plead her case. "We need at least three or four, or maybe it's five—I don't remember—to make it work right, or…or—"

"Or the dead *stay dead*? That sounds like a much better idea anyway," Levi said. "And which is it? Three? Four? Five? What *is* the quorum for a séance?"

"Now you're making fun, Levi." Chess pushed herself up from her kneeling position. "Like I said, we don't need non-believers. Anyone involved in a séance needs to be open to the spirit world or—"

"Yeah, yeah, I know—or it won't work." Levi's voice was comically weary as he added, "The truth is I'm torn, Chess. My better judgment says run. But Syd just ran, and office protocol dictates that I'm *never* on her side in anything." Levi held a look of troubled contemplation.

Chess held her own look. Of hope.

"Count me in." Levi reached up for a fist bump, but instead accepted the hug she gave him while squealing her appreciation.

"You two seem to have forgotten, I just nixed the use of my office for a séance." Samantha walked to her desk chair and sat down. "And has everyone completely forgotten that I am on the payroll of this place? Beside the fact that I'm leery of this sort of thing, how long do you suppose I'd be in the good graces of Vanderlaan University if I started hosting séances?"

"Dr. Hayes—" Chess began.

"No, Chess, let it go." Allie entered the conversation again. "Samantha's right. She can't be part of this. She's faculty and Vanderlaan would blow a gasket if they found out she was part of a séance. I get it. My parents have been tiptoeing around college administrators for decades. No, we have to leave her out of this."

"We?" Chess clapped and began bouncing again.

"Yeah, I'm in." As the squealing began, Allie held up a hand. "I'm not spooked either, plus it only makes sense that if there's going to be a séance, it should be held in my room. In case that's, you know, where she died. But," Allie continued, "I can't do it until after I finish my Jung paper. Let's plan for…" She took her planner out of her backpack and flipped through a few pages. "How about Monday?"

"Monday? I can't wait six whole days."

"It'll be fine, Chess," said Levi. "That'll give you time to put together the special effects. What do we need again? Candles for ambience? Audios of screams? Flowers for the dead?"

"Flowers!" Samantha grabbed her purse and ran for the door. "I haven't watered Rob's flowers *once* since he left!" She motioned rapidly for her entourage to exit with her. "I gotta water the sunflowers or tiger lilies or daffodils or…*whatever* is in my backyard right now! Let's move it, folks, before he makes me the dead body in his next novel."

Chapter 14

Monday, September 17

Chess was pleased with the ambience in Allie's room. Stratton Hall room 377 was dark except for the flickering of four candles: one taper candle, previously all of ten inches high, now burnt to a six-inch stump, was supported by a tarnished brass holder; one pillar candle, five inches in diameter, sat on its own ample base with each of its three wicks burning proudly; and two coffee mugs served as makeshift holders to the votive candles that flickered alongside their more impressive counterparts. They each did their duty in providing subtle illumination from the floor of Allie's fourteen by fourteen dorm room.

Chess sat with three friends in a circle around the flames, holding hands to create an atmosphere conducive to the visitation of a spirit. Two sitters, Jeff and Allie, had already confessed their open-minded expectation to Chess, their earnest leader. It was Levi, however, who squirmed and occasionally peeked around the room with one eye, which necessitated Chess's whispered, but stern, warning. "Levi, if you don't sit still, we'll never get a message to or from Annika. If you can't behave, leave so we can do this right."

"I'm sorry." Levi winced. "It's just...I think I'm sitting on a..." He pulled out something from underneath him and held it up. "…a flashlight."

"Oh, that's mine." Still whispering, Chess quickly grabbed the flashlight. "I brought it in case we didn't have enough candles. Sit still. What are you doing now?"

"It's hard for me to cross my legs like you all. I'm taller. I get all tangled up."

Chess broke the circle long enough to whack Levi across the legs multiple times in quick succession. "Figure it out!"

"All right. All right!" Levi situated his knees and ankles.

Chess took a deep breath.

Each of the four repositioned themselves and rejoined hands.

"Annika," Chess began, "we ask you to join us. We have questions only you can answer. Can you hear us? Come to us, Annika."

Silence.

"It's almost midnight," whispered Levi. "Maybe she's asleep."

Allie shushed Levi, as Chess continued, "Annika, we're all here to learn. Even Levi. Would you give us a sign if you're with us? Anything will do, just—"

Crash!

All four sitters yelled and jumped, letting go of each other's hands.

Chess quickly instructed, "Join hands again. Don't break the circle." With a jagged breath, she said, "Was that you, Annika? Are you with us? Was that a signal? We're here. We're listening."

Shuffling noises and muffled voices came from outside the door, first getting louder, then fading.

"Annika, we have some questions. Were you murdered?"

"Well, *that's* rude. Annika? Levi here. Chess should have started with an easier question. Is this the room you lived in?"

Silence.

"She's not talking to you, Levi. Annika, was this your room when you were alive?"

More muffled noises from outside the room.

"Thank you, Annika. Were you—"

"That wasn't Annika." Levi leaned into Chess. "I think they're cleaning up whatever they just dropped down the hall."

"I know that, Levi." Chess spoke with the controlled patience one would use with a three-year-old who could not understand why dessert must wait until after the broccoli. "Maybe Annika spoke to us through the noise down the hall. It doesn't have to be either-or."

Chess took a deep breath and began again. "Annika, we know you died in this room. Please tell us, was your death a murder?"

Allie screamed.

"What's wrong now?" A weary Chess opened her eyes as the last flicker from the wick of one candle dissolved into complete darkness.

"Want me to relight the candles?" Jeff offered.

"No," said Chess. "If Annika wants them out, they stay out. Join hands again. For people who aren't spooked, you all sure are jumpy."

Silence.

"Annika. We've received your message—you were murdered in this room. Can you tell us who murdered you?"

"Doesn't matter, Chess."

"Of course it matters, Levi."

"But it's not what we're here for. No reason to dig up memories that are dead and buried. Oops, sorry, Annika—forget that last part. Just tell us this: Did you have anything to do with us living where Samantha used to live?"

"And does it have something to do with your death?" Chess quickly added.

More silence.

Jeff whispered, "I think we asked her too many questions. We've scared her off."

Levi chuckled. "We scared off a ghost. Now *that's* impressive."

"Shh. Let me try," Allie said. "Annika, can you tell us anything about the room connection we have with Samantha?"

Silence.

After a full minute, Allie spoke, "Chess, this is silly. Let's call it a night." Illumination flooded the room. Allie stood at the light switch. Jeff and Levi rose and offered hands to Chess, who accepted and pulled herself up.

"That was useless," stated Levi.

"No, it wasn't!" Chess brushed herself off. "We made contact! You all heard the crash when I asked her for a sign. That was Annika!"

"I don't know," said a weary Allie. "Somebody down the hall dropped something, then somebody walked by the door, probably to see what happened. Let's not lose our heads over this."

"I'm with Allie," Jeff said. "I like to keep an open mind, but nothing tonight convinced me we were talking to anyone but each other."

Allie shook her head. "We tried, Chess."

Three soft raps drew attention to the door. Allie opened it to a young woman wearing pajamas. Her hair was pulled back in a ponytail, with blonde bangs coming barely above her red, oversized eyeglasses. "I'm sorry to bother you so late, but I'm looking for a broom. We broke a glass down the hall. Do you have one? A broom, I mean."

"No, but there should be one in the closet at the end of the hall. Are you new? I'm Allie Donnel."

"Hi, Allie. Yeah, I just moved onto campus. My name's Annika." When no one else offered an introduction, she added, "Well, nice to meet you. I have to go find that broom."

They all stood—motionless—looking at the closed door.

Allie's mouth poised for a response that didn't come.

Levi turned his head, as if he had misheard the name and expected it to be repeated.

Chess squealed. Her hands flew to her mouth.

Jeff crossed his arms and cocked his head to the side. "Now there's a plot twist."

Chapter 15

Tuesday, September 18

Samantha arrived on campus early enough to make coffee before her first class. At the outside door to Prescott Hall, she met Sydnee who carried a pencil and a travel cup sporting the logo of The Campus Cafe.

"You're here early, Ms. Baldwin."

"I've got a make-up exam with Dr. Simpson this morning." Sydnee crossed her eyes in disrespect of the hour.

"And you aren't the only early bird." Samantha addressed the rest of her entourage sitting outside her office door. The fact that they looked sleep deprived and were the very four who had been planning a séance when she saw them last wasn't lost on her. Samantha scrambled in her purse for keys, unlocked the door, and motioned everyone in.

"I'll just camp out here till he comes in." Sydnee plopped down on the sofa. Samantha's casual, "Feet off," caught Sydnee just as her feet moved toward the table, at which point they went back to the floor. "What are you all here for?"

Silence.

Samantha put her purse in a filing cabinet and walked to the coffee maker to begin her single-serve morning brew. She glanced at her assistants, who looked at each other with some non-verbals Samantha couldn't quite interpret—all of them, that is, except Sydnee who sipped her beverage and seemed oblivious to the others.

Allie spoke first. "We held the séance last night."

Samantha pushed the "on" button of her coffee maker. "I've got a class in twenty-two minutes. Talk fast."

Chess took over. "We talked to Annika—"

"Oh brother." Sydnee rolled her eyes and head.

"—and she gave us several signals to let us know she heard us. Then—"

"Chess, we don't know those were signals." Jeff directed his attention to Samantha. "Something crashed and then people moved around outside the door. Who's to say—"

"—then after it was over and the lights were on, she came to the door."

"Who?" Samantha asked.

"Annika."

"Chess, come on." Sydnee laughed and sipped.

Levi walked over to a chair and sat down. "Not *the* Annika. Just *an* Annika."

"Someone named Annika came to Allie's door last night after the séance?" Samantha picked up her coffee, poured hazelnut creamer in the cup, and stirred.

"Yes," Chess said while the other three nodded their heads. Each of the four fixed their eyes on Samantha as if she could tell them what to believe about séances, the spirit world, and visits from Annikas past or present.

"Hmm." Samantha licked the coffee stirrer and put a lid on her cup.

"Well?" Allie pushed.

Samantha offered a slow shrug. "I don't put stock in talking to dead people. But I have to admit, it is strange. What's the plan? Will you have another séance?"

"What would you do, Dr. H?" Jeff's voice, almost a whisper.

Samantha stared for a long moment. "I don't know."

"Dr. Hayes…" Sydnee shook her head.

"No, really, Syd. I don't know. I might. I might not." She tossed her coffee stirrer in the wastebasket.

Jeff asked, "Do you know this Annika, Dr. Hayes? Have you had her in class?"

"I don't remember a student by that name. Did she say how long she's been here?"

"Only that she just moved onto campus," Allie answered. "We didn't talk long enough to find out much about her."

"None of us knew her though." Chess shook her head and looked to the others for verification.

"You know any Annikas, Sydnee?" Samantha walked to her desk, picked up her notebook for class, and placed it in a canvas bag.

"No, I don't. That's an odd name though. Can't be too many of them around."

Allie said, "Last night after everyone left, I went down the hall to see if anyone was still up so I could ask about her. No one was. But I don't think she lives on my floor anyway, because there haven't been any vacant rooms all year. And no one has been without a roommate. So, she probably lives on another floor and was just hanging out with friends last night."

"Still, someone will know her." Chess responded

with confidence.

"I'll go back to the dorm after class and snoop around."

"It's a busy day for me," Samantha said. "But we can talk about it tonight."

"Tonight?" Levi asked.

Allie sighed. "Do you ever write anything down? You know they have these cool things called *calendars* and you can write things on them so you don't forget to show up places. You should try it, Mr. Corliss."

"Oh, yeah, we eat at Sam's tonight. I'll be there."

Samantha slung her canvas tote over her shoulder, picked up her coffee, and headed for the door. "In the meantime, Levi, ask Student Services if we have an Annika on campus."

"I'm on it," Levi said as he followed Samantha and the others out the door.

****

Chess's great-aunt Ruth resided at The Fountain of Youth residential facility, referred to by most in the community simply as *The Fountain*. Comfortable, if not luxurious, it was located on the outskirts of town, boasted well-manicured grounds, and was surrounded by a picket fence. The home itself was a brick and siding composite built to resemble a large, single-family dwelling. Rocking chairs and two swings on each side of the wrap-around porch completed the impression of *home*. Inside, the rooms were clean, reasonably spacious, and the hallways wide enough for the movement of wheelchairs for the less ambulatory residents.

Chess was devoted to her only living biological relative and visited her faithfully once a week even if only for a few minutes. Chess had lived with her aunt after her mother died when she was three years old. But when Ruth had been unable to care for an active toddler, Chess was adopted by Pamela and Charles Seeley, the only ones she could remember calling *Mom* and *Dad*. Then five years later the twins were born, surprising everyone. Chess had loved her little brothers from the very beginning and they adored her.

And yet—she couldn't shake the niggling doubt: would her parents have adopted her if they had known they were about to have twins? Naturally, Dr. Hayes had encouraged her to talk with them about her fears. But Chess couldn't. What if they lied to spare her feelings? Or worse—what if they admitted it? No, she couldn't risk it.

Meanwhile, Aunt Ruth had maintained a constant presence in Chess's life, attended school plays and graduations, and spent every Christmas and birthday at the Seeley's. Chess treasured this only remaining link to her family of origin.

On this day, Chess filled her in on the extraordinary incidents of the past week while she set up the checkerboard for their weekly game. "And then we had a séance, and you will never in a million years guess what happened."

Aunt Ruth chuckled. "You spoke to John Kennedy?"

Chess laughed as she set out the rows of red and black checkers. "No, silly. Someone named Annika actually came to Allie's room. I kid you not. Walked right in and asked for a broom."

"A broom? What'd'ya think, is she a witch?"

"No. I think she was a message from *the* Annika."

Chess nodded her conclusion.

"Might be, darlin'." She made the first move. "There's more things in heaven and earth than is dreamt of by most people, to paraphrase one of the greats."

"Shakespeare." Chess moved one of her pieces.

"Shakespeare." Aunt Ruth confirmed with a nod. "What does your professor say?"

"She wasn't there. But we told her about it today and she thinks it's creepy."

"Scares the bejeezus outta me." She spoke calmly and softly as she eyed the checkers through her bifocals.

Since Ruth held a lot of respect for anything that took the "ordinary" out of ordinary life, Chess was confident in her aunt's answer to the next question. Before she had a chance to ask it, however, a screech came from somewhere outside her aunt's door. *"Who is she? I don't even know her!"*

Chess contemplated her next move. She was used to the abrupt interruptions to their conversations. "New resident?"

"Mm hm," Ruth said. "Her name's Liv. Just moved in. Real confused." She shook her head.

"That's sad." Chess continued, "So would you have another séance if the Annika thing happened to you? I mean, would you be afraid to? Or would you want to get to the bottom of it?"

"No, I wouldn't. Be afraid, I mean." She jumped two of Chess's checkers. "What could she do to me?"

"I know, right!" Chess giggled at the response she expected. Then after a two-part jump, announced, "King me!"

"Oh, you." Ruth placed another checker on Chess's

piece and studied the board. A few well-calculated moves later and Chess had lost another game to her aunt. After a hug and the promise of a rematch next week, Chess headed back to campus.

One day, however, there would be no more "next weeks." Or, like Liv, Aunt Ruth would not recognize her when she visited. The thought was like a punch in the gut. Her last living relative. When she was gone, would Chess ever belong anywhere?

****

Len Titus drummed his fingers on his desk. How could he be expected to work under these conditions? He shoved his chair back and marched out of his office, into the hall. The incessant chatter, sprinkled with whoops of laughter, came from the student break room. Snack and soft drink machines with a couple of tables and some chairs provided a place for students to congregate briefly between classes. Today, however, their little tete-a-tete had dragged on longer and was noisier than usual.

He stopped at the door, took in the assemblage before breaking it up. Just as he thought. Not a one of them could afford this much time away from their studies, at least not in *his* classes.

"People work here and your"—he rolled his hands as if he didn't know the word for people having fun—"foolishness is too loud. Take it outside."

"We're sorry, Dr. Titus. We'll leave." The apparent ringleader of this troupe hopped out of her chair, gathered her backpack. "My roommate, Chess, held a séance last night and I was telling them about it."

"A séance?" Len stepped aside so they could trail out. "Surely you don't believe in séances, Julianna."

"No, I don't." A glance at her peers. "But *she* does." Another burst of laughter.

A young man added, "You wouldn't catch me messing with that stuff." He addressed Dr. Titus, "They tried to contact the student who died on campus a long time ago. Anita somebody—"

"Annika," Julianna corrected him.

"Whoever. Then she showed up," he whispered, "in the room!"

Amid laughter and continued chatter, the students left Shelley Hall. Len was sorry he had run them out so quickly. He would have liked to have known more. Wasn't Chess one of Levi's friends? Bet she's part of that posse over in Prescott. He walked back to his office and sank into his chair. *Is Samantha behind this?*

Chapter 16

Tuesday, September 18

Her crew would be here any minute. Dinner was ready: the salad on the table, the lasagna cooling, the apple pie out of the oven. The breadsticks would go in when they arrived. She was straightening the clutter in the den when Rob called. Another week before his book tour ended and, if the frequency of his phone calls was any indication, he was ready to be home. He chuckled when she told him about the séance but stopped with the addition of Annika to the story. Rob whistled his surprise. "And she has the *same name* as the one who died years ago?"

"Yes. And I don't know what to think." As they talked, Samantha made a half-hearted sweep through the den to pick up remnants of this morning's newspaper still strewn on the floor. "They were all a little scared."

"Even Levi?" Rob laughed.

"Especially, Levi. He didn't say much, an oddity for sure."

"What about you? A little spooked?"

"To tell you the truth," Samantha lowered her voice and sat on the sofa, "a little bit. And I'd *love* to have been there for the séance. Can you imagine?" They laughed together for a few more minutes.

"I'll let you go. I know you have your hands full

getting ready for the kids." Before hanging up, she promised to call later after everyone left.

She distributed the accent pillows more equitably on the sectional sofa from where Millie had arranged them for her afternoon nap. While Millie yelped her rebuke, Samantha scooped her up with one arm, tussled her blonde tresses with the other, and carried her to the adjoining kitchen.

"You stay here, Millie. Help me listen for the doorbell." From her doggie cushion perch, Millie alternated her gaze between Samantha and the front door. "Yeah, you know we're having company, don't you?" Samantha took six stoneware plates and as many salad bowls from the cabinet and set them on the table. "What do you mean I never cook unless we have company? I'll have you know—"

Dong.

"This isn't the end of our discussion, Mildred." Samantha did a walk-run to catch up to her pooch who was now in full chase down a short hall to the front door. She paused briefly to pick up Millie and to glance out the window. All five dinner guests stood on her front porch, Allie's and Levi's cars parked in the semi-circular drive a few feet behind them. Opening the door, she greeted each of them amidst the noise of Millie's happy barks.

Samantha handed Millie over to Levi who joined in the barking while Sydnee reprimanded Millie for encouraging her two-legged friend. They followed Samantha toward the kitchen with guesses of what was for dinner and offers to help.

"You can set the table if you'd like," Samantha said to Allie and Jeff as she nodded toward the dishes stacked on the counter.

"And you two," she said to Chess and Sydnee, "can put ice in the glasses and pour the drinks. I'll take an iced tea." It wasn't that she needed drinks poured so quickly—the lasagna needed a few more minutes to set and she hadn't even put the bread in the oven. She merely wanted to forestall any talk of séances and not-so-dead visitors at least until dessert.

And she did. Dinner was eaten enthusiastically amid talk of exams and papers due the next week. When Samantha bemoaned the fatigue of grading papers from first-year students, she received no sympathy from this group. Levi simply mimed playing a violin while Sydnee suggested she not *assign* papers if she didn't want to *grade* them. Samantha dismissed them with a laugh. Then looking at the clock, she jumped up. "I need to give Millie her medicine."

The rest had eaten enough meals at Samantha's to know the drill. Jeff and Sydnee filled the dishwasher as Chess cleared the table and Allie put leftovers in the fridge.

"Aw...you sick, Mills?" Levi gave her a sad face as he engaged her with a rope toy.

Samantha got her dog's medicine from the cabinet. "She had a rash earlier this week and still has an ear infection. And you know she's always had problems with her liver."

Samantha retrieved her not-quite-empty glass of iced tea, just as Chess reached for it in her table-clearing mission. Samantha took it to her kitchen island where she prepared Millie's medication against the happy background noises of talk and laughter, the clank of dishes and silverware, and the low, guttural growls of a dog and her playmate. As she listened to Sydnee instruct Jeff on proper glass arrangement in a dishwasher, Samantha peeled back the foil from the last of the blister packs and prepared to place each capsule into the piece of cheese Millie would eagerly devour as her evening treat.

This was the scene when Allie held up a glass bowl and asked, "Hey, Samantha, can this go in the dishwasher, or do you want us to wash it by hand?"

"Dishwasher is fine," she replied as Sydnee and Jeff engaged in a tussle over the appropriate placement of utensils. "Don't hurt yourselves, you two. Those knives are sharp."

Unfortunately, at that very moment—with Millie's medicine in hand—Samantha's attention was distracted just enough that she popped Millie's evening cocktail into her own mouth. And with one swig of tea, she downed one pill for an ear infection, one for a skin rash, and one for a failing doggie liver.

"Oh, no!" Cough. Sputter. "I can't believe I did that!" Choke. Gasp. "It was right there, and I wasn't thinking!" Gag. Wheeze. "Why did I do that!"

Activity ceased as all eyes were now on Samantha. Millie even surrendered her rope to Levi as she tilted her head in perplexed attention. Levi stood up with his newly acquired chew toy and joined the others in awed silence.

"What did you do?" Levi whispered, as if secrecy would help.

"I took Millie's medicine!" Samantha's voice squeaked.

Allie ran to Samantha and the now emptied packages of canine capsules. "Which ones did you take?"

"All of them, Allie! I took all of them!"

"Why did you do that!" said Levi, who also came to stare at the island which was now devoid of any doggie pills.

"Because I'm a fool, Levi! Why would anybody take their dog's medicine?"

"Okay, let's keep calm and figure this out." Allie pointed both index fingers at Levi and said, "Get your cell," and to Samantha, "Do you have emergency numbers for situations like this?"

"Situations like this?" Samantha sputtered. "Heaven help us—there *are* no situations like this!"

"Call 911," Sydnee said, "and ask for the number for poison control."

"Right! That's good, Syd." After getting the number, Levi punched it in his cell and announced, "It's ringing." He then turned the phone on speaker and placed it on the counter.

"Poison control. How can I help you?"

"Oh," squealed Samantha, "I've just done the stupidest thing. I took my dog's medicine. I'm so embarrassed."

"More common than you might think," she replied matter-of-factly. "Tell me what you took. Do you have the label there? Read off the name of the medication."

Allie and Levi gathered up each of the boxes and read the drug information to the poison specialist. She told them that each of these medications is also prescribed to humans then patiently answered their questions. No, she would not die. Yes, she might feel queasy. Yes, food on her stomach would help. No, it did not have to be a doggie biscuit.

With reassurances offered, Samantha thanked her repeatedly before ending the call. Everyone breathed a sigh of relief. Jeff and Sydnee resumed dish placement. Allie and Chess finished clearing the table. Levi and Millie continued their rope tussle. After giving Millie her meds, Samantha finished her tea and hoped her lapse in attention would not be her students' main take-away this evening. Nor the topic in her classes this week. While she was certain Levi could weave her blunder into a heck of a story, she'd prefer he didn't. What they needed was redirection.

"Levi," Samantha said, "did you learn anything from Student Services about any Annikas on campus?"

Levi shook his head. "No Annikas. Not in the dorms. Not in any Vanderlaan housing units."

"But she only just moved in, remember?" Allie said.

"Yeah, but Student Services would have assigned the housing. And they haven't given a room or apartment or house to anyone in the past month. Not to an Annika, not to anybody."

"Well, I did my own checking," Samantha said while she reached for a knife to cut slices of the apple pie. "After we talked earlier today, it occurred to me that any student living on or off campus would have a university email. But I couldn't find one for anyone named Annika." Samantha cast a nonverbal question to Jeff as she pointed to his pie with the ice cream scoop she now held in her hand.

Jeff nodded. "Maybe Annika is a middle name?"

Samantha tilted her head slightly. "Could be, but even middle names come up if you search the address file. Which I did. No Annikas." She handed the dish of pie a la mode to Jeff.

"No Annikas at Vanderlaan." Allie squinted as she summed up the findings.

Chess took the dessert offered. "So that means the Annika we met last night was not who she said she was." She giggled. "And that means she was someone else. Another Annika!"

"Or at least someone who pretended to be." Levi kept the possibility of a hoax ever-present.

"Why would anybody do that, Levi?" Chess took a bite of her dessert and gave Samantha a thumbs-up. "Allie, did you learn anything from the other residents on your hall?"

"No. Blair and Valesca did cop to breaking a glass last night and said that several went in search of a broom, but neither of them knows an Annika."

"Allie, why did you not lead off with that! This isn't, like, dessert news. It's, like, appetizers as we walk in the door news! What's wrong with you?" Chess swatted at Allie.

"Ouch! I don't know, Chess. Maybe it spooks me a little."

"Well, I'm not spooked." Jeff shook his head and pointed with his gooey spoon. "There's something in all of this that's not right."

"My point exactly," Chess said. "This cannot be explained except that we have been visited by the spirit of Annika."

Sydnee's response came slowly. "I'm almost convinced."

"Seriously?" Levi quickly asked.

"No, not seriously!" Sydnee threw a wadded up napkin at Levi. "And Allie, I'm surprised at you. You are the smartest person in this room—"

"Hey!" Samantha and Levi responded in chorus.

"—except maybe for Dr. H," Sydnee conceded. "And you actually believe you talked to someone who is dead!"

"Don't judge, Syd. We asked her to communicate with us and then there she was." Allie put her hand up toward Sydnee. "I know you're going to say it wasn't the same Annika, but it was *an* Annika and don't tell me that isn't beyond weird. Maybe if we had tried to communicate with a Jennifer or a Sarah or a Katelyn, your point would be well-taken. But her name is not that common. It's *Annika*, for heaven's sake!"

"Okay." Sydnee took a deep breath. "I get it. But don't lose your head. There's always a rational explanation—"

Chess shook her head. "Not for everything."

"—for everything." Sydnee nodded.

"So, what do we do from here?" Jeff said.

"I'm game for another séance." Chess looked hopeful.

"No, Chess. No more of that." Levi got up and put his now empty but sticky plate in the dishwasher. "I say we learn more about the first Annika—the one who died twenty years ago."

Allie said, "And tomorrow I'm meeting with the dorm director. I thought she might know something about Annika from last night."

"Oh! I'll go with you, Al," offered Chess. "If you find out anything scary, you shouldn't be alone."

Allie and Samantha exchanged smiles.

For the rest of the evening they relaxed, played with Millie, and said no more about séances or pharmaceuticals.

Although Levi did ask Samantha to stay off the furniture.

Chapter 17

Wednesday, September 19
The next day Samantha went to her office no worse for the wear. Not only had she not experienced any side effects from her canine cocktail, but she had slept well and arrived at her office early. In her first class, she intentionally joked with her first-year students about the benefits of sampling one's dog medication. Might as well create the narrative herself and defuse any teasing Levi might have up his sleeve. As she predicted, her students found her medicinal mishap humorous and several expressed a touching concern for Millie.

By the time she met with her second class, her story had spread. Her students' good-natured laughter assured Samantha that owning it was indeed the best way to handle such situations. She concluded her story by saying that conducting her own individual drug trial had certainly given her the buzz she needed for her morning classes. Students groaned in good humor as they took out notebooks and laptops for the day's lecture.

After class, she met with a prospective student and his family. She highlighted for them the advantages of a degree from Vanderlaan and the career opportunities for psychology majors. She had lunch with a colleague who happened to be on her tenure committee. Although she was curious as to the status of her application, she

120

did not ask and was proud of her restraint.

She didn't see any of her research assistants outside of class, however. The ebb and flow of the semester sometimes resulted in her office being empty. She loved the constant stream of students, but the occasional time alone in her office to catch up on work wasn't without appeal.

She was curious, though. Who was the Annika from the séance? What happened to the Annika from twenty years ago? Were they connected in some way? And what about synchronicity? The fact that four of her students lived in rooms where she once lived couldn't be a mere coincidence, could it? And if they labeled it synchronicity, did that make it any less incredible? What was synchronicity anyway? The work of a higher power? Something supernatural? If so, what was it meant to accomplish?

Samantha had questions aplenty, but no time to ponder them, much less settle on an answer. Room connections, synchronicity, and Annikas past or present would have to wait. Even so, Samantha looked forward to discussing all of it with Debra. And while she was at it, she had something else to run by her therapist. Something disturbingly familiar.

****

Samantha began her session with Debra by relaying their discovery of the room connection and their attempts to make sense of it, including the story of the séance, the appearance of Annika, and her students' futile efforts to find her since that night.

"Wait, wait." Debra repositioned herself as if she needed more grounding to take in what she was hearing. "You have four rooms in common with as many students, a student who died in one of those rooms, and a séance which seems to have conjured up a girl with the same name as the student. Samantha," she concluded, "this is incredible. What do you make of it?"

"It is the most bizarre thing I have ever experienced. And I have no idea what's going on. I keep expecting a logical, scientific explanation to surface, something to explain this whole thing. Instead, each new incident leads us farther away from logic or science.

"Then Allie brought up the possibility of synchronicity."

Debra nodded. "Carl Jung."

"Right, and the story of his patient's scarab experience. And I can't quit thinking about it." Samantha touched her scarab pendant in reference and played with it as she spoke. "I feel like I'm in the middle of a transformative experience myself. I just don't know what kind or where it will lead."

"I know you don't dismiss everything science can't explain."

"Of course not. There's also faith. But as far as religion goes, this is still kind of out there."

"Does there have to be a basis in one or the other?"

"Well…sure. If neither science nor religion can explain it, what else do we go on?"

"Maybe you go on your own experience and let that expand your understanding of reality."

"Expand my understanding of reality…" Samantha played with the scarab pendant while she hesitated. "Then there's something else. This whole thing with Annika. It's…familiar."

"Really? What part?"

"Christine said the girl in the dorm, Annika, died about twenty years ago. I knew someone about that time—a college-aged young woman—who died. It was back when I taught at Hayward. It was such a busy time. Elyse and Lucas were little. Rob and I were each building our careers. Then the college asked me to supervise a couple of graduate student interns through the counseling center while they were short-handed. It was a lot, but I wanted to be indispensable at Hayward." Samantha smiled and rolled her eyes.

Debra smiled.

"Alayna, one of the interns, had a client who had a history of depression and a bad case of homesickness. Didn't have many friends. Alayna shared with me that her client—I think her name was…Grace…maybe?" She nodded. "Grace. She had said a few things that concerned Alayna. She was appropriately cautious, asked all the right questions, and decided that her client was depressed but not suicidal. Then when the semester was over, the client left school. Alayna referred her to someone in Owenton—that was Grace's hometown." Samantha shrugged. "But she didn't know if Grace would follow through, and she never saw her again.

"Then over the summer, the center filled their staff positions, and they didn't need me for supervision any longer." Samantha turned her gaze to a tree outside the window whose leaves fluttered in the breeze. "But for some reason, I continued to think about Alayna's former client. It even occurred to me to follow up with her, but we didn't have a forwarding address and the number she had left was no longer active. I don't know…there wasn't really a reason to contact her." She turned back to Debra. "I just had this feeling I couldn't shake, you know?"

Debra nodded.

"Then, Alayna—she had graduated and moved by that time—she sent me a note that Grace had died. Not long after she had left Hayward. Alayna had heard about it from the colleague she referred the client to, who had read about it in the paper."

Debra looked up. "Suicide?"

Samantha shrugged. "Alayna didn't know. But it's odd, isn't it? Alayna's client and this Annika both were young college students, died about the same time, and suicide was a concern for each."

"That is odd." Debra tilted her head. "And when you heard about Grace's death, how did that—"

"—make me feel? Like if I had tried harder, I could have located her, noticed something was wrong, and intervened."

"And she wouldn't have died?"

"If she had been suicidal," Samantha said with a firm nod, "I would have gotten her some help. If she had been sick, I would have urged her to see a doctor. I could have done something."

"You might have," Debra said. "But you didn't have an ethical obligation to someone who was no longer your intern's client and who showed no signs of needing intervention even when she *was*."

Samantha wanted to feel as convinced as Debra sounded.

Debra continued. "In that situation I wouldn't have done anything differently than you did."

Silence.

"It was during that time I began reacting with such

panic to the sight of blood. Like I experienced when Chess hit her head a few weeks ago. As if I'm—" Samantha bit her lip and shook her head.

"Feeling responsible for things you can't control?"

"And then trying to control things I shouldn't."

"Hitting it right isn't easy," Debra said. "But this isn't all on you, Samantha. Ultimately your students have the responsibility to take or leave any advice you give them."

"Yeah, but it still scares me because there's this invisible boundary for when to speak up and when to keep quiet. I never know for sure where the line is." Samantha paused, hoping Debra would have some magic words to supply the answer.

Oddly enough, she didn't. Debra did, however, present an observation. "It's odd, isn't it?"

"What is?"

"You had an experience twenty years ago in which you worried you hadn't done enough with someone who later died. Now you're concerned about when and how much to intervene while drawn into a story of another young woman who died about twenty years ago. The whole thing is odd. Synchronistic."

"Yeah, it is." Samantha reached up to touch her scarab pendant. "I wish I knew what it meant."

Chapter 18

Days passed without much new information surfacing about either Annika. No one had seen the one from the séance; she seemed to have vanished after she left Allie's room that night. Chess suggested that someone contact the parents of the Annika from twenty years ago. But aside from the fact that it would require more time than any of them had to investigate their whereabouts, none of them wanted to intrude on her family merely to satisfy their own curiosity. For now, at least, they would focus on their classes and research.

Samantha, too, busied herself with class preparation and the bottomless stack of papers to grade. She and Rob texted or talked every day. Book sales were great, book signings well-attended. He had several ideas for his next novel and often asked Samantha's opinion about this plot or that character. Not only did she love that he wanted her input, but the more they talked about his next book, the less they spent on the pitiful state of his chrysanthemums. *I have to do better*, she promised herself.

She had just finished talking with Rob when Murphy from her Abnormal Psych class appeared at the door. He had timidly asked her the day before about study tips since he had done poorly on the first exam. She had told him to come by her office anytime and they would talk about study strategies. She invited him in, picked up her latte from her desk, and offered him a water or a soda, which he declined. Samantha sat down on the sofa next to the chair he now occupied. "What's up?"

"Dr. Hayes, you need to know something that was said yesterday after class. I don't want to make too much of it, but you know the student who sits in front of me in Abnormal?"

Samantha nodded. "Rochelle."

"Rochelle. She's been really annoyed with you these past few weeks."

Like I haven't noticed Ms. Pencil Tapper and her snide comments. "Mmm, I know." Samantha took a sip. *Where is this going?*

"And I know you just kind of don't let it get to you, but yesterday after class, she told me she wanted you dead, and I just—"

Samantha's coffee spurted out of her mouth.

She grabbed a tissue from the box on the side table to wipe off her now latte-colored sweater. "Dead! She wants me *dead*?"

"Yeah. She said you insulted her grandson the other day in class and—"

"Whoa! Wait! What? I insulted her grandson?"

"I don't remember any insults, but that's what she said. Then she said you would be sorry and would pay. So…I just thought you needed to know." He waited as Samantha mopped up. "What are you going to do? You need to be careful, Dr. Hayes."

"I will be, Murphy, and thank you." As Samantha got up and tossed the tissue in her waste basket, Murphy got up and headed to the door.

"Will you be all right?" He hesitated, as if unsure how long one should stay after a death threat delivery.

"I'm fine, Murphy." She smiled to reassure him. "She probably won't do anything, but you're right, I needed to know."

Samantha took a deep breath but forgot to let it out until she began to feel faint. This was her best attempt at remaining calm.

Alone in her office, Samantha sat at her desk and resumed sipping what was left of her latte. *Was this threat an idle rant from an annoyed student or does Rochelle pose a danger? Does she truly believe I insulted her grandson? Or is she just angry that I demanded respect?* Samantha didn't know the answer to any of these questions, but Rochelle's threat to Samantha also threatened the safety of others on campus. Accordingly, precautions had to be taken.

The rest of Samantha's morning was taken up with contacting those on campus who needed to be informed of such things—campus security, the Dean of Students, and the chair of Samantha's academic area. Security wanted to speak with Murphy since he had actually heard the threat and, of course, Rochelle would be called in and questioned. Hopefully, Rochelle would come in with little fuss so campus authorities could quickly assess the level of risk she posed. Since Samantha needed to be present for some of those meetings, she cancelled her morning classes and dismissed any thoughts of research for the afternoon.

However, despite their efforts, university personnel could not reach Rochelle. She had not answered her cell nor shown up for her morning class. And while campus officials discussed their next step and security kept a presence around Prescott Hall, Samantha went back to her office to salvage at least a portion of her afternoon.

Later in the day, Levi and Jeff came by to see why class had been cancelled. They had heard Samantha was on campus but not in class and wanted to know why. Allie came over as soon as she received Levi's text telling her what had happened.

"She threatened you! She actually said she wanted you dead?" Allie burst into the office with fire in her eyes and an edge to her voice usually reserved for sexist comments made by extended family members at holiday dinners.

"She did, Allie, but it doesn't mean she was serious."

Jeff sat silently on the sofa as Levi paced around the office. While he usually found the humor in any situation and happily presented it to the rest of them, this time Levi was without a wisecrack or one-liner.

"But, Samantha, she could be," Allie said. "You need to be careful. Why are you even on campus? You should go home and lay low for a while."

"It's not a bad idea, Sam," Levi agreed. "Until they talk to her, classes and research can wait. Just go home." He added, "Did you tell your husband?"

"No, there isn't any reason for him to know. He needs to focus right now on his book. Besides he'll be home in another week." She took a deep breath. "Let's not make this bigger than it is. She's not done anything and probably won't."

Sydnee burst into the office. "Who is this Rochelle and what's her problem?" An unusually quiet Chess followed. Jeff moved over to make room on the sofa.

"What I don't get," Allie said, "is why she thinks

you insulted her grandson. I was in class that day and you didn't say anything about her grandson. Did you talk to her later and then—"

"—then challenge his finger-painting skills?" Levi said.

Samantha smiled faintly. "She actually did come by later that day to ask a question. She was annoyed we had spent so much time on the room thing, and she might have taken offense at my response." Samantha shook her head. "But nothing was said about her grandson."

"I've had other classes with Rochelle. She's a little smart a—"

"Syd—" Samantha warned.

"I was about to say smart *aleck*—She's a little smart *aleck*. But what did you lecture on that day?"

Samantha closed her eyes, then popped them open again. "Childhood disorders."

A flurry of activity ensued as Allie, Chess, and Levi scrambled to get their notebooks. Samantha also grabbed her class binder and flipped through her notes for that day's material.

Chess began the overview. "Okay, you finished up the material on ADHD, covered separation anxiety, and talked a little about autism but didn't get finished."

Allie asked, "You think Rochelle's little darling has one of those?"

"Did she say anything about her grandson having any problems?" Samantha pinched the bridge of her nose and squinted. "I don't think she did."

"No, but she might not say anything even if." Allie slammed her notebook shut. "But no, Samantha, you didn't insult anyone."

"Yeah, but you could've said something she *perceived* as an insult." Levi said as he perused his notes.

"You said that kids with separation anxiety tend to be immature," offered Chess. "Could that have made her mad?"

"Enough to kill?" Sydnee said.

"Now *that* would be immature," Levi mumbled.

Allie shook her head. "You said nothing a reasonable person could take as an insult."

"Yeah, but *reasonable* is not this woman's strong suit," Sydnee said.

Chess said, "It's like Liv, the woman who lives at The Fountain. She blurts out things that don't make a bit of sense. She yells, 'I don't know her' when nobody's there. Or one time she kept saying 'She lied. But I'm no better. She lied. But I'm no better.'" Chess stopped thumbing through her notes. "It's so sad. Like she feels guilty about something she can't fix."

Samantha tossed her class binder aside. *Why can't we ever just talk about the weather in here?*

"It sounds like she has Alzheimer's," Allie told Chess.

Chess nodded, then twisted around toward Samantha. "I might want to work with elderly people. What do you think?"

Samantha smiled. "I think you'd be great."

When her phone rang and caller ID flashed *Dean of Students*, Samantha shushed everyone. "Hello, Monique...Yeah, I'm good. You?...You did. What did he say?...Did he say where she is?" Samantha sighed, closed her eyes, and dropped her head to the back of her chair. "What are we supposed to do? What am *I* supposed to do?…Okay…Yeah, I know…Thanks, Monique. You too."

Samantha hung up. "They brought in her husband who claims she is emotional and high-strung and difficult to deal with but is completely harmless." She looked up at five sets of skeptical eyes. "He claims she was out sick today and can't come in to talk about this. Meanwhile, we wait to see if she says or does anything else.

"But," she continued, "I don't expect you to sit here with me. If you're afraid of what she might do, I completely understand, and I want you to go back to your rooms or the library or anywhere else you feel safer, just—"

For the first time, Levi cracked a smile. "*You're* not scared but if *we* are, we shouldn't be here? Maybe a little projection, Dr. Freud?"

"Maybe a little," she conceded. "But I need to take my mind off this. So if you stay here, we can't talk anymore about it, okay?"

"Fair enough." Jeff nodded. "What can we do to help?"

"Well, first thing would be for Allie and Levi to look at the printout of the statistics we ran the other day and see what's significant. And explain as much as you can to Chess." Those three promptly moved to the research table and grabbed highlighters for the task they'd been assigned.

"Jeff, where are you and Syd on your project?" After Jeff brought Samantha up to speed, she suggested they make out a list of points which could feed into the discussion section of their manuscript.

Before long, all of them were busy at work and talk

of Rochelle had ceased, as if she no longer posed a threat to anyone.

Chapter 19

Wednesday, September 26

The next couple of days were difficult. Samantha wasn't certain whether to be relieved or alarmed that she hadn't seen Rochelle since hearing of her threat. Did Rochelle's absence from campus signal her retreat or did she plan to surprise Samantha one day when she least expected it? Rochelle's husband claimed that she was away, although he didn't say where. Meanwhile rumors ranged from her lying low out of embarrassment to her being hospitalized with a psychotic break. But after she had been out a full week, word on the street was that Rochelle would not return at all.

Likewise, the mystery of Annikas past and present had been placed on the back burner as nothing new had surfaced there either. Samantha was as curious as everyone else about Annika and Rochelle, but she was grateful to focus on her actual job rather than the death of one student and the homicidal tendencies of another. So although nothing had been resolved, life returned to a degree of normalcy as days passed without incident.

On one such afternoon, Jeff and Sydnee worked in Samantha's office as she graded quizzes. Although little conversation ensued, Jeff looked at his cell occasionally, after which he would smile and tap a response. After each text, Sydnee would grin and say, "Aw...Jeff's in love," to which he would respond,

"Back to work, Baldwin."

After three or four interruptions, however, Sydnee said, "Tell her you have homework and to quit bugging you."

"She's not bugging me near as much as you are. Besides, it's none of your business."

"Ah, so it is a 'she' and, of course, it's my business. You two wouldn't even be a thing if it weren't for me."

"Sure, we would. I would have asked her out. Eventually."

"But see, with my help you bypassed the *eventually* part and are now a happy couple."

As the cell vibrated once again, Sydnee grabbed Jeff's phone. His reaction was not quick enough to keep her from running with it to the other side of Samantha's office.

"Syd! What are you doing? Give that back!" Jeff ran after and cornered her between the sofa and a wall of bookshelves as he spread both arms and legs and bounced left and right to stop her should she run again. "Syd, I swear. If you read my texts—"

"Sydnee!" Samantha attempted to rectify the situation.

"I'm not reading anything, Jeff." She laughed as she ducked underneath his left arm and flopped on the sofa with his cell tucked behind her. "But if I did, what would I find?" She batted her eyes.

Jeff took a deep breath and gritted his teeth.

"Sydnee, give Jeff back his cell phone." Samantha got up from her desk. *What had gotten into her?*

"You don't have to fight my battles, Dr. H." Jeff waited, hands on hips. "Sydnee, give me my phone."

Sydnee tossed it in his direction. "Settle down. I'm just kidding around."

He snatched it mid-air. "It's not kidding around! It's an invasion of my privacy. Why do you do things like this?" He glanced at the text then stuffed the cell in his pocket. He sucked in a jagged breath, held up his hand as if to signal his impending response. Instead, he threw his hand down and stomped out of the office.

Samantha sat down on the other end of the sofa. "What *on earth* was that about?"

"I know, *right*? Gets mad over nothing, then storms out. I'll be glad to leave when he gets back so you can talk to him, Dr. H. I just—"

"No, Syd. What was with *you* back there?"

"*Me*? You're worried about *me*? I just wanted him to open up a little."

"*That* was your attempt at getting him to open up?" Samantha shook her head. "Sydnee, has it ever occurred to you that ripping his personal property out of his hands and running with it might not be the best approach?"

"It didn't work, did it?" Syd said as if she had executed a failsafe plan that, against all odds, had gone wrong. "He's just so secretive these days."

"Secretive?"

"Come on, Dr. H. I set him up with Maddie and now he won't even say one word to me about it. He hasn't thanked me or even let me know how they're doing. And when I bring it up, he treats me like the enemy."

"He doesn't treat you like the enemy—"

"When it comes to Maddie, he does." Syd sat up straighter. "Anytime I mention her name, he gets secretive."

"I don't know about secretive. Maybe *private*? But this isn't new, Syd. He's never been one to share a lot. You know that."

When Sydnee didn't respond, Samantha tapped her on the hand. "There's nothing wrong with keeping some things private."

Sydnee nodded and took a deep breath. "I get it. I'll talk to him, Dr. Hayes."

"Hey, you got a minute?" Christine burst through the door then immediately backed away. "Sorry, Samantha. Just come down when you're free."

Sydnee immediately got up and insisted that Christine come in. She excused herself, saying she wanted to find Jeff.

"Sit down, my friend," Samantha said, "and remind me that twenty-year-olds get older and wiser."

"Umm…sometimes they just get older. Take a look." She handed Samantha a sticky note on which was scribbled a note to Christine from the department chair asking her to send Samantha's tenure application on to the university tenure committee.

"Ooh, the department approved my tenure application, and they've sent it to the next level. That's good news."

"Keep reading."

"…to the University Tenure Committee Chair, Dr…Len Titus."

"I'm sorry, Samantha. I didn't want to tell you. But—"

"I'm sick." She bent over and put her head in her hands. "I'm going to throw up. Since when is he the chair? Last I heard it was Ray Chaney."

"Dr. Chaney's on sabbatical, remember? And word on the street is that Dr. Titus pushed to take his place. Samantha, you could get him taken off the committee. Tell Dr. Easton about the history between you two."

Samantha looked up but kept her face in her hands. Her voice shook. "Monique knows. We've talked."

"But not the whole story."

"Of course not." Samantha slid her hands to the back of her neck and rubbed. "And I can't tell her."

"I know, I know." Christine waved a dismissive hand. "You promised your friend. But, Samantha, she should have fought it then, and you should now. Just tell Monique that Len stole Barb's work and she's afraid to call him on it for fear of not getting tenure. And ask—*no*—*demand* that he be sanctioned. Then"—Christine propped her feet on the table herself—"he won't be a threat to you or Barb."

"If Barb would back me up, sure. But she won't. It's too risky and she's afraid." Samantha pointed a finger at Christine. "And no, I won't proceed without Barb's okay. It would be wrong. Plus, Monique can't do anything without proof, which I don't have without Barb." She sat up, shook her head. "No, I can't say anything."

"Doesn't it just eat away at you, though?" Christine balled her fist and hit the arm of the sofa. "To not confront him?"

"Who said I didn't confront him? Please."

"He *knows* that you know?" Christine's eyes bugged.

"Yeah." Samantha flopped her head back on the sofa and squeezed her eyes shut. "Which is why I'm now at risk. He wants me out, Christine. If he can get rid of me, and then Barb next year when she's up for tenure, no one around here will know what a dishonest, underhanded piece of slime he is." Samantha slapped her hands on the sofa. "I just have to reason with Len— to assess my performance objectively or recuse himself."

Christine's eyebrows arched. "You plan to reason with Len Titus?"

"Yes." Samantha got up, grabbed her sweater, and put it on. "Right now. I'll be back as soon as I can, but would you keep a lookout for Jeff? Tell him I need to talk to him today so not to leave before I get back."

****

Samantha could not understand her outright fondness for lost causes. She routinely reminded her grown children to eat healthy foods. On more than one occasion, she voted for political candidates who had no chance of winning. She frequently wrote letters on behalf of students who had failed all their classes but still pleaded for "just one more chance" with Vanderlaan's academic council. And today? Today she had tried to convince Len Titus to be a reasonable human being.

The walk back from his office to her own, even amidst the coolness of the autumn day and the vibrant colors of the leaves across campus, did nothing to calm her. She flew into her office as angry as she had left his. She immediately regretted slamming the door when she saw her office was not empty. Jeff sat at the research table with his laptop while Christine stood at Samantha's desk with the mail.

"I see *that* went well," Christine said.

"That man is just—" Samantha caught her breath

and walked to the fridge to get a water.

"Need me to leave, Dr. Hayes?" Jeff asked.

She took a deep breath and let it out. "For a few minutes, Jeff. Thanks."

As he slipped out, Christine sat on the sofa while Samantha tried to compose herself and sat in one of the chairs.

"He didn't offer to resign from your committee."

Samantha shook her head.

"He will stay on it. As chair."

Samantha nodded.

"He's as vindictive as ever, and you're worried you won't get tenure."

Samantha let herself cry. She never cried in front of a student and seldom with any of her colleagues. But with Christine, sure. "He could keep me from tenure. After all the experience I have and the work I've done here, if I'm denied, I'll have to leave."

"I don't understand this whole system. Why don't you just not apply?"

"It's job security, Christine. No one *has* to apply, but then I could be let go for any reason, or *no* reason. But to apply and get denied...is serious." Samantha shook her head. "I never thought it would come to this—Len Titus—chair of my tenure committee." She continued with renewed energy. "And he pushed for it. Did I tell you that? He specifically *asked* to chair my committee."

"But he won't have the final say, will he? I mean, isn't the final decision made by the trustees?"

"Yes, but they depend to a great extent on the recommendations of the committees." Samantha growled. "If it were just up to the trustees, I'd be fine.

I've only met the Chair, Eleanor Waters, but she would be *worlds* easier to convince than Len Titus."

"What will you do?"

"I don't know." Samantha took a deep breath, glanced at her cell, and jumped. "I have to talk to Jeff. It's getting late."

"Okay, let me know if I can help. Here if you need me." Christine scurried out.

"Can I come in? Is everything okay?" Jeff asked as he paused at the door.

"Sure, come on in, Jeff." She took a long drink of her water. "Sit down. Talk to me. About this afternoon and Sydnee."

"I'm sorry that happened in here, Dr. Hayes. Really. I just—"

"Whoa. I'm not fishing for an apology. Did you and Sydnee talk about this after you left the office?"

"We did. She apologized. Said she just wanted to know how Maddie and I are doing." Jeff shook his head as if the whole thing confused him. "I get that, but she needs to back off. Maddie and I will tell her more when we're ready."

Samantha squinted. "You still trying to prove a point to Sydnee?"

"Well, I *was*. But it's getting dangerous." Jeff chuckled. "Maybe I should thank her for stepping in. But if I do, she'll never learn." He was getting himself worked up again. "I don't know. I'll think about it, Dr. Hayes."

"Nothing wrong with giving credit where it's due." Then throwing him her mom-look and an index finger she said, "And trying to teach people lessons can backfire, young man."

With a knot in her stomach, the truth of those words hit her. *Yes, teaching lessons can backfire. It did with Rochelle. It did with Len.*

Chapter 20

Sunday, September 30

Samantha was thrilled to have Rob back home. She listened to his recap of the book tour and his plans for his next novel. He relayed the basics of the plot and a few places where he was stuck. He didn't know enough about killer bees but would meet next week with someone who could fill him in.

"Hey, I brought you something." He tossed her a book. "Remember Isaac? Taught at Hayward when you were there? He's written a book, a campus mystery type thing."

"Nice!" She turned it over to read the back cover. It was definitely her kind of book, although Rob's expendable cash would be better spent on a neighborhood teen to water plants in his absence. She placed it on her nightstand and brought him up to date on the happenings at Vanderlaan. Since they had talked frequently while he was away, he already knew about Len's shenanigans and the eerie coincidence of the two Annikas. However, she had successfully kept Rochelle's threat and subsequent disappearance from him. This, she shared as he unpacked.

Rob stopped with toiletries in hand. "She's threatened you and no one at Vanderlaan is *doing* anything?"

"They're *doing* something, Rob. They talked to her

husband and notified security. They just can't *find* her."
Samantha dismissed his skeptical look with a wave of
her hand. "She's harmless. I'm more concerned about
Len's sabotaging my tenure. That's the real threat right
now. And yes, I'm well-respected on campus, and no,
he isn't the whole committee, but the man is powerful
and really hates me."

"The school values you too much to let Len get by
with this. Have you talked to anyone higher up?"

"No, I don't want to look like I'm not a team
player. He could use *that* against me, too.

"Len *is* cantankerous." Rob got up and carried his
luggage to the closet where he stowed it away. His
muffled voice carried. "But this student who's
threatened you—she sounds like a nut job. And the fact
that no one has seen her lately doesn't reassure me in
the least." He reappeared. "Are you okay, really? I
mean are you scared to be on campus?"

"Nah, I'm good. Besides, 'nut job' isn't the
technical term."

"What would make her blame you to begin with?"

"Oh, I don't know her well enough to say. Maybe
she really is a threat, but she probably just misspoke."

Rob's eyes sparkled. "But speaking of people who
can't be found, anything new on the mysterious and
elusive Annika?"

"No." Samantha laughed. "She hasn't been seen
either. I'd be sure Levi was pranking me, but Allie, Jeff,
and Chess saw her too, so…"

"Yeah, Allie wouldn't prank." He closed the closet
door, and they headed downstairs to the kitchen.
Samantha dished up the vegetable soup she had made
for dinner and took cornbread from the oven.

"But what I don't get," Rob said as he poured glasses of tea, "is how I never thought of something like this for a book."

"What? Annika?"

"The room connection in general." They carried their dishes of food to the table. "As mysteries go, it's not bad."

"Hmm, there's a thought. If this were one of your books what would be behind the room connection?"

Rob slathered butter on his cornbread. "I'd make it a setup. Someone playing a practical joke. Like you said, Levi might do that. Even Sydnee. But the others?"

"No way," Samantha said.

"So outside of a joke," Rob chewed as he looked off in the distance. "I'd have someone you trust trying to frighten you and your students, make you all so paranoid you couldn't function. Anybody you suspect who'd do that?"

Samantha took her turn at the butter. "I don't feel frightened or paranoid. And no, we don't have any suspects. Not really." Samantha told him about her conversation with Kelly and her indignation at Samantha's suggestion that she had placed students in her former rooms.

"She's the only one who would know where I lived and be in a position to assign rooms. But when she said it back to me"—Samantha grimaced—"it sounded so ridiculous, I was embarrassed for even asking."

"Might've made it sound ridiculous to throw you off?"

"I don't think so," Samantha said. "We're not close enough for it to be a practical joke. And she certainly doesn't *dis*like me, so she'd have no ulterior motive."

She shook her head. "It's not Kelly."

"When it comes to motive," Rob said, "I'd give another look to that student who threatened you. Bet she'd love to mess with you and not as a harmless practical joke either." Rob munched cornbread.

Samantha paused eating, head atilt. "I can't imagine her taking time to pull a practical joke on *any*body, much less me." She went back to her soup. "Plus no one seems to like her very much so I don't know how she'd ever get Student Services to go along. Rochelle isn't exactly a sympathetic character," Samantha said pointedly.

"Rochelle?" Rob put down his spoon. "Is her last name Pierce?"

"Yeah. You know her?"

"She used to work over at the high school,"— Rob's eyes widened—"with *Kelly DeVore*. Remember Kelly was a guidance counselor before she came to Vanderlaan. I think Rochelle worked in her office." Rob motioned with both hands. "And *there* it is. Rochelle wants to mess with you and got Kelly to play along."

Samantha rose to pour another glass of tea. "Rob, that doesn't make a bit of sense. Rochelle would have had to know my students before they even came to Vanderlaan. And she didn't. Plus, I asked Kelly about it, and she's not involved." Samantha came back to the table with her tea.

"No"—she shook her head—"when it comes to motive, Len Titus is my pick," Samantha said. "But it's hard to imagine him going to such lengths. And he would still have to enlist Kelly's office to make it happen." She shrugged. "And Len's been on the outs with Student Services ever since they got him to sponsor the Math Club then he talked the club into disbanding. No, they'd be more likely to put him in a room, lock it, then spread the word he'd moved to Siberia."

"Well, if those are your only suspects, I'd say you're left with Chess's ghost theory."

Samantha laughed. "She'll love that."

"Or," Rob said, "deciding which of your suspects you don't know as well as you think."

Although she stood by her argument that such an arrangement was impossible, the thought troubled Samantha. *Was someone setting her up or targeting her students for harm? If so, who? How? And for what purpose?*

"You know what else this reminds me of?"

"I do." Samantha nodded. "But not while we're eating."

"Okay, but have you—"

"I have."

Rob stopped with his spoon halfway to his mouth. "Have what?"

"Talked to Debra about it."

Rob's head tilt conceded that she had indeed read his mind regarding the similarities between the deaths of Annika and the other student twenty years ago.

"She thinks the similarities have triggered my anxiety over…you know…"

"Uh huh," Rob pointed his spoon at her. "Uh huh. The unresolved, *unwarranted*, fear that you could have done something when—"

"When I couldn't have. I know." Samantha waved her hand in dismissal. "Eat your soup. It's good, isn't

147

it? I used more basil this time and—"

"And you should listen to Debra—"

"I am." More hand-waving dismissal. "We're working on it."

"Still." Rob stopped and took on his serious face. "I want you to be careful."

"I will."

"More than usual. Until they find her, or she shows up to class, or whatever. Don't assume her absence is a good thing."

"Will do." Samantha saluted him.

After dinner, Rob took their bowls to the dishwasher as Samantha pulled a handful of paint color chips from a kitchen drawer. "Now to more pressing concerns. You still planning to paint the kitchen while you're home? I have colors all picked out."

"What's it gonna be? Firecracker red? Electric lime? Sunburst yellow?"

"I want one of these orange shades." She fanned out the orange options on the granite countertop.

"Couldn't talk you into sandy taupe or oatmeal beige, could I?"

Samantha giggled and shook her head. "Orange. Just think how inviting it'll be on cold winter mornings."

"And in the heat of summer?"

"It'll be nice to have sunny weather inside where it's not so humid, don't you think?" Without waiting for his response, Samantha held her top three picks up against the cabinet. "This one." She nodded in satisfaction.

"This one it is." Rob circled the one she wanted.

Their banter over paint colors was a constant in

their relationship. While their styles differed, their solution was to alternate who chose the color each time a room needed a fresh coat. The last room to receive a make-over had been the den, which now sported Rob's choice of woodland beige. While Samantha feigned annoyance at what she dubbed his "impressive commitment to color," she celebrated being one step closer to an orange kitchen. Rob now accepted her decision with equal grace.

"At least it'll cover what I couldn't get last time."

When they moved into this house four years ago, it was in pristine condition. All except for the wall next to the kitchen door which boasted the letter "C" in crayoned scrawl about knee level. After sandpapering and applying several more coats, Rob gave up when the marks reappeared. But this time—with this color—Samantha hoped he'd get it.

"And while I'm painting our kitchen this hellish—I mean *heavenly*—shade of orange, you will be…"

"Going toe to toe with Len Titus."

"And?"

"Avoiding students who would have me dead."

"And?"

"And…talking to Debra about feeling responsible for things I can't be responsible for?"

He looped his arm around her and kissed her forehead. "Yes. Thank you."

"It's early. Want to watch a movie?"

"Sure." Rob pulled away and headed toward the back door. "Just let me go check my sunflowers first."

Samantha winced. *Sunflowers!*

Chapter 21

Monday, October 15

Two weeks passed. No one had come up with a
rationale for the room connection. Rochelle continued
to lay low, although no one was sure exactly where. For
all they knew, she was holed up with broom-searching
Annika since no one had tracked her down either.
Samantha wished Len Titus would disappear as easily,
but no such luck. He remained a foreboding presence in
Samantha's life, holding her career hostage as her
nemesis and chair of her tenure committee.

Amid these unresolved issues, her classes
consistently reminded her of everything she loved about
her job: teaching students the knowledge and skills
needed to successfully transition into their adult lives.
And class periods when the lecture topic coincided
perfectly with the decisions they were making—those
were the best. On those days, her lecture was merely a
springboard for discussion through which the real
learning took place.

On this particular day, she had almost finished a
unit for which they would be tested during mid-terms.
While an exam in the near future generally increased
their level of attentiveness, the fact that today's topic hit
close to home didn't hurt.

"And while those who agree with Erikson are
convinced we all go through the same stages at roughly

the same ages, some critics suggest that men and women progress through these stages differently. They claim that the male identity forms prior to achieving intimacy with others; they say female identity develops alongside intimacy with others."

"Not just *others*. You mean men, right?" Allie quietly asked in the last few minutes of her professor's lecture.

"That's often what happens. The idea is that women are often encouraged to achieve a sense of identity through a boyfriend or husband."

"But doesn't that make it harder to actually *have* an identity, if you make it all about another person?" Samantha was pleased to see Shayla, one of her new students, connect the dots.

"Exactly, which some argue is the problem. Without an identity these women will seek fulfillment in others rather than themselves. This could account for the higher number of women diagnosed with depression and anxiety disorders."

"But why do women let that happen? I mean, why do they listen?" asked a student whose name Samantha didn't yet know.

Allie answered, "Because women don't realize it until they are in a relationship with several children. The point isn't 'Why do women listen?' It's 'Why does society teach boys to *be* their own man and girls to *find* one?' "

"Good question. Why do we?" prompted Samantha.

"If men would just stop expecting women to cater to their every need," said another female student.

"I don't expect that," Levi said. "A lot of guys

don't. But when they do, why don't girls—"

"Women," corrected Allie.

"Women," Levi conceded. "Why don't *women* just follow their own dreams and not give in to a guy who's a taker. It's not easy, but forming an identity isn't easy for any of us. I can't say I know for sure who I am or what I'll become."

"That's not uncommon at your age," Samantha said. "Most college students are searching, and this time of your life is often a process of deciding what feels right and what doesn't."

Levi continued. "Psychology feels right for me, but what will I do with it? I don't know. I don't know where I'll be after college or who I'll be at that point. It's as hard for guys as it is for girls—women."

"I wouldn't say it's *just* as hard for guys," Jeff stated. "Society tells us to get a job so we can support a family. That seems to make it easier for men to derive a sense of calling for our lives, a way to contribute to the greater good."

"Yeah, but that's a career, not an identity. There's probably a difference?" another student asked.

"Yes, there is a difference. Although how you spend forty hours a week for the next forty years has a lot to do with how that identity unfolds. Values feed into it, too—deciding what you believe in, stand for, what you will invest in and commit to. All of that makes up an identity."

"Was your identity set before you married your husband, Dr. Hayes?"

"Yes." She smiled. "By the time I married Rob Donovan I had an identity. So did he. That's one reason our marriage works. Well, that and the fact that he tolerates my love of pasta and I get his love for 60s protest music."

Laughter did not quite muffle the sounds of their desks as they scraped the floor.

"Not so fast!" She halted their movements. "Remember to get your presentation outlines in before our next class and take a look at that study guide you begged me for. It should be your best friend as you prepare for mid-terms. Okay, get out of here. See you Wednesday."

As students shuffled away from their desks with bags and books, Monique stepped inside the classroom door. While several students waved and said good-bye to their professor as they left, Samantha's mind whirled with possibilities. *Which student complained about what grade? Has Len put the kibosh on my tenure application already? What has Rochelle done now?*

As the last student left and Samantha gathered her things, Monique walked toward the front of the classroom.

"Monique, hello. What's up?"

"Samantha, I wanted you to hear this from me before word gets out to the rest of campus." Monique's eyes met Samantha's. "A few hours ago, Rochelle Pierce died."

****

Samantha grabbed the desk to steady herself.

"She had a stroke last night and a massive heart attack early this morning. Her sister called my office to let us know."

"She was only…how old? Maybe in her forties?"

"Forty-six, her sister said. I expressed our sympathies, of course, and will pass along the information to the rest of campus. But I wanted you to know first."

Samantha nodded. "I appreciate that."

"I know the whole Rochelle thing has been a trying experience for you, Samantha. If there's anything I can—"

"I need to get back to my office." Samantha abruptly moved toward the door.

"Samantha—"

"Thanks, Monique," she called over her shoulder as she bolted from the room toward her office.

Relieved no one was waiting for her, she unlocked her office door, slipped inside, closed and locked the door behind herself. She left the lights off, pulled a bottled water from the fridge, made her way to the far side of the sofa where she sat down. Anyone who peered through the window of her door would assume she was not in. Her students would hear about Rochelle's death any minute now, but she had to sort through her own feelings before she could help them process their own.

A stroke. A heart attack. That means Rochelle hadn't been well for some time. Did that contribute to her unfounded accusations? She was almost delusional. Delusions...Do they indicate a physical problem? Sometimes. Should I have recognized that in Rochelle?

She ran her hands through her hair and rubbed the back of her neck. She gulped her water and let out a shaky breath. *Did my calling attention to her threat put undue pressure on Rochelle? Pressure that led to a heart attack? But what else could I have done? If she had tried to hurt me in my office or in class it would have put my students at risk. I couldn't ignore that!*

She stood up and paced, careful to stay out of view of anyone outside her door. *It's the same story all over again—Grace. Len. And now Rochelle. I can't keep doing this. If I don't know when to butt in and when to butt out, what's the point?* She crawled onto the sofa again, wrapped her arms around her folded legs—her makeshift fetal position.

I need Rob. She snatched her phone and punched in his name. *Text? Call?* She threw her cell onto the sofa. *Neither.* He was in his meeting right now—would be for another hour at least. Another swig of her water, this time choking her as it went down, forcing up a cough she tried to muffle with a pillow. She caught her breath hoping no one had heard her.

Bzz. Bzz. Bzz. Her phone snapped her back to attention. One text from Allie and one from Levi, each asking if she had heard the news about Rochelle. The third was a reminder of her appointment with Debra in fifteen minutes. *Debra! Good timing.* She grabbed her purse and hurried from her office, ran out of Prescott to her car, and sped off campus.

Chapter 22

Monday, October 15

Samantha was uncharacteristically quiet as she entered Debra's office. No peppy banter. No recount of her week. Not even mindless chit-chat about the weather. All unusual for Samantha.

After they each took their seats, Debra broke the silence. "You're quite the chatterbox today."

"She died, Debra. The student who wanted to kill me died."

Debra closed her eyes briefly as she settled in her chair.

"She had been out for several weeks. Ever since she made the threat, no one on campus had seen or heard from her. Her husband told us she was sick, but she was *really sick*. She had a stroke and heart attack." Samantha took a deep breath and let it out. "She threatened me and, I'll admit it, I was scared. I didn't want to let on to my students because they were all over the place worried, but yeah, I was scared.

"And I was relieved when she didn't return to class." Samantha hesitated. "Then when I heard about her stroke, I remembered that delusions can precipitate a stroke." Tears stung Samantha's eyes. "I knew she had problems. I mean look at the expectations she had for me and for the other students. But I never thought about her being *physically sick.* If I had known she was about to die…"

"If you had known she was about to die…what?" Debra asked.

Samantha shook her head. "I don't know. I didn't know her outside of class. She never came to my office or confided in me…"

Debra slowly nodded her head. "So you're saying you couldn't have known this was more than a student with unreasonable demands?"

"No." Samantha sniffed and wiped her nose. "And I get it. I can't be responsible for what I didn't know. But the fact that she could be so young and on the verge of death, and meanwhile, I'm just upset to be accused of something I didn't do."

"And you didn't like being falsely accused?"

"No, of course not!" Samantha punched the pillow next to her on the sofa. "I hated that she said things that weren't true. Everyone who knows me knows I didn't say anything inappropriate to her, but—" Samantha growled in aggravation.

"But what?"

"But it would have been nice if I had some inkling that there was more here than met the eye, that she was sick, and maybe not even responsible. Maybe I could have gotten her some help."

"Like, maybe sent her to a doctor to find out she had a life-threatening condition?"

"Yeah, and then—"

"Whoa, back up. Where was she when she died?"

Samantha looked up.

"I mean, was she at home? In the hospital? On a beach in Aruba? Where was she?"

"In the hospital. She had been admitted for tests."

"So, she got to a health care professional—without your driving her there. She was admitted so they could assess her condition. And…?"

Samantha nodded and took a shaky breath. "And she died anyway."

"She did. Samantha, you were her teacher, not her therapist, not her cardiologist, not—" Debra put her hands up. "—anyone who could have stopped her body from doing what it was going to do." Debra leaned forward and persisted. "I get that you feel bad for Rochelle. It's a horrible thing that happened. But you're not to blame."

Samantha sat silently and processed Debra's words. "I want to believe you. It's just…"

"Just what?"

"We talked about this last time. I keep going through the same circumstances again and again. Twenty years ago with Alayna's client and now with Rochelle. In each instance, I didn't intervene and look what happened. Is it any wonder I intrude with my students? I have to, Debra. When I don't, bad things happen."

"Are you saying that if you held back—didn't intrude with Levi, Allie, and the others, that someone would die?"

Samantha let out a breath. "No, Debra…Maybe…I don't know." She shook her head. "I do know I can't keep a position of responsibility with my students when I have no idea where the line is."

"The line?"

"The line." Samantha drew a line in the air in front of her. "How far to go. When to push. When to stop. I don't know where it is, Debra." She shrugged and gained speed. "And then there's Len Titus. I found out that when I pushed my friend years ago to speak up about Len's behavior, he not only lost his job but went into a depression that cost him his wife and who knows what else, because I pushed."

Debra shifted positions and shook her head. "Samantha, you're jumping to a lot of conclusions here. From what you told me about Len Titus, he deserved to lose that job." When Samantha opened her mouth to object, Debra continued. "And if it prompted his wife to leave him, my guess is that it was the final straw and not your fault."

"But I could have behaved differently, maybe with more compassion or at least just stayed out of it."

"Sure." Debra shrugged. "Or you could do exactly what you did which led to his dismissal and Hayward giving the job to someone better for their students. And besides, he did find another job and, as of yet"—Debra knocked on the wooden table next to her chair—"hasn't died."

Samantha took a deep, shaky breath. "Of course not. But it does scare me that something I do for my students could alter the course of their lives."

"It could." Debra nodded. "And if you do *nothing* for your students, it will alter the course of their lives. If you did nothing when Len caused trouble at Hayward, students' lives there would have been altered—and in a bad way, I might add. Samantha"—Debra leaned in— "every choice we make changes the world in some way. And we don't always get to decide what the change will be."

At Samantha's moan and head flop onto the sofa back, Debra sped up. "We don't, Samantha. That's life.

All you can control is your intention to influence others for the better."

"I know that." Samantha raised her head and held Debra's gaze. "But what I don't know is how. Because I can't keep doing this."

"Doing what?" Debra squinted.

"Not trusting myself—wondering if and when I've crossed the line."

"But what's the option? Unless you plan to resign—" Debra snapped to attention.

"I might not have to actually resign." Samantha told Debra that Len was chairing her committee. "If Len gets his way, I'll be out of a job. And who knows." She picked up a pillow and slumped into the sofa. "Maybe that's what this whole room connection is about—that my time here has come full circle and I need to leave."

Debra spoke quietly. "I can't imagine that *that's* what it's about."

Samantha broke eye contact. "If I just don't fight him on this—just go quietly…"

Debra was silent.

"I know you don't agree." Samantha put her palm up to forestall Debra's response. "And I know what you're going to say. Fear shouldn't make the call. And I agree. Of course, I don't want fear to win. I don't want *Len Titus* to win. But what else am I supposed to do?"

"Well, you could—"

"Yeah, I could fight back." Samantha rubbed the back of her neck. "But that means I openly oppose the man who chairs my tenure committee, no less. Of course, he has a lot of enemies." She spoke quickly as she flicked her head back and forth. "But he also has a lot of power. We can't forget that."

"Sure." Debra nodded. "And if—"

"If I do fight, I'll have to learn to trust my own good intentions while I learn where the line is and how to stay within it."

"And don't forget—"

"Oh, I won't." Samantha rattled off in sing-song style what Debra had told her countless times. "My students are ultimately responsible for what they do with my advice."

Debra smiled. "Right. And you have to trust them—"

"Trust them?" Samantha stared. "To do what?"

Debra seemed surprised at the opportunity to finish a sentence. "To decide for themselves how much or little of your advice to take."

"Mmm…never easy for me." Samantha reached for the scarab on her necklace.

Debra cracked a smile. "That scarab you wear symbolizes transformation. You ready for this one?"

Samantha released the breath she had been holding. "I don't know that I have a choice."

Chapter 23

Sunday, October 21

Samantha committed to another appointment with Debra early next week. Transformations didn't come easily so the sooner she got started, the sooner she'd get control of her life again. In the meantime, however, on this Sunday afternoon Samantha took a break from grading mid-terms to watch a psychological thriller. She had curled up in her favorite sweats and was just about to diagnose the main character when four rapid chimes of the doorbell broke her attention. Before she could get to the door, three decisive knocks followed. A glance out the window revealed a familiar car and two familiar students.

"Chess. Sydnee. Come in."

"Dr. Hayes, you're home! Sorry to bother you on Sunday afternoon but we have an idea."

"I can't wait to hear it." Samantha laughed as she led them into the kitchen. "Sit down. Can I get you two something to drink?"

"No." Chess waved her arms. "We're fine."

Sydnee stopped short. "I want something to drink."

Chess let out a sigh of frustration as Samantha got a soda for Sydnee from the fridge.

"Okay, I'm all ears," Samantha said as they took chairs around the kitchen table. "Tell me your idea."

"Well," began Chess with the eagerness Samantha

adored. "Today Syd and I went to the art fair over in Cannville. A couple of my art friends have a booth where they sell jewelry they make."

"Chess asked me to go. I'm not a big fan but"— Sydnee shrugged—"why not."

"I don't get why you're not a fan, Syd. You decide you don't like something and then you just close your mind to it." Chess waved her hand to illustrate.

"Chess." Syd tapped a finger on the table. "Stay on topic."

"Right. So, while we were there, we ran into Brent and Jacob."

Samantha nodded. "From my Lifespan class."

"Yes," Chess continued. "They were there because Jacob's mom has a booth. She does pottery. And we all walked around for a while. Then—" she paused to take a breath, "—Brent mentioned how weird the room connection thing is and we're like 'yeah it is.' Then he's like 'are you guys creeped out?' And I'm like 'we're not creeped out but yeah we're intrigued.' Then we, like, walked around and—"

"No, Chess. We didn't *like* walk around. We *walked around*. Honestly." Sydnee swigged her soda.

Chess tapped her fingers to her closed mouth and giggled apologetically. "Sorry."

Samantha wondered if she would, like, ever hear the end of this story. But other than watching half of a movie and eating a bag of cookies she had nothing better to do.

"Then we batted around ideas on what it means. And Jacob said"—Chess held up an index finger— "what if this is all about Dr. Hayes and what *she's* supposed to learn and has nothing to do with *you* all learning *anything*." Chess concluded with wide eyes and a nod.

Was this all that stood between her and a movie with cookies? Because if they left now, she might be able to work in a nap before the day was over.

"What do you think?" Chess said.

"Well, we sort of already knew I was part of it, so…"

"Not *part* of it, Dr. Hayes. Maybe it's *all* about you." Chess leaned in. "Like maybe you are the one who's supposed to learn something here. Maybe this whole thing is for you, not us."

Again, the doorbell rang. This time only once. As Samantha rose to answer it, Sydnee quickly explained, "Oh, and we texted the guys and Allie and asked them if they could meet us here so that's probably them right now."

Samantha shook her head and smiled as she opened the door to Jeff, Levi, and Allie. As the newcomers followed her to the kitchen, Samantha walked to the fridge, opened it, and sent a questioning look to the group. All shook their heads, except Levi who caught the soda Samantha tossed in his direction. As Chess brought the others up to speed, Samantha pulled in another chair and sat down with them.

"Okay, so you think I'm supposed to learn something from each of you and that's why we have this room connection?"

"Yes. But what is it that you need to learn from us, Dr. Hayes?" Chess studied Samantha intently.

"Um, the best way to choose a career? How to study for three exams while writing four papers? Oh wait, I've done all that."

"Yeah, but you did all that decades ago—" Jeff began.

"*Eons ago*," muttered Levi as he strolled to the pantry. There he found the bag of cookies, which he held up in a non-verbal request for permission. Samantha nodded as Levi brought the bag over, took out a few for himself, and placed it in the middle of the table.

"No." Levi munched. "You already know that stuff. It has to be something you haven't done already, something you still need to learn."

Jeff spoke up. "You mean something beyond academics then? Something more to do with…what? Her personal life?"

"Yeah. Maybe some struggle Dr. Ancient here hasn't resolved yet."

Jeff sat back and turned his attention toward Samantha. Syd and Chess stared, too, as if the answer might suddenly appear on her forehead. Levi continued to munch.

Allie reached for a cookie. "In that case, you would know more about what this is than we would, Samantha."

Samantha got up to put on some coffee. *How much do I want to tell them?* "Sure, I'm definitely learning some things through this situation. Some of it fairly personal." Before they could ask for details, she moved on. "For one thing, this room connection doesn't fit neatly into *any* part of my belief system."

She took several mugs from a cabinet and creamer from her fridge as she continued. "I'm a social scientist. I respect empirical evidence. I've built my career around research and teaching what research uncovers.

But this"—Samantha took spoons from a drawer—"this defies science." She gestured with a spoon. "Not that I discount everything science can't prove. You all know I believe in a higher power."

"But the room connection doesn't seem to fit in with that either, does it, Samantha?" Allie said. "At least I don't see how."

"Don't be too quick to dismiss the possibility of this being spiritual," Jeff said. "I was raised to believe too, Dr. Hayes, and I don't see anything that indicates this *isn't* of God."

"Except for the séance stuff," Sydnee said between bites of a cookie. "Any church I ever went to didn't want us messing with that crap."

"Well, I don't go to church much, but I don't see how holding a séance makes me less religious," Chess said.

"No, but Syd's right. Christianity has traditionally disapproved." Jeff got up and poured some coffee. "I, however, try to keep an open mind regardless of what organized religion says. I mean, the church has been wrong before. You know, the universe rotating around the earth and all that."

"True." Levi took the coffee Jeff handed him and grabbed two more cookies. "But I don't buy that this is supposed to make us more religious or something."

"Who said anything about that?" argued Jeff. "Not all spiritual phenomena pull us toward religion. Sometimes things happen that make us better people but not necessarily more religious."

"Yeah, like synchronicity." Allie sat up straighter. "There could be a meaning, and it could be spiritual, but it wouldn't have to be religious."

"Nah, you're all making something out of nothing." Sydnee offered Samantha one of the few remaining cookies and shook her head to the offer of coffee. "I don't buy religion at all. Or séances. I believe what I can test and prove. This room connection is a fluke. It's a waste of time to make it more than that."

Levi shook his head. "How can you say that? There is overwhelming evidence that *something* is going on here. I can't explain it scientifically, and I don't know where I stand with religion. But no way is this a coincidence."

"Me neither, Syd," Allie said. "And I don't know what to do with it either. Like Samantha, my belief system doesn't allow for this kind of thing."

"If I look at this from a cognitive perspective"— Jeff leaned forward, his fingertips forming a steeple— "I'm stuck with a mental framework that doesn't work anymore. Not the part that trusts a world of cause and effect. Not even the part that fits in with my faith. I'll need a completely new mindset."

"A completely new mindset..." Samantha leaned against a cabinet with her coffee. "I was told recently to let this expand my understanding of reality." *Debra also says not to let fear make the call. And I'm afraid all right. Len would love nothing more than to get me fired. He warned me about pandering to paranormal bunk and suggested that my job depends on it. Will he block my tenure? Can I take him on? Do I even have a choice?*

No, I don't. Samantha pushed herself up from the cabinet. "We need answers. Jeff, I'm with you. A completely new mindset is exactly what I need."

Sydnee popped the last cookie in her mouth. "Not me. I'm good."

Chapter 24

Monday, October 22

After a short mid-term break, Monday morning ushered in the second half of the semester at Vanderlaan. Each of Samantha's students now had a mid-term grade which she had dutifully entered into the university's online grading system over the weekend. As of this morning at 9:00 students could access their standing in each of their classes.

While most of her students would be pleased, a few would find their less than stellar performance had landed them less than stellar grades. By early afternoon, these troubled scholars would appear in her office to bemoan the fate that dealt them such a hand. And as she had done every semester, she would help each one assess what they could do differently to salvage the rest of their semester.

But her office hours weren't until early afternoon. For now, she entered the classroom to several who busily tapped on their cells in the last few moments before class began. A pocket of students to her left discussed auditions for the school's upcoming production. Still others peppered her with questions: "Dr. Hayes, are mid-terms posted yet?" "Do you give extra credit?" "Can I come by this afternoon about my grade?" To these she answered: "Yes," "No," and "Any time after 1:00." While the sudden zeal for a quality education was all too predictable, she would be available for those who needed extra help.

On this day Samantha's lecture focused on middle adulthood. While most of her students had parents in midlife, they were often surprised to learn that this stage included challenges they had never before considered. The hour went by quickly for Samantha and ended, as it usually did, with her trying to cover the last bit of material before class was over.

"For those in midlife, increased responsibility for others often leads to greater caution and less risk-taking. This is one reason we don't see as many people in their forties and fifties die because of reckless behavior. However, they are more likely than younger adults to die from disease or health-related problems."

"But they're not just croaking right and left, are they?" asked Brent. "My mom and dad are kind of old, but they aren't decrepit yet."

"How old are they, Brent?" Samantha asked.

"My mom's fifty-four and my dad's fifty-six."

Moans and laughter came from Samantha and several in the class who were not much younger than mid-fifties themselves. "That, my child, is not old."

"But my mom lies about her age." Brent enjoyed the performance. "She's like, 'I'm only thirty-nine,' when everybody knows she's way older."

"See, people play that all wrong. If I lied about my age, I'd add on a few years, not take any off." She sat on the side of her desk. "Because if I'm, say, fifty and tell you I'm forty, you'd be like, 'Wow, she looks bad for forty.' But if I say I'm sixty," she paused for effect, "then you'd think, 'Wow, she's hot for sixty.' "

As everyone laughed, Brent asked, "How old are

you, Dr. Hayes?"

"Eighty-four." Her abrupt answer brought more laughter. "Okay, that's it for today. See you Wednesday."

As students packed up and left the room, Jeff made his way to Samantha with his laptop open. "Hey, Dr. H. I just wanted to tell you what I found out about Annika. I looked through some old issues of *Vanderlaan Life* for a paper I'm doing for my journalism class. While I was on the website, I decided I'd see what was reported about Annika when she died. And look what I found." He turned his laptop so Samantha could see the screen. "This is from twenty years ago. Almost to the day." Jeff pointed to the date at the top of the article.

Samantha chewed her nail as she read parts of the article aloud. "The body of *Annika Lavelle*"—her eyes met Jeff's—"was found Saturday morning, the twenty-third of October in Stratton Hall on the Vanderlaan campus...twenty-one-year-old Lavelle was not a student...visiting her cousin...investigation ongoing...possibly accidental death...rumors of suicide."

"Can you pull up the next issue? How often did they print this back then?"

Jeff leaned in, touched the back arrow to return to a list of publication dates for the university newspaper. "It came out twice a month back then. See the one with the story about her death is the second issue for October, on the twenty-sixth. Then the next several were in November, the ninth and the twenty-third, and the last of the semester on December sixth. And nothing in any of these"—he motioned to the screen—"is said about Annika. At all. I read each one, Dr. H., and that's it."

"So, they start out with 'girl dies in dorm, possibly an accident, rumors of suicide,' then report nothing else at all?" Samantha went back to her thumbnail and began to pace. "Just like it never happened. What's that about?"

"You know what I think?"

Samantha sincerely hoped it wasn't *that I talked to her Sunday night in Allie's room.*

Jeff pointed to his laptop. "I think after this article they were told not to print any more stories about it. Maybe they didn't want the bad press. It wouldn't exactly attract donors and prospective students to campus."

"True. And Christine mentioned that her family had some clout. They could have kept things on the downlow." Samantha stopped and took her thumb out of her mouth. "What about the local paper—the one here or the one from her hometown? They'd surely have a write up about something this big."

Jeff nodded and clicked on another tab. "Not much there either, just—"

Monique Easton rapped on the classroom door, commanding their attention. While she had a good working relationship with her academic dean, Samantha's gut tensed. The last time they had spoken, Monique had told her about Rochelle's death. Students for the next class were also trickling in, reminding Samantha that another instructor would need this room in a matter of minutes.

"We need to leave, Jeff. Another class needs the room, and it looks like Dr. Easton needs to speak to me. Come by my office later?"

Jeff agreed, put his laptop into his backpack, and slipped out as Monique came in.

"Hello, Samantha," Monique said. "I just wanted to tell you that Rochelle's memorial service is scheduled for tomorrow at 11:00. Several from the university will be there. Maybe you'd like to sit with us?"

"Sure, Monique." Samantha relaxed slightly. "I'd like that. Thanks for asking."

Monique went on her way as Samantha gathered her notebooks, stuffed them into her canvas bag, and scurried toward her office. She slowed her walk as she thumb-punched Rob's name on her cell. His brief, albeit warm, greeting was cut short by Samantha's hurried question. "Could Annika actually *be* Alayna's former client?"

"I'm good. And you?"

"Can't decide. But could they be the same person? Their names were different but…"

"And you ask because…"

"Because…" Samantha took a deep breath and switched her cell to the other hand. "Because the circumstances are so similar. They died the same semester, same age, and with each there was talk of suicide."

"And if they are one and the same, you could find out what happened and, once and for all, put your conscience to rest."

Samantha came to a stop, physically and verbally. She let a group of students walk by before she continued. "Or once and for all face up to my part in it."

****

Samantha's afternoon was as she had expected, busy. Students with appointments came by to discuss their grades. Students without appointments did the same. She met with several privately, and for those who came in blurting out their academic woes to all present, there wasn't the need.

She occasionally spied one of her entourage peeking through her office door window, as if to remind her they were there with news to tell. She would love to promise each distressed student the grade they wanted and send them on so she could learn the latest from Jeff's investigation, but professionalism prevailed. Finally, when the last student wiped her last tear and promised a more valiant effort than she had thus far exhibited, Samantha was free to motion in her merry band.

"Shew, just tell 'em to work harder or drop out." Sydnee's answer to academic problems had all the sympathy of a concrete block.

"She can't do that, Syd," Chess scolded. "How would you feel if she said that to you?"

"She wouldn't." Sydnee dropped her backpack and lay down on the sofa. "Because I don't fail. Or even come close. Meanwhile"—she positioned a pillow under her head—"I'm employed full time and still have energy to offer my services to you would-be sleuths. Feel free to use me as a model for your students, Dr. H. You know, girl pulls herself out of poverty by sheer grit and determination. That kind of thing."

"I'll keep it in mind." Samantha saluted as she stepped over Sydnee's backpack and plopped into a side chair. "Now, everybody get settled and tell me what you found out."

Levi stared at Sydnee's feet until she moved them. He then staked claim to that side of the sofa.

Jeff began the discussion. "Information published in the local paper was sketchy, just like in the campus paper. They reported Annika's death on campus, that she was not a student herself, but was visiting her cousin. Pretty much what we already knew."

Samantha said, "If her family's influence went beyond the university, they might've kept it out of local papers, too."

Jeff moved forward in his chair and continued. "They did give one more piece of information. They added her cousin's name—Laura Lavelle."

"So when Jeff sent me the name, I did some digging." Levi took the story. "Student Services has record of a Laura Lavelle who lived in Stratton that semester. In—"

"Let me tell it." Allie waved her hands. "In room 331." Allie reached over and tapped Samantha on the arm. "Our room, Samantha! But we've searched online and can't find a Laura Lavelle. She probably married and changed her name, but still you'd think we'd find something."

"The article went on to say that Annika and Laura were both from Chandler," Jeff said. "You know of it, Dr. Hayes?"

"It's about seventy miles north, right off the interstate." *And not where Grace was from.* "What did Chandler's paper report?"

Levi nodded. "I pulled up her obituary online." If he could make career decisions as quickly as he could follow the trail of an untimely demise, he'd be set. "Same info with the addition of her parents' names, Aaron and Olivia Lavelle. Still, cause of death not reported." Levi shrugged. "That's it."

Chess looked from one to the other. "What do you mean, 'that's it'? That's a lot." She bounced in her chair, pulling both legs underneath her in the process. "We have now established that Annika died in Allie and Dr. Hayes's room. The room where we talked to her the other night—"

"Forget that stupid séance!" Sydnee pulled the pillow from under her head and threw it at Chess.

"*You* forget it, Syd." Chess stood on her knees, caught the pillow, and hugged it. "The way I see it, our next move is to contact Annika's cousin—this Laura person—to find out what really happened."

Everyone turned toward Chess. Allie said, "Why Annika died?"

"Yep." Chess lobbed the pillow back to Sydnee and plopped from her knees to her backside. "And if they've seen her since."

Chapter 25

Tuesday, October 23

The next day was Rochelle's funeral. Samantha had cancelled her 11:00 class so she could attend and was grateful to slip in almost immediately before the service began. No sense dragging this out. After speaking briefly with Rochelle's husband and sister and taking the obligatory glance at the dearly departed, Samantha spotted Monique and the rest of the Vanderlaan contingent toward the back of the crowd. Several faculty members, administrators, and a few students nodded to her and made room for her at the end of their pew.

Samantha took a steadying breath. She had prepared for the worst, although what that would be she didn't know. Had she expected Rochelle's husband to yell at her for insulting their grandchildren thereby pushing his wife into a cardiovascular event? Or maybe Rochelle's sister would eye Samantha suspiciously, point an accusing finger, and scream, "I'd still have my sister if it weren't for you!"

Whatever she had expected, it hadn't happened. Rochelle's tearful husband had thanked her for coming. Her sister had held Samantha's hand in both of her own and expressed Rochelle's love for her classes, professors, and the friends she had made there.

Regardless, Samantha would feel better when it

was over and she could scoot on out to her car. She didn't plan to go to the graveside portion of the service. Leave that for Rochelle's family and close friends.

Just as the organ music began, her colleagues motioned her to move farther down the pew, opening a space for a late comer.

"Hello, Samantha."

Grrr… "Hello, Len."

"Rochelle was a psych major?"

"Mm hm. She started out in math, didn't she?"

"She did. I heard you and she had some problems a week or so ago." He peered over his glasses.

She turned slightly toward Monique to fend off an unwanted conversation with Len.

He persisted in a whisper. "She was all business, that one. Didn't like it when others goofed off in class. And she didn't take it well when people criticized—"

"You don't know what—" Surprised herself at the volume of her own voice, she lowered it. "You don't know what you're talking about, Len. I never—"

"Yeah, yeah, of course. Students say things all the time that aren't accurate." He leaned in. "For that matter, even faculty members say things that aren't true. We know how that can end up."

"Len, this isn't the time or the place—"

"Just expressing my appreciation of the deceased."

"No, you're just pushing your weight around. How dare you use a student's funeral to threaten me."

"Who's threatening?" He raised both hands as if proving his innocence. "I was referring to your friend years ago who freely offered her opinion about me at Hayward."

Monique shot a look of perplexed annoyance at

Samantha and Len which stopped Samantha from her next response.

Len's reference to his short stint at Hayward was a threat to Samantha and her tenure application. But how far would he go with that? Monique knew Rochelle's accusations were unfounded. She would have Samantha's back if Len tried to push this beyond the tenure committee.

Then why could she not shake the uneasy feeling that Len's whispered taunts were about to become louder and harder to ignore?

****

"He is the most hateful person, Debra. And he scares me to death." Samantha recounted the scene at the funeral and her continuing fear that Len would sabotage her tenure. "But regardless of what Len does to me, I have to get to the bottom of this room connection. I'm committed to finding answers—for my students' sake as well as my own."

"Does Len have a stake in this situation with Annika or Grace?" Debra asked.

"No, he just has a stake in my leaving Vanderlaan. Plus," Samantha added, "Annika and Grace were two different students." Samantha reported yesterday's findings along with her realization that since Annika hailed from Chandler and Grace from Owenton, miles apart, they were obviously not the same person. "Rob wanted them to be the same person so I could get to the bottom of it and admit he's right."

"About not blaming yourself for Grace's death?" Debra shrugged. "I'm with Team Rob on this one. And same person or not, with their circumstances being so similar, learning more about Annika might help you resolve your feelings about Grace."

Samantha offered a noncommittal shrug.

Debra continued, "How much do your students know about this part of the puzzle?"

"About Grace? Nothing. I wouldn't share that kind of thing with them."

"Oh, I know you wouldn't give specifics. But you might have told them about a client you once had that you still feel guilty about."

"Nah, it never came up. Let them think I have it all together." Samantha chuckled.

"What would they think if they knew you didn't?"

Sam considered for only a moment. "Levi would try to tease me out of it, but then Chess would scold him. Allie and Jeff would reassure me."

"And Sydnee?"

"She would push for every last detail then pronounce that I'm nuts to feel any guilt at all."

"That sounds like Sydnee." Debra nodded, although she only knew her through Samantha's stories. "So, they wouldn't want you to feel guilty without cause, and would do what they could to help you see it more realistically."

Samantha stopped her nod midway. "But it is realistic for me to feel guilty. I could have listened to the part of me that said to act. And I could have acted quicker."

"I've read that part in the code of ethics."

"What part?" Samantha squinted.

"The part about acting quickly once you've read the client's mind." She sipped on a cup of tea.

Samantha tried unsuccessfully to stifle a laugh. "I know, Debra. I do. And my guilt over Grace probably drives a lot of my protectiveness with my students."

Debra clapped her hands in silent applause.

"Oh, and we found out Annika actually did stay for a short time in what is now Allie's room."

"And your former room." She nodded. "Why am I not surprised?"

"You were right about one thing—"

"Probably more than one, but—" Debra motioned for Samantha to continue.

"This requires me to expand my understanding of reality."

"What? For Annika revisiting 331 Stratton? Or your guilt over Grace?" Debra smiled.

"Mercy, you're persistent!" Samantha laughed. "Both, okay? Both."

"I'm glad fear isn't calling the shots." Debra leaned forward and whispered, "But level with me."

"I usually do." Samantha lowered her voice too.

"What about this Annika person who showed up in Allie's room after the séance?"

"The truth?" Samantha spoke in her regular voice. "Totally. Freaks. Me. Out."

They both laughed as Debra admitted the same.

Samantha's cell buzzed several times in quick succession. A glance would have sufficed, if she hadn't seen a few lines of Clarence Whitmer's text flash across the screen. She tapped the screen to read the entire message.

—*Check your email. Now! Len Titus just sent out something to the tenure committee.*—

Chapter 26

Samantha phoned Clarence as she walked to her car. "I'm not *on* the tenure committee. Why would I get an email sent to them? For that matter, you're not on the committee either. How do you even know about an email?" Questions tumbled from Samantha as she held her cell in one hand and scrounged through her purse with the other.

"Overheard it in the faculty lounge. Len called a meeting and requested you be there. You didn't get an email?"

"I'll check it if I can just find—" Samantha's shoulder held her cell to her ear while she used both hands to dig through her purse.

"Find what?"

"My cell. It's not in my purse." Samantha grunted in exasperation. "Did I leave it somewhere?"

"Samantha?"

"Wait, Clarence. I—"

"Samantha. Look in your hand."

Silence.

Her voice was low and ominous. "Tell anyone and I'll deny it."

"Hang up and check your email."

Samantha ended the call and tapped the email icon on her cell. Len's message appeared. He had called a meeting of the tenure committee for Monday of next week and requested Samantha be present to provide information regarding a "matter of concern."

A matter of concern. Well, that narrows it down. How was she supposed to wait until then to see what Len had up his sleeve? She wouldn't, that's how. Samantha pulled her car out of the parking lot and sped toward campus. She would talk to him today.

*****

Out of breath, Samantha walked into Shelley Hall. She slowed her stride when she saw Len's office door open and the light on. To walk in gasping for air would completely undo the calm determination she hoped to convey. A deep breath and she started toward his office.

This time she didn't bother to announce her visit with raps on the door. She merely stood at the entrance to his office and waited. When he didn't look up, she began, "Len, what is this about? I won't be blindsided at the meeting you've called next week."

His head shot up. "Samantha, I don't have time to discuss this now—"

"You'll make time. What will happen at this meeting?"

"If you must know, several disturbing facts have come to my attention."

"Such as?"

"Such as"—he leaned back in his swivel chair—"the fact that you encouraged your students to hold a *séance*, of all things, to speak with a student who died twenty years ago, and planted the idea of the university being *involved* in her death."

Samantha stared at Len and blinked. "I

encouraged…Wait. What?"

Len waved a dismissive hand and mumbled, "Your students are all talking about it, Samantha. Don't deny it."

"They're talking about the fact that they live in rooms I used to live in. Sure. Why shouldn't they? It's odd. But no, Len." Samantha shook her head. "I never said or even thought for a minute that the university was involved in a *death*! And I didn't encourage my students to hold a séance. I didn't *dis*courage it if that's what you mean."

Len sat up straight in his chair and pointed a spindly finger. "Close enough. Need I remind you of the conservative base of support this school draws from? One whiff of faculty-sponsored séances or *worse* and you can kiss funding for our research good-bye."

"Research funding? I don't exactly drain the coffers when it comes to research. Most of it—"

"Maybe you don't. But what about the rest of us? Your new age escapades could very well sink it for the rest of us. And your judgment leaves something to be desired too. Word has it that you gave Rochelle a difficult time—something about her grandchildren? And joking with students about taking drugs to help you teach your morning classes! What were you *thinking*, Samantha?"

"You can't be serious! I don't know where you get your information, Len, but Rochelle was delusional. And *drugs*? I know you don't like me, but you *know* me better than that!"

"As chair of the tenure committee, I have a responsibility to the Vanderlaan community to ensure we don't put someone like you in a position to embarrass us all."

"A position to embarrass?" Samantha closed her eyes and took a deep breath. "So, you'll be telling them I'm an embarrassment to Vanderlaan and shouldn't receive tenure."

"I merely want them to know what we can expect from you in the future should we approve your application."

In contrast to the pounding of her heart, her words came quietly. "Fine. Let me tell you what you can expect from me *now*." She placed both hands on his desk and leaned in. "I'll be at your meeting next week. And the meeting after that. And the meeting after that. I will let them know the truth behind these claims and I won't quit until they see you for the deceitful, manipulative man you are."

As she pulled away and turned to leave, Len said, "I'm glad you're taking this calmly, Samantha. Regardless of what you may think, this isn't personal."

"Oh." She turned back as she reached his office door. "Don't mistake this for calm, Len. And trust me, this is very personal."

****

That night Samantha didn't sleep well. Despite her insistence that Len would not sabotage her future at Vanderlaan, she worried he might. Her bravado with Len was real enough, but she didn't underestimate his influence on campus. So, throughout the night, for every burst of resolve to fight to the end she was hit with the realization that he would do the same. This would not be easy.

She and Rob had discussed it through dinner and afterward while they settled in for the night. He maintained that Len could not turn the entire committee against her. She was too well liked and contributed too much to the university.

Samantha was almost convinced until Rob went to sleep. But as she lay there replaying her run-in with Len, she recalled the calm coolness of Len's accusations. He obviously thought he had the facts straight.

But how could he? She turned over to her side. Students didn't hang out in his office like they did hers, and he certainly didn't exude passion for his students' lives outside of their grades in his classes. Still, one could learn a lot simply listening to students talk before and after class. Sure. That could be it.

She flipped over to her other side. She didn't mind campus talk about the room connection. It was bizarre, and students were interested. Did she mind that the séance had evidently captured the attention of students at large? That was trickier. She had not suggested a séance. In fact, she had refused to participate and put the kibosh on their holding it in her office. But the fact that some in the campus community associated the séance with her students and the room connection they shared gave her pause.

She shifted her weight, turned on her back again. And how in the world had her story about Millie's medicine gotten turned around into something so reprehensible? And surely he didn't believe anything Rochelle had said. But Len was right about one thing: the financial base of Vanderlaan would not tolerate faculty hosting a séance. And if they believed she had made light of drug use or accused the university of being involved in a student *death* they would grab their checkbooks and run. It was enough to quash her dreams of tenure.

But she hadn't done any of those things. Samantha yawned. She would make that clear when she met with the committee…

She could explain it all…

And she would…

Right away…

She finally dozed off. And dreamt of Millie leading a séance, paws outstretched to Rochelle on one side, Len Titus on the other.

Chapter 27

Tuesday, October 23

That night, sleep didn't come easily for Len Titus. When he finally drifted off, a visitor led him into troubled sleep.

He would never finish this stack of papers. Bad enough he spent more time grading this mess than his students put in working the problems. The knock on his office door reminded him that the process would take longer due to these incessant interruptions. "What do you want?" he growled.

"Dr. Titus," she began tentatively. "I'm sorry to interrupt. I know you're busy. I just hoped that I could talk to you for a minute. It's kind of important."

Why do students always have issues to discuss when I'm trying to get out of here early? "Sure. Sit down." He motioned to the empty chair next to the door. "I don't have much time, but if you can talk while I work, go ahead."

But she didn't.

He glanced up. His eyes shot to hers. His chest tightened. "What do you want?"

"I want to tell you the truth. If you're ready to—"

"No! You need to leave." He jumped up, waved toward the door.

She stood. Whispered, "If you aren't ready, I can't stay. But I'll be back."

He bolted upright. Gasping. Disoriented. He fell back onto his pillow, clutched the blanket to his chest. It had been a while since Len had dreamed of her. Always hinting that he was culpable, that he was the reason. But everyone had nightmares occasionally. It was normal. Best forgotten.

But he couldn't forget. Not since he had actually *seen* her. Once while participating in a panel discussion on academic integrity, he had seen her face in the audience. And that time on campus when all the first-year students gathered for orientation. He had been asked to convene a session on campus safety and there she was, a face in the crowd. Those were the times that made him question his sanity and made forgetting impossible.

He closed his eyes, willing himself to sleep. *It was only a dream. It's over.*

But it wasn't. Night after night his sleep was disrupted with the same message, the same messenger.

Night after night Len sent her away.

Chapter 28

Wednesday, October 24

Samantha arrived at Prescott Hall earlier than usual. Before leaving her house, she had sent a text to each of her office entourage, asking them to come by her office before the workday started. All texted back with a thumbs-up emoticon. All except Levi who sent a sleepy face. But, along with the others, he would be here any minute.

Samantha pushed her coffee maker's *on* button and waited impatiently for the caffeinated beverage she craved after last night's difficulty sleeping. As it finished, Allie and Chess came into the room with energetic greetings. Levi and Jeff came in with Sydnee not far behind. All expressed curiosity at the urgency of such an early meeting.

"Rumors are circulating about the séance and Annika's death. Word on the street is, I encouraged you to hold a séance, you used my office for it, and that we are trying to find evidence of the school's involvement in Annika's death."

"But you didn't. And we aren't," Allie said slowly as she turned her head slightly and leaned forward.

"Involvement?" Jeff said. "We were curious about why the campus paper didn't say more, but I wasn't thinking they had anything to do with her death."

"I haven't said anything, Sam. Honest." Levi, now

awake, sat upright.

"I told Maddie," Jeff added, "but no way I said any of that."

"I believe you all and I'm not worried about Maddie." Samantha leaned forward in her chair and took a breath before continuing. "And what I said in class about taking Millie's medicine got twisted. So now I'm also"—she made air quotes—"making light of drug use."

"Drug use!" Sydnee exclaimed. "You?"

Samantha replied calmly, "People blow things way out of proportion and rumors get started."

"But you called us here before sun-up. There's more to it than that," Sydnee said.

Samantha shrugged slightly. "This is not a good time for the powers-that-be to think I'm a threat to Vanderlaan's good name or that I encourage students to use drugs while conversing with dead people."

"I knew it!" Allie jumped up and ran her fingers through her hair. "This is about tenure, isn't it?"

"Allie, this will be fine." Samantha wanted to divert attention away from the risk to her job. And if that lowered the decibel level of Allie's voice, so much the better.

"I've seen my parents tiptoe around tenure committees. I know what this means, Samantha."

"What? What does it mean, Allie? Dr. Hayes?" Chess looked from one to the other.

Allie answered before Samantha could. "Chess, if a faculty member applies for tenure and is denied, they have to leave."

Chess's eyes widened and her mouth hung open. "You get fired?"

"Nobody has fired me, Chess. It's fine. There's no need to worry at this point."

"At this point?" Chess's voice cracked. "Dr. Hayes, are you telling us you might get fired because of rumors about Annika and our séance?"

"It isn't likely to go that far—"

"Not likely, but it *could*?" Chess's eyes teared as she looked back and forth between Samantha and Allie.

Samantha hesitated. "Yes, it could, but there's a tenure committee meeting next week. I'll go and explain the truth behind the rumors. But until this all blows over, don't say any more about this around campus. Except to clarify inaccuracies when you hear them."

Allie agreed, as did Jeff who promised to pass along the same to Maddie.

Sydnee said, "I have no friends outside this office anyway. I'm too busy for friends. Or gossip." She nudged Levi. "And don't play innocent with me. You haven't said anything because you don't want to admit you went to a séance and were freaked out," Sydnee lowered her voice an octave, "by Annika."

"I wasn't freaked out." Levi squinted at Sydnee. "I was *intrigued*."

"I haven't, except with you all," Allie said. "I didn't mean to upset you, Chess. I just wanted you to know this is serious." Allie sat on the edge of the sofa and put an arm around Chess.

Chess shook off Allie's arm. "Don't you see? None of you even talked about this outside this room. No one except me. I'm the weak link here. I told my roommate and several girls in my dorm and most of the students in my classes."

"Dang, Chess," Levi mumbled.

"I didn't know it was a secret!"

"It wasn't a secret." Allie slapped Levi on the shoulder. She tilted her head toward Chess, beckoning the others to do their part.

They all quickly joined in a chorus of, "Of course, it wasn't, Chess."

"And I never said we held the séance here or that you encouraged it or that the university did *any*thing to Annika. I promise, Dr. Hayes." Chess's voice shook.

Samantha leaned forward in her chair again. "Chess, you haven't done anything wrong."

"But if it means you lose your job…" Tears spilled down her cheeks.

As her eyes met Allie's, Samantha nodded toward the door.

Allie gave an almost imperceptible nod and motioned to the others. "I have class. So do you three."

"No, I don't."

Sydnee remained seated until Allie took her by the arm and insisted, "I'm pretty sure you do."

As the last of them left, Chess took a deep breath. "If you're mad and want to kick me out of"—she waved her arms toward the now vacant chairs—"your research team, your office, I understand."

"Chess, I'm not mad. I just want to make sure you're okay."

"I didn't mean to, but I've messed things up for you—"

"No, you haven't." Samantha shook her head and pushed a box of tissue closer to Chess. "And no one wants you to quit our research *or* this office."

"I'm not part of this group. I came in later than the others. I'm not part of this *stupid* room connection." Chess picked up the pillow next to her on the sofa and punched it.

Samantha smiled at the flicker of energy her pillow punch revealed. "And that's important to you."

"Yes! I want to be part of this group. I don't want to be the throwaway." Tears welled in her eyes again. She whispered, "Not here."

Samantha spoke quietly, "You haven't spoken with your parents, have you?"

Chess's head jerked up. "No, not yet."

"Talk to them. And in the meantime, you are *not* the throwaway here. Or anywhere."

Chess nodded, crumpled her tissue, and tossed it in the wastebasket. "I'm fine. And I have to go to class. Will you tell us when you hear more?"

With assurance that she would and instructions not to worry, Samantha sent Chess on to class. She held her coffee mug and slowly breathed in its aroma as she leaned against her desk. It was true—the séance, Annika—none of it was a secret. Chess's behavior was not the least bit out of line. She had merely shared a strange turn of events with their friends and classmates. She was no more responsible for the campus rumors than Samantha was herself. *But if she just wouldn't have talked about it!* Samantha closed her eyes and took a deep breath. *What's done is done.* After Monday's meeting, everything would blow over. It *had* to.

She took a sip as she glanced at the wall clock.

Coffee spurted out her mouth. She grabbed class material in one hand and a napkin in the other as she ran for the door. *Late for class! I'll lose this job yet!*

Chapter 29

Friday, October 26

The remainder of Samantha's week was uneventful. She taught her classes, met with students who needed help, and prepared several exams she would give next week. Her office crew was scarce, too, as they busied themselves with papers, exams, and work. Although she loved a busy office, she was relieved no one was around to bring up Monday's meeting. Not that it was ever far from the corners of her mind. It persistently vied for her attention. But it was easier to keep at bay when no one asked questions that required her reassurance. This time next week the ordeal would be behind her and she would be one step closer to tenure at Vanderlaan. In the meantime, she would simply do her job.

She had jotted down a response to each issue Len said would concern the committee. Since the rumors were unfounded, she simply wrote out the facts and an unequivocal denial of each breach of conduct of which she had been accused. While notes wouldn't be necessary, they gave her the same sense of security that lecture notes provided in class. Rarely needed, but at the ready.

On Friday evening, Samantha and Rob visited one of their favorite local spots. The Patio featured the best pizza and steaks around. Even on a weeknight, you couldn't eat there without seeing several neighbors, city officials, and students alike. The scarcity of available parking suggested there would be more than a few familiar faces here this evening. As they walked across the lot, gravel crunched beneath their feet as the coolness of the autumn air blew across Samantha's face. Her chest felt lighter, and her breath came easier than it had all week.

"What's with you and no jacket?" Rob pulled her close. "It's October, woman!"

"I wouldn't need one if you'd walk faster." She put her arm around him, as much to pull him along as for the warmth. "We need to get in there before their tables are all gone. And their desserts."

"Let me guess, chocolate cream pie?"

"Definitely. But I think I'll start with—"

"Pizza. With *everything* on it," Rob teased. He'd heard it almost every time they had visited The Patio these past four years.

As they entered the restaurant's wooden double doors, the aroma of sizzling onions and peppers greeted them along with the savory waft of Italian sausages. The soft lighting invited her to let go of what remained of her week's stress. A top-forty song that Samantha didn't recognize rang out with a message of hope for love gone wrong but didn't quite drown the laughter and bits of conversation that emanated from each table.

"Hello, Dr. Hayes, Mr. Donovan. Will it be a booth or a table tonight?" The host showed them to a table and handed them menus they would not need. As she hurried back to seat the next group, their waiter appeared. After they ordered drinks and declined appetizers, she disappeared with the promise of a speedy return.

But Samantha wasn't in a hurry. She sat with her face in her palms as Rob gave her a rundown of his work this week. One major kink in his plot had required a rewrite of several scenes. Although it had taken some time and additional research, the plot was now solid. She could always tell how his manuscript was progressing by the amount of time he spent talking about it. When a character or plot was in trouble, he barely spoke. But once he worked it out, he would give her more specifics than she could follow. From his detailed explanation tonight, this week had been a good one.

Rob and Samantha's neighbors from across the street paused on their way to be seated. Rob modestly accepted their compliments of the asters and black-eyed Susans now in bloom along their driveway.

While their waiter's prediction of a swift return was a bit optimistic, she did come back with their drinks, apologies, and her tablet, ready to take their orders. After she tapped in their selections and assured them of their "good choices," she hurried back to the kitchen.

"I see Levi's dating." Rob nodded toward the front of the restaurant. "Who is she?"

Samantha turned in the direction of Rob's gaze. Levi and his date were sitting at a table near the restaurant entrance with another couple. "Shayla. She's in my development class." Samantha waved when Levi glanced in her direction then turned back to Rob. "That doesn't surprise me. They've been talking for a while now. I wondered how long it would take for one of them to ask the other out."

"Hey, Sam. Mr. Donovan." Levi sat down next to Samantha and pulled out his cell phone. "Guess what I found today?"

"Your favorite teacher at a restaurant?"

"Yeah. Yeah." He tapped at his cell. "Look at this." He held it up within a couple of inches of her face. She slid it out to bring it into focus.

"Can you see me in the military?"

"The *military*." Samantha's eyebrows arched. "I didn't know you were considering that as an option."

"My uncle suggested it, so I told him I'd look into it." Levi swiped the screen a couple more times. "There are so many benefits, and it would give me more time to make decisions about grad school."

"Well, that certainly gives you something to think about, Levi." She took the last sip of her soda. Followed by a long drink of her water. She swallowed while holding one hand to her chest and the other toward Levi, as if she would be a more active contributor to this conversation if it weren't for all these beverages in the way. She put her elbow on the table and rested her chin in her palm, sending a couple of forks off the table and into Levi's lap.

Without pause, he returned them and continued. "I gotta get back. I'll come by next week and we'll talk more about it, okay?"

"Absolutely!" She was more than thankful to postpone this conversation to another day.

Levi stood up and stopped. He bolted toward his table, ran past it, and out the door of the restaurant.

"I hope this isn't their first date," said Rob. "Some girls would find that off-putting."

Samantha and Rob scurried to the table where

Levi's friends sat with mouths open. While they murmured about his peculiar exit, Levi stumbled back inside with jagged breath. With nods of assurance toward The Patio's manager, Levi sat down and grabbed a glass of water.

"I saw her, Sam." Another gulp and exhale. "I saw Annika. From the séance. I didn't catch up with her, but it was—" He shook his head. "At least I'm pretty sure, it was her."

Chapter 30

Monday, October 29

"I'm just saying, she couldn't get away fast enough." Levi explained Friday evening's encounter with the elusive Annika to Sydnee and Chess. Samantha listened halfway from her desk while she counted incorrect answers on an exam.

"Did you see her, Dr. Hayes?" Chess asked.

Samantha held up an index finger while she mouthed her count. "I did not." She wrote the percentage on the top of the page, flipped it over, and picked another ungraded one from her stack. She continued.

"How long did you chase her?" Sydnee asked.

"I didn't *chase* her. Man, Syd." Levi recited in sing-song fashion, "White girl chased down by black man on county road." He shook his head. "What could go wrong?"

"Okay, not *chase*, but you followed her and she—what?—ran away?"

Levi nodded. "When I called her name, she looked back over her shoulder then ducked into a group of college students who piled into a car. And she was gone."

"Wow," Chess whispered. "Who was she?"

"Someone named Annika who for some reason didn't want to talk." Sydnee crushed her coffee mug and shot it into the wastebasket. She headed to the research table where she turned on her laptop.

"But why?" Chess slumped into her chair and put her feet on the coffee table.

"Feet off the table!" Levi swatted at her ankle boots.

Chess jumped. Her feet came down. "What's wrong with you, Levi? You put your feet anywhere you want."

"But Sam doesn't let me by with it. And it's my job to mentor you. Speaking of which"—Levi swiveled his neck—"Sam, I don't want to join the military."

"You don't?" She paused ever so slightly. "Whatever you think best, Levi. Any progress on what you *will* do?" she added casually.

"No." Levi slid his laptop out of his backpack, turned it on, and tapped.

"Hi, guys." Jeff walked in and slid his backpack onto the floor.

"Hey!" Sydnee protested.

"And gals." Jeff claimed a spot next to Chess on the sofa. "It's quiet in here. What did I interrupt?"

"Dr. Hayes, exams. Syd, research. Levi, won't enlist."

Jeff nodded at Chess's summary of the past few minutes. "Got it."

"Did you know there's such a thing as a laughter psychologist?" A wide-eyed Levi carried his laptop to Samantha's desk.

Samantha stopped, pen poised in mid-air, to look at the screen which now claimed the center of her desk. "And this professional would do what, exactly?"

"Make people laugh, of course." Levi bent and

scrolled down. "Think of all the people who need a good laugh. Sick people. Stressed people. People in jail. I could be a one-man show of laughter and good will."

"If anybody could do it, my money's on you." Samantha chuckled and waved her hands toward his laptop which he removed.

"Ooh, no way!" He exclaimed before he made it back to the sofa. "Do you know about scatology, Sam?"

"Scat—what?" She continued to mark exams.

"Scatology. Scientists who study…um…excrement."

"Levi!" Chess pretended to dry heave. "Get off that website."

"Yeah, I probably don't have the classes for it. Or the stomach." Levi tapped a few seconds more then stopped when his cell buzzed. "Sam? Guess what?"

Samantha peered over her reading glasses. "You want to study the excrement of people who died laughing."

Levi paused as if contemplating, then shook his head. "No. I just got a text from Allie. She's found Laura, dead Annika's cousin."

All eyes in the room cut to Samantha who put her pen down and pushed the exams aside.

"This isn't the right time to make contact though, is it?" Jeff's eyes darted from Samantha to Levi and back again.

Chess's voice trembled. "Levi, text her. Tell her not to do anything that puts Dr. Hayes in jeopardy!"

"She wouldn't do that, Chess." Sydnee looked up from her laptop, fingers paused above her keyboard.

"Who wouldn't do what?" Allie sauntered in and dropped her bag and jacket on the floor.

"You wouldn't try to find Laura while Dr. H. is up for tenure," Sydnee recapped.

"You told them, Levi!" Allie stopped, eyes wide. "What's wrong with you?" She walked toward Samantha. "I would never do that to you, Samantha. I didn't tell Mr. *Blabbermouth* here," she said through gritted teeth, "for him to announce it. I did find her though. At least I'm pretty sure it's her. A Laura David. It didn't give a maiden name but she's the right age and from Chandler. I won't contact her though until you get tenure. I promise."

"Thank you, Allie." Samantha squeezed Allie's arm and let out a breath. She stacked her newly graded exams with her class material for tomorrow and reached into the drawer of her desk for the lunch she had packed. She pulled the peel from an orange and wished it were a banana when its sticky juice dribbled down her fingers. She grabbed a napkin from the same desk drawer and mopped up as best she could.

Christine walked in and pushed a piece of paper at Samantha. "I just took a message for you. I wanted to transfer the call, but he said not to."

Samantha took the note, met Christine's eyes. "He's postponed the tenure committee meeting for another week."

Her students each chimed in with variations of, "So you have to wait another week?" "Why would he postpone?"

"Probably just a schedule conflict with one of the committee members." Samantha swiveled her chair around to a stack of mail. With her back now to her office entourage she could sort through it freely, decide what to keep and what to throw away. It was usually easy. But not today. Like this ad for a conference. It promised to "Guide You through the Tenure Process: When to Apply and When to Relocate." Could one conference do that? She didn't know. Samantha tossed it aside, gritted her teeth, blinked back the tears, and kept sorting.

Meanwhile, Christine slipped out of the office. Her students moved on to a discussion of exams and papers due this week.

Schedule conflict, nothing. Len Titus just sent me a message. My tenure is in his hands. And it will be granted—or not—on his schedule.

Chapter 31

Saturday, November 3

For the rest of the week, Samantha busied herself at work so she wouldn't obsess about the meeting Len had postponed until Monday. It worked, but it was only a stopgap measure. "I was so busy I couldn't enjoy anything. Even my students," Samantha complained to Rob from her perch on the tarpaulin-covered kitchen table.

Rob cut in Samantha's choice of volcanic eruption orange paint around the side of the cabinets. His pace of speech mimicked his cautious precision with his task. "It'll be over soon. The committee can't put off meeting forever." Once he had the roller in hand, their conversations would speed up considerably.

"Sure you don't want some help?" Samantha's socked feet dangled from the table, so certain was she of his answer.

"Need I remind you about the last time you painted?"

"We needed new carpet anyway."

"Yeah, but *you* need to channel your enthusiasm. Painting requires more restraint than, say, mentoring students. You need patience for the process."

"Hmm. Thank you, Debra." She hopped off the table. "Let me know when you want to break for lunch. I'm going upstairs to edit the rough draft of an article."

"Which one of your merry band wrote this one?"

"Jeff."

"Ah, then maybe it won't require a lot."

"Here's hoping. I'll be in my office if you change your mind about my help." Before she could get to the staircase, the doorbell rang and altered her destination. A glance out the front door's side window revealed Allie and Chess, donned in sweats and hoodies, perfect attire for a chilly morning.

"Hey, ladies! Early for a Saturday morning, isn't it? Don't students sleep until noon anymore?" Samantha began to laugh at her own wisecrack but saw Allie's red, puffy eyes and stopped. "Come on in. Want some coffee? How about a cinnamon roll?"

"We're good, Dr. Hayes. Allie needs to talk."

They trooped down the hall to the kitchen, stepped carefully over the tarp and around table and chairs.

"Mr. Donovan, this is the coolest color! Did you pick it out?" Chess asked.

"What do *you* think?"

"I think it wasn't you." She giggled.

"It'll be beautiful." Allie's lips smiled. Her eyes did not.

As they continued to the den, Rob turned on the radio. Samantha mouthed *thank you* and closed the door behind her. Samantha sat on the couch next to Allie. Chess scooped up Millie and took the chair that had been her perch.

"My parents called this morning. They aren't coming back to the States for Christmas." Allie took the tissue from the box Samantha offered. "They were asked to speak at some human rights conference that'll keep them in England or Germany or *somewhere* over there my entire winter break." Allie growled and tore the tissue. "I need them to come home. To help me sort through my grad school questions. To help me make decisions and to spend the holidays with their *only child*!" Allie threw her hands in the air. "My parents don't get that *occasionally* we need to be in the same country."

"And Allie would just hop on a plane to go there since, you know, she's, like, loaded. But she needs to take a class over break to be able to graduate in May. And it's the *only* class that Whitmer doesn't offer online because he says—" Samantha reached over and placed a gentle hand on Chess's knee. "But you know that, Dr. Hayes; you're her academic advisor." Chess mimed zipping her lip.

Samantha propped her elbow on the sofa back and leaned her head against her fist. "How did you respond when they told you?"

Allie broke eye contact and fiddled with her tissue.

"Let me guess—you said it was fine." A smile tugged at Samantha's lips.

Allie blew out a breath. "It *has* to be, Samantha. This is important to them, to their careers. What they do makes a difference. My parents live for this sort of thing."

"You didn't tell them you're upset."

"No," Allie mumbled into her tissue. "But do I need to tell them everything? Can't they just have—"

"A crystal ball?"

Allie folded her arms and shook her head. "No. It doesn't take a crystal ball to know that even grown kids need family."

"Maybe so. But I've met your parents, Allie, and

208

they adore you. My gut says they're just new to this parenting an adult child. Trust me. It's hard. I mess up on a regular basis with Lucas and Elyse."

"I agree." Chess leaned in toward Allie from her chair. "I mean the part about your parents adoring you. Not the part about Dr. Hayes messing up a lot with her kids. She probably never messes up. She's a cool mom."

"Ha! Well, this cool mom has a suggestion: Call your parents and level with them. Tell them you need them to come home. You're making decisions and need their input." Before Allie could object, Samantha continued. "I know they do important work, but you're important too. You're their daughter. I bet they'll get it."

After a full minute of sniffling and wiping her eyes, Allie pulled herself up from the deep cushions of Samantha's sofa. "Can I do it here?"

"See, Al?" Chess turned toward Samantha and added, sotto voce, "That's what I told her. To just call them and get it out there."

"And you, missy"—Samantha waggled a finger at Chess—"need to take your own advice. Talk to your parents." While Allie took her cell from her pocket and Chess opened her mouth to object, Samantha rose from the sofa and walked to the door to the kitchen. She paused.

"You okay?" asked Allie.

"Hmm? Oh yeah. It's just that at some point in the course of Rob painting a new color I've chosen, I want to scream, 'What have I done!' I just never know when it'll happen."

She yanked open the door, like jerking a bandage

from a wound.

She relaxed, walked into the kitchen giggling. So far, no regrets.

Chess followed close behind and closed the door after her. "She needs privacy. I'll make my call later."

Although unconvinced, she let it go. Rob picked up the roller and cut a swathe of Volcanic Eruption across the far wall. He shook his head and didn't quite stifle a laugh.

"No comments, Donovan." Samantha chuckled.

"I didn't say a word."

While they waited for Allie, Samantha and Chess each sipped coffee and offered their supervision to Rob's efforts. Chess filled them in on her weekend plans which centered on finishing a paper due Monday and studying for a test scheduled Tuesday afternoon. If she could work it in, she wanted to see Aunt Ruth, too.

Allie returned within a few minutes. "They'll be home for Christmas. They didn't seem to mind." A smile crept across Allie's face. She wiped her nose and stuffed her tissue in her hoodie pocket. "They were glad I called."

Samantha smiled. "Feel better?"

"I do. Tha—"

Samantha followed Allie's gaze to the far wall, as Allie declared, "That's orange."

Rob deadpanned, "My wife picked it out. We love it."

Allie tilted her head, right, then left, as if a different angle would change the shade. "It'll be fine." Her creased forehead contradicted her words. She motioned to the front door. "Ready, Chess?"

"Wait. Wait. Tell them what you found out about

Laura." Chess held her hands up to Samantha. "We won't do anything yet, because we can't get you in trouble. But she found this blog. Laura is a nurse and gives health tips and—"

"*You* wanna tell it?" Allie said.

"No, no. You." Chess waved her on.

Allie tapped on her cell and turned it so Samantha could also look at the screen. "See, Laura David. I was pretty sure before that she's the same Laura, but now I'm positive. Look." She scrolled down and tapped on a blog dated a couple of months before. "Here it is. She tells about a cousin who died twenty years ago and how it was so sad because she was so young. And she gives her name—Annika."

"Annika Gra—" Samantha's stomach did a somersault. "Annika *Grace* Lavelle."

Chapter 32

For the remainder of her day Chess debated Dr. Hayes's insistence that she talk to her family about her fears. By Sunday afternoon, she gathered her courage and went to The Fountain to see what she could learn from her aunt. After Ruth beat her at gin rummy by an impressive margin, she asked Chess what was wrong. "Not that I'm complaining but this has been too easy," she teased. "Are you letting me win or is something bothering you?"

"Do you think the Seeleys would have adopted me if they knew they were about to have twins?"

Ruth sat back and studied Chess's face briefly. "Probably not."

"Aunt Ruth! I can't believe you just—"

"Well, I don't think many people *would* adopt one if they were about to have two more. And it has nothing to do with the value of the child." She took the deck of cards Chess had collected from their last hand and placed them on her nightstand. "But that's not really what you're asking, is it? What you really want to know is whether Charles and Pamela were as happy to have you *after* the boys came along as they were before."

Chess nodded. Tears fell. "I want to belong some place, Aunt Ruth. At home. With my friends. I'm always the odd one out. Never one of them." Chess

212

sniffed.

"Have you spoken to your parents about this?"

She let out a growl of frustration. "What's with everyone wanting me to talk to my parents?"

Aunt Ruth smiled and squeezed Chess's hand. "Is that what your Dr. Hayes said?"

"And Allie. And Levi." She laughed from a tear-streaked face.

"Because it's the best answer and we all know it." Aunt Ruth reached out for a hug that Chess gladly gave.

"I'll talk to Mom and Dad first chance I get," Chess promised. With plans for a rematch next Sunday, Chess tossed her jacket over her shoulder and turned to leave.

Chess came to an abrupt halt at the door where she almost ran into Liv, the resident with dementia. "Oh, I'm sorry Miss Liv. I didn't see you there. How are you today?"

Unflustered and particularly lucid, Liv said, "Don't worry, honey. Parents will do anything for their child. Unless it's too late, of course. And it will be for some." Liv looked away, as if lost in another time. Then, as if returning to the present, she sought Chess's eyes. "But for the ones we can still help, we'll do anything." She smiled, seemed satisfied to have made her point, and took her leave.

Chapter 33

The fact that Grace and Annika were one and the same sickened Samantha yet came as no surprise. She could barely think of anything else the rest of the weekend. Hadn't she known from the moment she heard about Annika's death that she and Grace were the same person? She couldn't explain the names being different or that they hailed from different hometowns; nonetheless, at some level, she had known.

By Monday morning Samantha had ruminated over what little she knew about Annika Grace and reached the same conclusion each time: she couldn't resolve this until she talked with Laura. And once her job was secure—or lost for good—she would do just that.

But on the bright side—literally—her orange kitchen erupted with a bold welcome befitting its name. One more coat and Rob would be finished. She stepped across the tarp to retrieve her lunch from the fridge, snatched her purse and coat from the hall closet, and left for the office.

Registration for next semester was in full swing. Before and after each class, a stream of students came by with questions about courses offered and pleas for help setting up their schedules. The chaos drove away her obsessions about Annika Grace and the tenure committee meeting scheduled for 5:00 that afternoon.

Oh, and a session with Debra afterward. Good timing.

About 4:30, Samantha closed her office door, turned off her lights, and sat at the far end of the sofa. She set the alarm on her cell for 4:45 so she could get to Shelley Hall a little before the meeting began. She wouldn't run in late, flustered and out of breath. No, she would be calm, with grace and confidence. She had nothing to hide. She would answer any questions they asked and put their minds and this whole debacle to rest.

She closed her eyes and took slow deep breaths. *I am an accomplished, professional woman. I am tenure material.* She repeated her mantra several times until her alarm broke in. She silenced the alarm. One more breath. *Let's do this.*

She jumped up, fluffed the back of her hair, and grabbed her coat. She stepped into the hallway and dug through her purse. No keys. She felt inside her coat pockets. Nothing. Growling, she stepped back inside, emptied the contents of her purse onto the coffee table. Not there. With one hand on a hip and the other around an empty shoulder bag, Samantha did a visual search of her desk. Aha! Under the stack of student files sitting catawampus. *How did they get there?* She lifted the files and grabbed—her stapler.

"Where are my keys!" She slammed the files and the stapler back onto her desk.

"Dr. Hayes?" The last student she had advised this afternoon stood at her door.

"Murphy. I'm sorry. I'm about to leave, kind of in a hurry and—"

He held out her keys. "I must've picked these up with mine when I left a few minutes ago. Didn't notice until I was almost to my dorm. I'm sorry, I—"

"No, no! It's fine." Samantha clutched the keys in one hand, her throat in the other. "Thank you for making the trip back." He prattled off additional apologies; she, a few more expressions of gratitude while locking up and fast walking toward the outside door of Prescott.

"You have an umbrella, Dr. Hayes?"

"An umbrella? Oh—" Water droplets glistened on Murphy's hair and face. "It's raining."

"Just started to sprinkle on my way over here. If you hurry to your car, you'll be all right." He glanced out the glass door. "If your car is close by."

Samantha's car was right outside the door. Shelley Hall was not. "I'll be okay, Murphy. I'm headed to a meeting, but I can stop at my car for an umbrella. Thanks again," she called out as they parted ways.

She couldn't avoid the drizzle but hardly got wet as she hurried to her car. She snatched an umbrella from the backseat and set out again, this time at a slower pace. By the time the downpour started, she was shielded under the domed umbrella Rob had insisted she keep in her car. She would arrive at Shelley, dry and on time. She wouldn't be early, but she wouldn't be late either. It was all good. She would meet the committee in a way befitting a candidate for tenure: with grace and confidence.

She would have, too, had her foot not slipped on the wet pavement. "Aaahhh!" Purse flew. Umbrella sailed. Her backside absorbed the squishy earth. Cries of concern rang out from a couple of students who scurried from their car. Collecting her jettisoned purse and umbrella, they helped her rise from her soggy place of honor.

"Can we take you somewhere?" Their voices muffled by the now torrential rainfall.

"No, thank you." Samantha's tears flowed as she assessed her need for bandages, splints, or adult daycare. "I can walk." Evidently her limp suggested otherwise to the student who once again clutched at her arm. "Are you hurt?"

"No," Samantha squeaked. "My heel just broke off my boot. I'm fine. Really." She sniveled as she accepted her umbrella and purse from her would-be caretakers. With another thank you, she hobbled off.

Wet and cold, she made her way to Shelley Hall. A quick detour to the women's room allowed her to squish water from her hair and sop mud from her derriere. She snatched tissue from one of the stalls to wipe away the smear of rain, tears, and mascara that dripped from her cheeks and chin. "Waterproof. Sure." She blew her nose, tossed the tissue in a trash receptacle, and swung open the door.

"Grace and confidence," she obediently recited to herself as she clicked and clonked down the hall to the conference room.

****

Six pairs of eyes stared at Samantha as she entered the conference room of Shelley Hall. No longer dripping, she remained cold and soggy. With as much grace as she could muster, she wobbled in and nodded politely to the people who would help decide her fate: to recommend she receive tenure and send her application to its next stop in the chain of reviewers or send her application on with a recommendation she be denied. While a recommendation either way would not determine her fate, it would influence the next committee. Enough committee denials and she would be told to leave.

The room held a mahogany finished conference table, surrounded by eight plush, black, executive chairs. Len Titus peered at her over wire-rimmed glasses from his post at the head of the table. Two familiar and friendlier faces sat on either side of him. Kathryn Day, professor of music, attended the same church as Samantha and Rob. Newcomer, Gregory Hill, taught business classes and currently served with her on another committee. Kathy and Greg were decent people who had no agenda other than teaching well and serving students. They were her allies. Each greeted her and expressed concern over the downpour which had obviously taken her by surprise.

Two men she did not recognize stood at a corner cabinet, helping themselves to coffee. One introduced himself as Dr. Lancaster, and although he offered to pour her a cup, his poker face made it impossible for her to determine if he was friend or foe. The other reached across the table to shake her hand and offer a warm smile along with his name, Charlie Bremer.

The last of the six looked up briefly, with a grimace, when Kathryn introduced her as Priscilla Wright, from the university library. Samantha retracted her outstretched hand when Priscilla shot her unhappy gaze back to what she had been reading. *If that's my tenure file, I'm sunk.*

"Let's get started." Len wasted no time. "Samantha asked to speak to our concerns as we consider her application for tenure. Since the inclement weather didn't detain her"—he gave her sodden attire the once-over still again—"I suggest we ask her our questions now. And she will leave before we move on to other applicants."

And why does he even keep those glasses on his nose? Does he ever actually use them?

"Your credentials are more than adequate, Samantha. Ph.D. from the University of Louisville. Twenty-five years as Professor of Psychology at Hayward before coming to Vanderlaan. Four years here. You've served on each committee you've been assigned, chaired a couple of them. Excellent evaluations from your students and department head. You do your share of academic advising. And you've published in several prestigious academic journals. Garnered a few for your students as well."

I sound like a real loser. Why don't they demand my immediate dismissal?

Kathryn had nodded throughout Len's soliloquy. "Which is why I don't know why we are even debating this."

Len held up a palm toward Kathryn. "In fact, my only concerns are that you evidently told your students you take drugs to help you endure your morning teaching schedule and—"

"Oh, Len, come on," Kathryn said. "There has to be an explanation for that." She directed her gaze to Samantha.

"Of course there is." Samantha nodded. "I told my classes that I had accidentally taken my dog's medicine and—"

A mirthless snort escaped Priscilla.

"—I made a joke about it the next day."

"Nonetheless," Len said, "there's also the recent

talk of your dabbling in the paranormal and—"

"Really, Len? Dabbling?" Kathryn rolled her eyes.

He swiveled his head toward Kathryn. "A séance on campus—"

"Excuse me, but I did not hold nor participate in a séance."

"You deny it?" Dr. Lancaster asked. "Because I heard you held a séance in your office to contact some girl who died forty or fifty years ago." He flung his arm back as if the past several decades were in the next room.

"I heard about the séance," Greg said. "Samantha, you're not a flake. What was that about?"

"Some of my students heard about a girl on campus who died *twenty* years ago." Samantha shot a glance at Lancaster. "One of them suggested a séance, several others agreed. It was not held in my office. I did not attend." She turned her gaze back to Greg. "That's all there was to it."

Len's head tilted and mouth opened as if he doubted her candor. "Not all there was to it, Samantha. Did you not encourage the kids to hold a second séance when they claimed to make contact with this America person?"

"America? What?"

"The girl, the girl." Len rolled his hand as if to accelerate her thought process.

"Oh! *Annika*." Samantha shook her head. "No, Len. *Annika* was her name. And, yes, a girl by that name *did* come by after their séance. And, no, I *did not* encourage them to hold another one. But yes, I *did* tell them I thought it was odd. Which it was." Samantha sat up in her chair to escape as much of the cold dampness against her back as she could. "And they aren't kids, by the way, they're young adults."

"You didn't host it, attend it, or encourage it." Greg turned to Len. "What's the problem?"

"The problem is her *presence* at these discussions *and* her joking about something as serious as drugs use." Len pointed a finger at Samantha. "Young adults or not, they are impressionable, and you let it get out of hand."

"Now she's responsible for what twenty-somethings do on their own time?" Kathryn whistled. "We're all in trouble. Why do you let your students party all night, Len? A couple of mine were picked up for shoplifting last term. Should I answer for that?"

"There is a difference, Kathryn. You and I don't mastermind the partying or the shoplifting."

"Mastermind! I didn't mastermind anything! I was simply in the room when they talked about it."

"Our donors will see a professor who leads impressionable young people into new-age crap and then insinuates that the Vanderlaan administration had something to do with the girl's death. Next thing you know, they pull funding, and our research budget consists of a box of paperclips and a ream of copy paper."

"Look," Lancaster said. "I just met you a few minutes ago, but you seem reasonable. Just apologize for your students' behavior and make your students quit. Problem solved." His eyes darted between Samantha and Len.

Without commenting on Dr. Lancaster's suggestion, Len continued his litany. "And what's this about these students having your old rooms? Did you have a hand in their room assignments? That didn't just happen, Samantha. How did you manage that and for what purpose?"

"Oh, puh-lease." Kathryn pushed her chair away from the table. "What are you saying, Len? That Samantha rigged dorm assignments so she could...what? Help young people make good career choices? This is ludicrous." She threw her pen to the table.

Samantha's chest tightened. How much should she say to the committee? "This isn't even about room assignments or séances. It's about—"

"We need to move on." Len placed both palms on the table. "It's time you left, Samantha, so we can discuss this privately. We have other tenure applicants."

"You haven't responded to my solution, Samantha," Dr. Lancaster said.

Because it was asinine. "They're adults." Samantha turned her head slightly to make eye contact. "What did you say your first name was again?"

He met her stare. Held it. Said nothing.

"You need to leave, Samantha." Len's voice was quiet, steady.

Her gaze switched to Len. Her tone mirrored his. "What are you afraid of? That I'll tell them why you would sabotage my tenure?" She rose and walked to the door. "Because I won't."

Chapter 34

Monday, November 5

She glanced at her watch as she left Shelley Hall. Ten after five. Good. Even with the limp, necessitated by her missing heel, she had time to go home and change out of her wet, muddy attire before her session with Debra. *Click. Thud.* Of course, the rain had stopped. *Click. Thud.* A clear evening lay ahead. *Click. Thud.* How nice. Now that there's *no* reason to need an extra dose of self-confidence. *Click. Thud.*

She reached her car, opened the trunk, and pulled out several plastic bags from the pile she had forgotten to take for recycling. She covered the driver's seat and settled herself there. Boots off. Heater on.

Once home, she dumped her boots, now matted with mud, in the garbage and peeled off her soggy garments. After a quick shower, she put on fresh clothes, opting for a more comfortable ensemble—jeans, a hoodie, and athletic shoes. Much better. No time for make-up or any more than a quick blow dry of her hair. She almost opted out of the bra. But with today's luck that would have all but insured getting pulled over by a former student turned police officer. No, sadly, the bra was in.

She shot a glance at the grandfather clock before jouncing downstairs. Was there time to make coffee? Probably not, but she would hurry. She stepped across the drop-cloth that still covered the kitchen floor to grab a travel mug and pop it under the single-serve coffee maker. A blob of creamer, a lid, and she was on her way.

****

Samantha arrived at Debra's office with coffee in hand and zero minutes to spare. She relayed her ill-fated trek to Shelley Hall and race home afterward to change clothes. She concluded with open arms to direct attention to her attire, and a slight bow as Debra clapped for a story well-told. Was it the telling of the tale or that she was now warm and dry, in a place where she would be the cared *for*, not the care*giver*, that gave her the first flicker of humor for the experience?

Samantha settled in. "You think clients trust you when they spill their secrets? No. It's when they come in sans make-up with a bra-optional attitude, *that* is when the therapeutic relationship is firmly established." She raised her cup to her lips. "They won't teach you that in a book, Debra."

Debra laughed and shook her head. "Not even *once* have I read that in a book."

Samantha inhaled. Exhaled. Took a sip of her coffee. In the flurry of activity required to get here, she had not allowed herself to deliberate over the committee meeting or her feelings about it. She could now do just that. She began with a recount of what had been said by whom and her fear of what it meant for her future at Vanderlaan.

"I underestimated the malice Len Titus holds for me. And the power he wields." She bit her lower lip. "Rob and I are at home here and assumed this would be our last stop. To start over somewhere else..." A tear rolled down her cheek. Then another. Samantha reached for the tissue box Debra kept at the ready.

"Okay, but we don't know it's come to that." Debra popped her leg underneath her. "You have allies on the committee. They might rein Titus in."

Silence.

Debra continued, "And if they don't…you *do* have some recourse."

Samantha pinched the bridge of her nose. Shook her head and took a swig of her now cooled coffee. "Not if you mean blowing the whistle on Len's plagiarism."

"I'm not saying you should or—"

"No, Debra."

"—or that you shouldn't. But, Samantha, letting Titus continue while the university loses *good* people like you…"

"If it were only me, I'd fight." Her voice broke again. She gave in to the tears that stung her eyes. "But it's Barb's career too. If I don't handle this well and she gets hurt—"

"If she gets hurt, it won't be Samantha's doing. It'll be Len's." Debra leaned in. "You've just been blindsided by someone who wants to hurt you purely for the sake of revenge. And yes, there is a risk. If you blow the whistle on Len, Barb might bear the consequences. But there is also the possibility that *he* will. Speaking up could free you *and* Barb." Debra sat back. "It's dicey, Samantha. I don't pretend to have the answer. I just hope you won't let fear make the call."

Samantha sniffed and dabbed her eyes for several moments. Then cleared her throat and tossed her tissue in a nearby wastebasket. "On a positive note, I'm killing it in the when-to-intervene-with-students category."

Debra didn't balk at Samantha's topic shift. "Great! What are they up to these days?"

"Levi is in an all-out exploration of every career out there—whether it makes sense for him or not. Some I like. Some I *detest*." Samantha laughed. "But I haven't put the kibosh on any of them."

Debra nodded her approval.

"Then Allie and Chess want more direction, which I'm doing. Mostly in the form of encouragement to talk to their respective parents." She shook her head and growled. "Just speak up, girls!"

Debra looked to the ceiling and offered a singsong, "No comment," and made a show of clamping her lips shut.

"Point taken." Samantha played with the rim of her travel mug. "I've stepped out of some choices, stepped in for others." A smile pulled at Samantha's lips. "Almost like I know what the heck I'm doing." She downed the last swallow from her coffee. "Only…"

Debra threw her head back and offered a good-natured groan. "How did I know there would be an 'only'?"

"Only…it doesn't resolve anything with the others."

"You still feel responsible for Rochelle?"

"A little. And a little for Len's experience at Hayward. And for Annika."

"Annika?"

Samantha related Allie's discovery of Laura and her own realization that Annika's middle name was Grace. That they were one and the same. "And once tenure is no longer a concern, we'll ask Laura what happened with her cousin." Samantha shrugged.

Debra stared out the window and chewed on the end of her pen. "You haven't said anything about the room connection in a while. Any ideas on how it ties in with Annika? Grace?"

"Only that it seems like some cruel, cosmic joke." *Did I say that out loud?* Samantha tapped a couple of fingers to her lips. "I didn't mean that." She closed her eyes. "Or maybe I did."

"What part of it seems cruel?"

"That I have worked my entire adult life to be there for everyone—my family, my friends, my students." She gritted her teeth. "And I worry constantly that I don't do enough, or maybe too much. Because that's the way life is. We never know do we?" She looked at Debra for confirmation. She received a shrug.

"Then I find out the students I've been closer to than any others—ever—have this, this surreal connection to me that no one can explain." Samantha got up and walked to the window, hands on hips. "And the only link we find is a girl who died years ago that I knew"—she waved her hands—"sort of, and always felt an eerie sense of guilt about her death.

"And"—she held out an index finger—"it all happened at the place where I ousted someone whose wife left him, sent his life into a spiral, and who just *happens* to *now* have the biggest say in whether I stay or leave." Hands on the windowsill, she turned back to Debra. "So, unless I wake up soon to learn this has all been a nightmare, then *something*—synchronicity or the universe or God or whatever—is telling me I hurt others more than I help them and I need a change."

Samantha shook her head and felt her scarab pendant move against her collar. "Is that what this was for, Debra? To tell me I need to quit?"

Debra swiveled in her chair toward Samantha. "I don't know what it means. But it *can't* mean you need to quit." Debra sat on the edge of her chair. "To *not* speak truth in this situation might be necessary. But, Samantha, it comes at a price. For your career, for your students' education, for your own peace of mind." Debra paused, sat back. "Is the price worth it?"

Chapter 35

Tuesday, November 6

It could be as much as two weeks before the committee would pass along her file to the president of Vanderlaan. Samantha would hear at that time whether they recommended she be retained with tenure status or not. Until then, she waited. Of course, she could also give Barb a heads-up, publicly call Len out on his academic theft, and demand he be removed from her committee. But she didn't. Maybe it wouldn't be necessary. Maybe it would work itself out somehow without putting anyone else at risk.

But she couldn't focus on tenure and committee decisions today. Too much to do in these next few weeks before Thanksgiving break. In addition to class prep and papers coming in faster than she could grade them, she needed to finish revising the manuscript her team had written. She hoped to send it out this afternoon to an academic journal.

While she worked, Sydnee and Jeff sat in her office, occupied with homework on their laptops. They hadn't squabbled in some time now. After a few minutes of quiet work, Jeff muttered that he needed an idea for a birthday present for Maddie. "I don't want it to be too personal. Just something fun that reflects her personality."

Samantha and Sydnee each held their fingers above

their respective keyboards and looked at him with their mouths open.

"What?" he asked.

"You have the nerve to ask me to help you pick out a gift for Maddie? You told me to butt out and leave it to you."

"I never said to butt out."

Sydnee answered with protest noises. Samantha raised an eyebrow.

"Okay, yeah. I did. More or less. But—"

"But *what*?" Sydnee crawled out of her chair and plopped down next to Jeff on the sofa. "You need my help? Old Sydnee butted in once and you want me to save the day again? Is that it? Speak up, Jeff. I can't hear you." Her hand cupped her ear.

"Gloating is beneath you, Syd." Jeff shook his head. "Most unseemly."

Sydnee shook her head while Samantha resumed typing.

"You got nothing? No ideas? I need help!"

"You can't have it both ways, Mr. Hannan." Samantha chuckled. "Can Syd help you or not?"

"I don't want it both ways," he mumbled. "It's fair to want gift suggestions but not want interference in the relationship."

Samantha tilted her head as she considered. "He's got a point, Syd."

"Yeah, well, I got a point too, Mr. I-Need-Help-No-I-Don't-Yes-I-Do." Sydnee could sass better than anybody Samantha knew.

"If you've got a point, I wish you'd get to it." Jeff was not without sass himself.

"Did it ever occur to you that maybe I didn't step

in for *you*?"

His eyebrows pulled together.

"That maybe I stepped in for *her*?" Sydnee added.

"For Maddie?" His head tilted. His eyes lit up as he whispered, "You knew *she* liked *me* and that's why you said something? That's why she called me as soon as she did!"

"Yes," Syd said with weary satisfaction. She took off her ball cap and slapped him with it, put it back on her own head. "That's why, you dim-witted, crazy man."

"And that's how she got my number?"

Syd smiled and batted her eyes.

He held up a hand for a high five which she returned. "Well played, Ms. Baldwin. Well played."

****

Samantha made final touches to their manuscript and called them to the research table. She reviewed with them the changes she had made and answered their questions about the journal where she would send it. The next goal for this project would be for them to consolidate the main findings into a poster to present at a regional conference in January. They agreed to finish it in the next few weeks so Samantha could print it over winter break.

Syd and Jeff packed up their gear and took off for class, just as Levi and Chess came in, conversation in progress.

"Just ask. What's the worst that could happen?" Levi's backpack slid off his shoulders onto the floor by the sofa.

Chess kicked off her shoes and flopped cross-legged into a chair. "They'll be hurt and try too hard to reassure me. I still won't know if it's the truth and I'll be more stressed than ever. No, not asking."

"What if I ask?" Levi put his shoe-clad feet on the table.

Samantha waved her hand toward the table on her way to the desk. "What if you take your feet off the table first? And what do you want to ask?"

His feet came down. "I want to ask her parents—wait." He asked Chess, "Can I talk about this?"

"Sure. She knows about it." Chess waved him on.

"Ask her parents what?" Samantha sat down at her desk and pulled a multicolored stack of note cards out of the top drawer. She needed to sort them for a class activity tomorrow.

"I would say, 'Hey, Mr. and Ms. Seeley. Chess feels like a fifth wheel. Could you maybe adopt *me* so she'll know you're cool with having more kids after the twins?' "

Samantha shook her head and continued her card sort. "He is right about one thing, Chess. You need to talk to your family."

Levi pulled his laptop out of his backpack, powered up, and muttered, "Just offering my services. I'd be a great big brother."

"I don't know how without backing them into a corner where they'll have to lie." Chess pulled her hair into a knot and let it fall again.

"Who has to lie?" Allie came in, put her book bag on the research table.

"My parents, if I ask them about wanting me after the twins."

"Ah." Allie dismissed Chess's statement with a wave of her hand. "They won't lie. You're worried for nothing. But wait—scratch that. Dr. Gordon says it's important to communicate empathy for the client, so," Allie paused as she tilted her head from side to side. Then in a slightly robotic fashion, she rephrased, "It's hard to ask a question when you're afraid of the answer." She looked at Samantha who nodded her approval. Levi offered a high five, which Allie accepted.

"It is." Allie sat on the chair next to Chess. Chess asked, "What would you do? Ask or not?"

"*I'd* ask." Allie shrugged. "Hey, you ever think you ended up with the Seeleys because of synchronicity? Like, this whole room connection thing?"

Chess blew out a gust of air. "Sure. I'm just as out of the loop there as I am here."

"No, no." Allie sat up straight. "I mean that you ended up with the Seeleys for some greater purpose."

"Jeff would say it's providence—the work of God," Levi mumbled as he continued to tap.

"Yes, and it could be the same thing." Allie leaned forward and tapped the arm of Chess's chair. "But the point is, there could be a higher reason you ended up where you did. Just like some higher purpose for us to all end up in Samantha's old rooms. We don't know yet what it is, but…" She shrugged.

Samantha caught her breath. Allie's words about the purpose of the room connection hit like a gut punch. What if the purpose was to show her the truth behind Annika's death and her own failure as a mentor? Should she leave Vanderlaan? Would she even have a choice if Len got his way? The busy-ness of office chatter and class prep couldn't alter the tenuous state of her job at Vanderlaan. Nor the precarious balance in her emotions. *Breathe. Just sort the cards and breathe.*

"I don't know. But I need answers." Chess slumped and hung her legs over the side of the chair.

"Speaking of the need for answers, can I ask an unrelated question?" Levi carried his laptop to Samantha's desk. "What do you think about this? A job as a technical writer for psychological pamphlets."

Samantha read from his computer screen. "Technical writer…describe psychological symptoms and treatment options in reader-friendly language." She went back to her stacks of cards. "You're certainly capable."

Levi waited. "You mean apply?"

"If you want."

Levi trudged back to the sofa with his laptop. "I need more than that. Do you think I should apply or not?"

"I don't know. What do you think?" Samantha tied a rubber band around each stack.

"That this is a big decision—graduate school or a job? And if I get a job, which one?"

Samantha swiveled her chair around to her computer. Typed in her password. Hit enter.

"You really won't tell me what you think?"

"You can't have it both ways." Samantha glanced over her shoulder. "I can give my opinion. I can keep quiet. Can't do both," she said with a tilt of her head.

"Samantha!" Christine burst through the door. She flapped both hands toward herself and jerked her head toward the hallway.

Samantha jumped up, bolted to her friend. Her stomach pitched to her throat. "What's wrong?"

"Dr. Titus's secretary just called." Christine caught her breath. "He just sent your file to the president."

Chapter 36

Tuesday, November 6

Although the continuation of her tenure application down the academic pipeline was a pressing concern, Samantha was eager to hear why it necessitated a private meeting outside her office. Christine relayed that her friend Lisa, the secretary for the math department, had just called to say Len Titus had sent the committee's recommendation to the president's office.

Lisa liked Len as much as anyone did. Which is to say, she didn't. At all. While she would never jeopardize her job, she was an ally of anyone on the receiving end of Len Titus's handiwork and made a point of tipping them off when possible. Lisa wasn't privy, of course, to the committee's decision regarding Samantha but had picked up a few tidbits from the rumor mill of Shelley Hall. She had passed along the same to her friend, Christine, who summed it up in whispers outside the door to Samantha's office.

"Lisa worked late last night and overheard them fighting after you left. She couldn't make out all of it, but it sounded like Kathy—Dr. Day—reamed Titus but good. A lot of yelling about due process and campus bullies." Christine made a visual sweep of the hall. "Then more yelling, this time from Dr. High-and-Mighty—"

"Priscilla?"

"I know, right? Who knew she could talk? Lisa said she and Titus ganged up on Dr. Day. After the meeting adjourned, they all came out slamming doors and stomped out of the building. Except Dr. Hill and the new guy, Dr. Bremer. They kind of tiptoed out. She caught a glimpse of Bremer though. Said he was literally shaking. Poor guy, probably wonders what kind of a circus he's joined."

Samantha leaned against the wall and spoke into prayer-folded hands. "Each committee is to let the applicant know what their recommendation is. Right away." Samantha looked back into the office at her computer.

"As in an email?" Christine asked. "That seems cold."

"Email, in person, pony express." Samantha shrugged. "I dunno."

"Want me help you get rid of your entourage so you can check emails in private?"

Samantha squeezed her friend's arm and pushed away from the wall. "I'll do it. Thanks." Samantha walked back into her office with a reasonably believable fake smile. She gathered her jacket and purse, pretending to close shop for the day, and was relieved to see her crew follow her lead. Within minutes all had gone.

Samantha locked the door. Darted to her computer. Clicked the email icon. A flurry of new messages appeared on the screen. Campus announcements. Textbook publishers. Student questions. Conference advertisements.

Nothing from the committee.

Her fists hit the desk and almost muffled the tap on the door.

Kathy.

Samantha's heart hammered. Breath caught in her chest. Before she could process what to do, she was across the office, with the door open, waving her colleague in. Just as quickly, the door was closed. They sat.

"Well?" Samantha leaned forward.

"I'm sorry, Samantha." Kathy handed her an envelope with Vanderlaan letterhead in the return address corner. The committee's recommendation—hand delivered.

She leaned back into the sofa. Let out the breath she had been holding. "The committee recommended I not get tenure." How could she expect the worst yet, when it came, still be surprised?

"It was awful, Samantha." Kathy rubbed her forehead, closed her eyes. "After you left, Len asked if we believed your version of the story. I told him you deserved tenure. That this was a witch hunt." Kathy swallowed. "Greg agreed. Said it wasn't right to make you responsible for kids being kids.

"Then Len asked the others to weigh in. Charlie hem-hawed about being new, not knowing the campus climate, blah, blah, blah." Kathy shook her head. "Fear talking. He already knows you don't cross Len. So, I said, 'Unacceptable. You're on this committee, Bremer. Speak your mind.' Long story short—he sided with Len."

Kathy took a breath. "I didn't handle it well, Samantha. I was so fed up. I screamed at Bremer, told him Len counted on the new hires being afraid, and if he would just stand up to the man—" She shuddered. "Then I called Len a few names I'm not proud of. And Priscilla blew up at me, said I was *a petulant child*." Kathy pinched her voice to mimic her haughty colleague. "She said Lancaster was right. That you had not owned up to your part of the séance gaffe and could we trust you to be level-headed with impressionable young minds. She threw her support to Len."

Kathy slumped in defeat. "Samantha, I let you down. If I hadn't lost my temper, maybe I could have convinced them. I'm sorry."

Samantha couldn't move. Her chest tight with breath it would not release. Knots and nausea competed for control in her stomach.

"What will you do?" Kathy asked.

"What *can* I do? Wait. See what the president and trustees say." She shrugged. "I'll be okay. And thank you for what you did." Samantha got up, walked to the fridge for water, handed one to Kathy and unscrewed the cap on her own. She took a long gulp, cleared her throat.

"Okay, so how long will it be? Another month? I can do that. The university will either decide for me or for Len. They either want me here or they want to pander to the great and powerful, Dr. Titus. It's as simple as that." Another draft. "Meanwhile, I keep my eyes open for jobs."

"That…would be a good idea." Kathy met Samantha's eyes. "There's more."

"More?" A mirthless laugh spurted from Samantha. "What else?"

"I ran into Len last weekend. He was out with someone."

"Who?" Where was this going? Samantha motioned with her water bottle for Kathy to speed it up.

"Eleanor Waters. Chair of the trustees."

****

"Can you *believe* he's dating the chair of the Vanderlaan trustees?" Samantha shoved the last of the laundry into the washer and slammed the lid shut. Rob stood, hands on hips, mouth open as she relayed the accounts of last night's meeting.

"And Kathy was sure it was Len and this Eleanor Waters person? And that it was a *date* date?"

"You mean does he *like* like her?" She delivered the middle-school sarcasm with a snarky smile.

Rob's jaw clenched. "I'm not the enemy, Samantha. I'm on your side."

She squeezed her eyes shut. Tears stung, then fell. "I'm sorry. I know."

He pulled her into an embrace, where she let herself sob for the first time since hearing the news.

"I'm just saying, it might not be what it seems." He walked them up the stairs into the kitchen. "For instance, this would *have* to be against school policy, for a tenure committee chair—or even *member*—be in a relationship with the head of the trustees?" He shook his head. "Wouldn't he have to recuse himself from your committee if they were dating? There has to be more to the story."

Rob poured coffee for each of them, set her spoon and salted caramel creamer on the table. She stirred in enough to ensure she would taste no coffee.

"Plus, didn't we meet this woman at the president's open house in August?" Rob sat with hands around his steaming mug. "She seemed too nice to date that little pisher."

"I'm just tired, Rob. Tired of the fight. Tired of defending myself. Tired of thinking about it." She played with the handle of her mug. "I might—"

"Don't say it."

"—pull my tenure application and resign."

"Samantha—"

"If I'm not *denied* tenure, I won't have to explain it at the next school."

"You also won't be granted something you've earned! You'd be letting Titus win. And how many times does he get to mess with people before someone stands up and says 'no'? And"—he pointed a finger at her—"you'd have to leave students you adore. You ready for that?"

She buried her face in her hands, elbows on the table. "No. But they'll graduate before long anyway."

"We'd have to sell the house." A smile tugged at Rob's lips. "Leave your volcanic eruption walls."

Tears welled again as her voice squeaked, "I love my walls."

Chapter 37

Yes, she would have to leave her students. Would they understand? Did she even understand it herself? It didn't matter. Now that the higher ups had her application, it was only a matter of time until the decision would be made for her with direr consequences than she was willing to pay.

No, the time had come. And before it became public, she wanted to give them a heads up. She texted the group asking them to come by her office late afternoon. By 5:00 everyone but Levi was seated in her office. Chess sat sideways in her chair, legs hanging off the side.

Allie opened the fridge. "Oh. Out of juice. And soda."

"Off my game. Sorry, Allie."

"I'll take a water." She flashed a warm smile and took the corner of the sofa.

Sydnee grabbed a handful of fruit candies from the dish and piled all of them in her lap.

Jeff stared. "Could you at least ask if anybody else wants any?"

Sydnee huffed, handed him her stash, and went back for more.

"Let the party begin." Levi walked in arms outstretched. He plucked a package of candy from

242

Jeff's pile and sat next to Allie.

Samantha wheeled her desk chair to the group. "There is no easy way to say this. I'm resigning—leaving Vanderlaan."

Blank stares.

"Because of me?" Chess said quietly. "Because of what I said about the séance?"

"No, Chess. This isn't your fault," Samantha said. "I applied for tenure. The departmental committee recommended it be granted. The university committee did not. And while the trustees make the final decision, they aren't likely to grant it if one of the committees recommends otherwise. I've decided to resign now rather than have that blot on my career."

Levi's jaw muscles tensed. "How can they do this to you after everything you've done for this school? For *us*. And this is how they repay you?"

"We need to fight this, Dr. H." Sydnee jumped up and paced. Her candy spilled from her lap onto the floor. "We can flood the president's office with calls. Or no! Wait!" She twirled around with her hand out as a stop sign. "We call each of the trustees. Demand you get tenure. If we each call—how many trustees are there? We can divide up—"

"No, Syd," Allie said. "That isn't how it works. A few students won't override an entire committee of her colleagues."

"Well, what do you suggest?" Sydnee's hands went to her hips.

"That you sit down." Allie bit her lip and stared ahead.

Chess's tears rolled silently down her face. A trail of mascara followed.

Jeff sat on the edge of his chair, hands steeple-like. "Couldn't you just stay and pull your application? No harm, no foul?"

Samantha tilted her head from side to side. "I could. But it wouldn't mean I could stay." She leaned forward in her chair, elbows on her knees, hands folded. "It's like this. A few of my colleagues don't like me. They've wanted a reason, *any* reason, to make me leave. When they heard about my interest in the student's death twenty years ago, they blew it out of proportion and used it." She reached to touch Chess's arm. "And if not this, it would have been something else. Trust me." Samantha paused. "For me to stay at Vanderlaan without tenure isn't the answer."

Allie said, "I don't understand. We find a connection between all of us and a girl who died twenty years ago." Tears welled in her eyes. "I thought there was some higher purpose. Something we were supposed to learn about ourselves, each other. That it would lead somewhere."

"I thought so, too," Samantha said more to herself than to them.

****

The student entourage left their teacher's office quietly. Sydnee detested restraint in general but found it almost unbearable when someone she cared about was suffering. Only as they reached the portico of Prescott, out of earshot of Dr. Hayes, did Sydnee launch into her plan. "We're going to The Campus Cafe to plan our next move."

"Next move?" Allie rolled her eyes. "There isn't going to be a next move, Syd." She pulled her coat tighter and clomped down the few steps that connected

Prescott Hall to the parking lot. Levi murmured for Sydnee to give him a minute as he hurried after Allie.

Sydnee led Jeff and Chess across the courtyard toward The Cafe. "This will not be the end. Dr. Hayes will keep her job or she'll go down while we're fighting." She flung open The Cafe door. "You'll see, Chess. I got this."

They each ordered coffees with varying levels of frothy enhancements and moved toward an open table. As they got settled, Levi and Allie walked in, bypassed the refreshments, and took seats with them.

Allie began, "I won't be party to anything that could get Samantha in any more trouble."

"Give me some credit, Al. We won't hurt Dr. H." Sydnee leaned across the table and tapped out a fast beat with her palms. "But we gotta work fast. I know the five of us can't turn this thing around but if all of her students did, it might make a difference." Syd put up a palm toward Allie. "Hear me out. We could rally all the students she's taught at Vanderlaan—to send emails or letters to the trustees saying how much she's done for us."

Allie took in a breath and shook her head. "I don't know, Syd. Samantha wouldn't want us to—"

"Does it matter if she wants us to?" asked Syd.

"Yeah, it kinda does," Jeff said.

"But if it means it would save her job…" Chess said.

Levi spoke up, "It might not save her job. But I don't think she'd mind." He turned toward Allie. "What could it hurt?"

"Maybe it wouldn't." Allie pulled her chair up closer to the table. "I guess we could try."

"Yeah!" Sydnee did a drum roll on the table. "And one more thing. I say we contact Annika's cousin, Laura, and get the scoop on what happened to her."

"Now, *that* she'd mind." Levi pushed away from the table.

Sydnee said, "What could it matter now? She's resigning. Plus, she doesn't have to know."

"But what good would it do?" Chess asked.

"Satisfy our curiosity for one thing." Sydnee leaned her chair back into a precarious two-legged perch. "And Dr. H. needs to know too. Haven't you noticed how she gets when Annika's name is mentioned? This bothers her for some reason. It's not gonna affect her job now. Why not find out what we can?"

Allie handed her cell to Sydnee. "This is Laura's blog. You want to contact her or should I?"

"Wait," Levi said. "Let's think this through. What do we say?"

Chess asked, "How about that we've read her blog and are interested in her story about her cousin's death, and we want to know more."

"Too blunt." Jeff shook his head. "This is her cousin, and childhood friend. We have to be more subtle."

"Why subtle?" Levi asked. "Just say we are curious about what would cause a student Annika's age to die."

"Should we say we go to Vanderlaan ourselves?" asked Chess.

Allie said, "That'd be okay. It might make her more likely to respond to us."

"Yeah, I agree." Jeff nodded. "How about—"

"Done." Sydnee plopped Allie's cell on to the

table.

"You've already sent her a message?" Allie grabbed her cell and swiped it on. "What did you say?"

Sydnee dropped her chair back onto its four legs. "I just asked how Annika died."

Allie grabbed her phone and read from the screen. *"Comment from Sylie: How did your cousin die?"* Allie raised an eyebrow. "Sylie? Who's that?"

"Combination of Sydnee and Allie, of course. Your phone. My message. Sylie." Syd stood up, felt in her jeans pocket for money. She walked to the counter and brought back her chocolate glazed pastry. "Give it a rest. She isn't likely to answer right away." Sydnee sat down, took her first bite, rolled her eyes in pleasure. "These things are so good." She gulped some coffee. "While we wait let's plan who will contact who."

"Whom," Jeff said.

"Yeah, yeah." She waved away his correction. "Between us five, we're in how many of Dr. H's classes?"

"All of them, except her Intro class," Levi said. "But I'm across the hall in Neuroscience that hour. I usually stick my head in the room before class starts, just to bug her. If one of you would make her late tomorrow, I'll give the students the info before she gets there."

"I'll be in her office first thing tomorrow and delay her if I can. But make it fast, Levi," Allie said.

Sydnee scribbled in a notebook. "Chess, you still in contact with the former student of hers from your hometown..." She clicked the pen several times, closed her eyes, trying to recall the name. "Snowy?"

"Her name's Rainey. And, yes, I am."

"Rainey! Could you let her know what we're doing and enlist her help? She'll know former students we don't. If she could contact them…"

"I'm on it." Chess saluted.

"Remember Richard?" Jeff asked. "The guy who spoke to Psych Club last semester? Graduated a couple years back? We've stayed in contact. I'll ask him to touch base with any alums who would send a letter."

"Good! He can—"

Allie's cell lit up and buzzed. She lunged for it, swiped it on. She looked up to the others. "Laura responded."

A cacophony of "What's she say?" "Read it!" "Let me see!" came from around the table. Sydnee was the only one though who grabbed for the cell herself. Allie swiveled in her seat enough to throw her grabby friend off balance. Syd's chair slipped backward and clattered to the floor. Syd clutched the table and managed to avoid an undignified descent.

"Man, Syd!" Levi set her chair upright. "You wanna get us kicked out of here?"

Without pause, Sydnee motioned for Allie to continue.

Comment from Laura: I haven't provided more details out of respect for my family, the shame and guilt that still surrounds Annika's death. One day I might write more. But for now, I honor their request.

Silence.

Allie read it out loud again and put the cell in her back pocket. She shuddered and hugged herself.

Chess whispered, "Suicide."

****

After her entourage left the office, Samantha typed

her letter of resignation, including a retraction of her application for tenure. She printed it on university letterhead, signed, folded, and placed it in an envelope. Of course, she could send it as an email but that seemed less than professional. She would do this right. With it sealed, she tossed it into the desk tray marked *outbox*. It would go out in tomorrow's mail and be delivered tomorrow afternoon.

Unless…A quick glance at her watch. She could make it if she hurried. She snatched the envelope from the outbox, pulled her jacket out of the closet, and left for Anderson Hall. She would deliver it herself to the president's office. Today.

When she arrived, however, their door was closed. Locked. Lights out.

She growled in frustration. *I want to get this over with.* She blocked the glare with her hands as she peered through the window, through blinds on the other side that were not quite shut. No one.

Wait. A mail slot. She could still leave it. His secretary, Joyce, would see it first thing in the morning.

Slide it through, Samantha. Be done with this right now. She held the envelope up to the slot. Stuck the corner in. Paused. Pulled it back.

Samantha leaned back against the door with a thud. It protested with a creak. *But I want to give it to a human being. Someone who can put it on the president's desk. Better yet, in his hand.* She sighed and pushed herself off the door. Another creak. She would wait until tomorrow.

"Dr. Hayes?"

Samantha jumped. Twirled around to the voice that

had come from behind.

A young woman stood in the doorway of the darkened office.

"Oh! I didn't think anyone was still here." Samantha's hand flew to her chest.

"I'm sorry. I didn't mean to startle you. I was about to lock up and thought I heard someone out here. Did you need to leave something?" The young woman offered Samantha a warm smile. Her eyes sparkled behind large red glasses, just under locks of blonde hair. She nodded toward Samantha's hand, which still held the envelope.

"Yes, actually, I did. I *do*." Samantha's heart pounded a jazzy rhythm.

This is so awkward. Should I leave it with this person I don't know, but who evidently works here? She knows me. Probably in a class of mine at some point.

"Will you see that Dr. Portes gets this first thing tomorrow, please?" Samantha handed her the envelope.

She smiled. "I will. Have a good evening, Dr. Hayes." She closed the door.

Relief. It was finished.

****

Samantha spent the evening staring mindlessly at the TV. She smiled when Rob's chuckle indicated something humorous had just happened. In light of the hoopla around the series finale of their favorite dramedy, Samantha was less than satisfied. So many loose ends. Plots and subplots without resolution. Inner journeys incomplete. Really, they needed one more season to finish this thing. But that was no longer possible. The decision had been made. This season—

this episode—was the last.

Maybe it was for the best. Some shows went on too long, way past whatever relevance they once held. Maybe this show had no more to offer.

Or maybe…someone—probably a bigwig with a lot of power—didn't like the show or its main character for some reason, and wanted it eliminated. Then that someone bullied others into siding with him against those who wanted to keep it around for another season or two.

Samantha shook her head. *So unfair. All those characters. All those unfinished storylines. All because of some bully.*

Meanwhile commercials for next season's replacement fell short of convincing Samantha to invest herself. Who needs another series with the inevitable disappointment when it too ends prematurely?

Not me. She folded her throw and placed it neatly across the back of the sofa. "Time to call it a day."

Chapter 38

Thursday, November 8

Samantha's brisk pace slowed as she approached Prescott Hall. Levi and Allie were ahead of her, going in the same direction. *Heading to my office, no doubt. Don't think they saw me. I could stop over at The Cafe...* But the weight of her book bag convinced her to not take a longer route than necessary. She steeled herself and resumed her normal pace.

"I know you have class in a few, but we just need five minutes." Allie's plea began as soon as Samantha approached her office door.

"I cancelled my classes today. Lots of work to catch up on. But five minutes this early in the morning?" Despite herself, a smile tugged at Samantha's lips.

"Let me assure you," Levi said in a sleep-raspy voice. "It wasn't my idea."

"He's here for moral support." Allie entered the office ahead of Samantha, flipped the light switch, and dropped into a chair. "*I'm* here because I can't handle guilt."

Samantha placed a mug under the machine and pressed the button for a one-cup brew. The hiss and gurgle of coffee and its soothing aroma brought tears to her eyes. How many mornings had started just like this? Students needing something before the day even got started. Her anticipation of the day ahead as she grabbed her coffee and rushed out the door. Samantha blinked and caught her breath. Sooner or later, Allie would have to handle guilt on her own. Sooner, rather than later, it would seem.

"I—*we*—did something yesterday you need to know about. Levi thinks you won't mind. Syd would blow up if she knew we were telling you."

"I won't lie. That's why I'm here," Levi said with eyes closed, head on the back of his chair, feet on the table.

"Yesterday we posted to Laura's blog. Asked her why Annika died." Allie hurried on. "We used a fake name. We didn't learn much, but I need to be open about it."

"It's fine, Allie." Samantha held her coffee as she sat down on the sofa. "It can't do any damage at this point even if you had used real names. But thank you for telling me."

Levi raised his head, finally alert. "You really did it. You resigned."

Samantha put her cup on the table and curled a leg underneath her. "I submitted my letter of resignation last evening before leaving campus."

Levi ran both hands over his head, stopped and held the back of his neck, and let out the breath he had been holding. "Man, I didn't think it would come to this. Even when you told us…"

"You're actually leaving Vanderlaan," Allie said.

"Not until May." Samantha hurried into a change of conversation. "Meanwhile, tell me what Laura said."

"Just that she wouldn't talk about it out of respect for her family. She mentioned shame and guilt."

Samantha shot a glance at Allie. "Not what the shame and guilt were about?"

"No, but I tell you what it sounds like to us— suicide." Allie leaned forward and counted off on her fingers. "Why else would a person her age die unless there was foul play? And remember the police didn't find any evidence of that. And according to the newspaper report, she was healthy. Plus, a suicide would account for shame and guilt, right? I mean, not that they *should*, but those left behind often *do* feel guilty. You know, for not recognizing the signs, not being able to stop it."

Samantha bit the inside of her lip. "Not able to stop it…" she repeated softly.

"You okay, Samantha?" Allie said.

"Sure." Samantha sprang from the sofa and moved to her desk. "You two are welcome to stay if you want, but I have tons of work to do. This week has—"

Jeff burst in with Chess close behind. "Hey, you weren't in class," he said. "What gives?"

"I didn't send the email?" Samantha jabbed in her password which brought up her unfinished email from the night before. The word *DRAFT* blinked at her silently, mockingly.

"I apologize, Jeff, Chess," she muttered. "I was sure I sent this out last night."

She snatched her cell from her purse. "Why didn't you text when I didn't show?" Three unread messages. She flung her cell at the desk. Its screen cracked against the sharp edge of a picture frame.

Office chatter stopped.

"It wasn't a big deal," Chess whispered.

"We weren't upset, Dr. H." Jeff stole glances at his

peers. "We gave you the standard fifteen minutes before we left."

Samantha held both hands flat against her face. *What's happening to me? Not sending emails I've written, throwing things, snapping at students?* She squeezed her eyelids against insistent tears. She caught her breath and shook her head. *Pull yourself together.*

She stood next to her desk surrounded by four of the five who had made these years the best of her career. They would soon become students she once taught, once mentored, in a place she once worked. So, what did it matter now anyway? *Go ahead—cry. Throw something. Hold a séance right here in this office, if you want! But why stop there? Invite the entire tenure committee! What difference would it make?*

So she cried. And not the sniffly kind where you dab the end of your nose and the corner of your eye. No. She cried the way you do when you're home by yourself, watching a sappy movie that makes you relive your first heartbreak. The kind that requires two boxes of tissues, a cold rag to the eyes, and coffee to clear the voice gravel.

And that's when it happened. These soon-to-be former students suddenly segued into something she had not expected—at least not for a few years yet— something akin to adult friends. Chess leapt across the room and led Samantha to the sofa. The others fell into a silent ensemble and within moments were seated around her with tissues and bottled water. They didn't speak. They didn't shush her with platitudes. No one ducked out amid mumbles of embarrassment. They simply sat with her while she cried. Even a few days ago she would have balked at this change of roles. But right here, right now, it felt good.

As Samantha's sobs subsided, Allie posed a question. "I've learned some things from my parents about campus politics. I assume there's more here than you can tell us. Am I right?"

Samantha wiped her nose and nodded. Unfortunately, the only things she knew for certain were off limits for discussion: the history of animosity between herself and Dr. Titus which had led to her resignation, and her failure to prevent Annika's suicide twenty years ago.

"I understand," Allie said. "Still, I guess I wanted this room connection to be bigger than campus politics. For it to mean something, have a purpose."

"I wanted that, too," Jeff said. "But for us to track one of those rooms to Annika's death, get the administration riled, then Dr. H. forced to leave…" He shook his head.

"And the Annika from the séance. Where is she? Did she just drop in to scare the holy—" Chess put two fingers to her mouth. "Sorry, Dr. Hayes, scare us to death, then drop off the planet? Why is it that *nobody* can find her? It's crazy that—"

"I'm sorry." They all jumped at Sydnee's voice. *When had she come in?* All eyes turned to the office door where she stood. "I never meant for it to go this far. I figured surely one of you would come after her when she left Allie's room. Or joke about it the next day. But instead you were all freaked out. And then I kind of enjoyed it." Sydnee sat on the arm of a side chair. "I got someone from work to come by Allie's room on the night of the séance. I told her to drop in long enough to tell you her name was Annika and then get out of the dorm fast so no one could find her." Sydnee looked down. "I didn't mean to hurt anyone. But there was no Annika at the séance."

Chapter 39

"No Annika?" Allie's stomach did a flip.

Sydnee closed her eyes. "I'm sorry. I didn't know how to tell you after you all took it so seriously."

"I thought I'd connected us to the spirit world," Chess whispered. "That was gonna be my contribution to this room thing."

"I wouldn't have thought that I'd buy in," Allie said. "But I must have because I'm oddly disappointed."

"You are *un*believable, Sydnee!" Levi jumped up and moved away from the others seated around the coffee table. "You staged a fake Annika then listened to us go on about it in this very office. And *still*, you said nothing."

"I just thought—"

"You just *thought* you'd have a big laugh at our expense. Well, guess what?" He leaned in. "No one's laughing!"

"Levi," Allie said. "Calm down. It's not that big a deal."

"Are you kidding me, Allie? You should be furious!" He turned back to Sydnee. "*You* were just setting us up."

Sydnee's eyes arched. "So, *that's* what this is about. You can't stand for people to know that you,

258

Levi Corliss, are afraid of a *ghost*! This is about you, Levi. Don't you dare make it about me."

Allie's head whipped around. "I'd say it's a *little* about you. You *are* the one who recruited a fake Annika."

"Wait," Chess said. "What was your point, Syd? Did you want to prove that spiritual stuff is all mumbo jumbo? Because it still doesn't convince me. Just because she was a fake doesn't mean there isn't a real Annika with a hand in this room connection."

"No, Chess, I wasn't trying to *prove* anything. It was a joke." She mumbled, "Of course, I knew sooner or later you would find out and it *might* make a point about—"

"Aha!" Levi said. "So you *did* want to prove something."

Sydnee's spoke through clenched teeth. "I said I'm sorry. Let's move on."

Allie walked to the door and looked down the hall. Samantha had left the room without explanation during Syd and Levi's row. "Where do you think Samantha went?" she asked.

"You think she's mad?" Sydnee asked.

Jeff said, "Dr. H. doesn't get mad that easily. Maybe she just wanted you all to work it out yourselves."

"This whole thing is hard on her." Allie gave Levi and Sydnee a pointed look. "And all this fighting isn't helping. She'll have to start over somewhere else. And whatever, or whoever, is at the bottom of this, she can't even talk to us about it. It's hard on all of us, but this is her *career*. So you two do your fighting outside this office. Got it?"

Neither Levi nor Sydnee responded, which seemed to signify a truce.

Allie looked into the hall. "It's not like her to just leave like that. Should I go see where she is?"

"Nah, she'll be back." Chess flopped back into her chair. "She left her coffee, and it already has caramel goop in it."

****

But Samantha didn't come back. She left Prescott Hall amidst the quarreling, punched in Debra's number on the way to her car, and drove over when Debra told her she had a free hour.

"I couldn't stay one minute longer while they fought over the stupid séance and the *fake* Annika and the *real* Annika. Honestly, that séance has caused me more problems than *anything* I've ever *not* been part of! I have never seen Levi angry before. I mean *really* angry. And Chess—she's hurt. Sydnee feels guilty. Jeff and Allie—they're stunned because they'd started to believe she—"

Debra held up her hand. "Slow down. I get that it was a blow to them. They're hurt, angry, probably a little embarrassed. But what about you, Samantha? What did you feel when Sydnee fessed up?"

Samantha squeezed the bridge of her nose and let out a shaky breath. "The truth? Relieved. Surprised. Disappointed. I don't believe in séances, communicating with the dead, but it did give me pause. And to be honest, I was intrigued. I'd let myself hope it would lead to an explanation of the room connection and…"

"And what?"

"And…what happened to Annika twenty years

ago." She picked at the fringe of a pillow next to her. "But we don't have to wonder about that anymore. Since I saw you last, my group corresponded with Annika's cousin, Laura. She wouldn't say much because evidently the family still feels some guilt and shame about the death. *Their* words—guilt and shame."

"Suicide?"

Samantha closed her eyes. Tears fell, nonetheless. "I had so hoped it wouldn't be, but I needed to know. Maybe now I can accept it and move on." She wiped her eyes and hurried ahead. "Speaking of which, I submitted my resignation last night. Took it to the president's office myself. He would have received it this morning when he came in. So, it's official. I'm leaving Vanderlaan."

Debra looked less than convinced.

"I can't *stay*, that's for sure," Samantha argued with Debra's silence. "Since I won't get tenure, my days are numbered. Better I choose to leave than the university make me." Samantha bit her lip. "And they would eventually with Len Titus fighting me at every turn. Besides, this whole tightrope act is exhausting. When to speak up. When to shut up. Or just wait until a student *dies*, like Annika. Or Rochelle." Tears fell again. "I wish I had never come to Vanderlaan. Never gone to Hayward, for that matter."

"Then Len would have had free rein at Hayward. And you would have missed out on a lot—to have never taught or mentored these students. Would you have preferred that?"

"Yes...Maybe...I don't know." She tossed the pillow to another chair. "I just hate this feeling. Whatever *this* is."

"This," Debra said, "is grief. You know, the reaction we have when someone we care about leaves. Normal response to loss? Any of this ringing a bell, Dr. Hayes?"

Samantha chuckled and dabbed her eyes.

"It has been sudden, Samantha. You've hardly had time to process any of it. Or look for another job. What will you do?"

"Hayward advertised a position. Maybe they'll take me back." She sniffed. "But this time it'll be different. I'll teach, I'll serve on committees, then I'll go home. I won't mentor. I won't have them over to my house." She shook her head. "It hurts too much." Samantha picked lint from her pants. "That's why I left my office today. I'm tired. And I'm done."

Debra turned her head slightly, her eyes narrowed. "What do you mean?"

"I mean I'm not waiting until May. I'm leaving at the end of this semester. In December."

"You're leaving next month!"

Samantha sucked in her breath and nodded. "I am."

Chapter 40

Thursday, November 15

Thanksgiving break would begin on Wednesday of next week, after which students and faculty would be gearing up for final exams. The end of the semester was always busy, but with her resignation and all that had led up to it, this one was particularly stressful. But aside from that, something else bothered her.

She had hand-delivered her letter of resignation to President Portes's office on Wednesday evening and followed it on Friday with an addendum stating her intent to leave at the end of this semester. On Friday, she had also personally spoken to Monique. Samantha expected her to be upset; she had not expected Monique to be completely unaware she had resigned. As a rule, communication along the chain of command at Vanderlaan was swifter. The rumor mill, even more so. Communication had broken down somewhere. Something was off.

Samantha hardly had time to mull it over. Her decision to leave early meant she had less than a month to finish her semester's work, submit final grades, and say goodbye to her colleagues and students. Of course, before she said good-bye to anyone, she had to tell her office entourage that these next few weeks would be their last together.

But to tell them, she had to quit avoiding them as

she had this past week. Samantha's sprint from class each day prevented the post-lecture discussions that had become their norm. Multiple stops of dubious importance on her way back to Prescott—the post office (to pick up mail Christine had already placed on her desk), the cafeteria to check out the day's menu (even though her lunch from home was tucked away in her desk)—all served to minimize time in her office, making her less available than ever before.

Just this afternoon, as she entered Prescott, Levi and Jeff stood outside her office with their backs turned slightly. She darted inside a well-placed restroom without being seen. She heard their voices only moments later as they left the building. Thankfully they hadn't waited long. Samantha would have hated to occupy the facilities long enough to raise suspicion among anyone needing to answer nature's call.

This couldn't go on. She knew that. She would stop procrastinating. She would tell them of her decision to leave Vanderlaan early. And she would do it right away.

Today, in fact.

Or tomorrow.

Early next week, tops.

****

Chess walked back and forth like a caged tiger, her stomach in knots, her hoop earrings jangling, while the rest of the office gang sat around a table at The Campus Cafe. They had come in response to her urgent text that Dr. Hayes would be leaving in December and her plea that they meet ASAP! She summed up the facts as she knew them, then concluded, "Candy and drink supply—not what it used to be. She's not restocking.

264

I'm telling you, she's outta here in a few short weeks."

"Your source?" asked Jeff.

"Dean Easton's son, Travis, overheard his mom, thought I already knew, and let it slip. But don't tell anybody! His mother will *kill* him. Then he'll kill me." Chess grimaced, then shook it off. "The way I see it, our only hope of keeping Dr. H. here is to change tactics. So, here's the plan. We each contact everyone from before and tell them if they haven't sent emails yet, to send them directly to Dr. Hayes rather than President Portes. At this point, *she's* the one who needs to be convinced."

Sydnee's forehead wrinkled as she turned her neck left and right to keep up with Chess's movements. "When did you get so bossy?"

"Should we be hurt that she didn't tell us?" Allie slumped slightly. "I would think she'd tell us before others. Especially me."

Levi said, "If she were going to tell anybody, it would've been me. But don't be hurt, Al. If you haven't noticed, she isn't telling any of us anything these days."

They agreed, Samantha had hardly been on campus at all the past week and bolted immediately after her classes before anyone could catch her.

"She's avoiding us," Jeff said. "You think it's that hard for her to leave?"

"That, or she's mad. We did hold the séance that got her in trouble," Levi said. "I've even wondered if I had anything to do with it."

"You?" Chess asked.

"Earlier this semester, Dr. Titus got upset with me. I talked to Sam about it, and she said it wasn't really *about* me. Said it went back farther than my situation. I didn't know what she meant, and she wouldn't explain. But then, remember when I overheard her say Dr. Titus was vindictive? I wonder if he's part of the campus politics she mentioned last week."

"She'd never tell us if that were it." Chess waved a finger. "And no one says a word about the emails to Dr. Hayes. Agreed?"

Heads nodded. Jeff and Allie slung on their backpacks and hurried out to the task Chess had set before them. Levi bemoaned missing lunch and went to the counter for pastries and coffee. Sydnee remained seated, watching Chess like a bug under a glass.

Chess took in a deep breath. "Was I bossy, really?"

Sydnee cocked her head to the side. "I always took you for an up-and-coming Levi. You know—the irreverent jokes, smart-alecky digs. But today?" Sydnee nodded. "You might be a Sydnee-in-the-making." Her smile held respect. "Well done."

Chapter 41

Monday, November 19

Samantha sat at her desk Monday morning before any of her colleagues arrived. Early morning was the best time to get work done and she had plenty of it to do. First, she tackled some committee work she had put off all semester. She was tempted to let it slide but hated to create more work for her colleagues than necessary. She finished it in less time than anticipated and reprimanded herself for procrastinating in the first place. Next, she answered a bevy of emails and deleted even more with barely a glance at who had sent them. She had quite the rhythm going with her index finger on the "delete" button when one email brought it to a halt.

Miguel R. Portes, The President's Office. Finally. An acknowledgement of her resignation.

But it wasn't an acknowledgement. He wanted to see her in his office at her earliest convenience. A glance at the time told her she would need to wait until after class to stop by his office. Her students would be here any minute.

On Saturday, she had sent a group text to her five, asking them to come by her office first thing Monday morning. She had put off telling them of her early departure for as long as she could. Time was running out. Maybe she had hoped for them to magically find out without anyone saying it out loud. As it turned out, that seemed to be the case. Over the weekend, one by one, each texted to tell her they all knew. *How had they found out?*

When the first text came in—from Sydnee, who else?—Samantha had smiled in relief. Now she wouldn't have to break the news. With the next three, she had chuckled at their sneaky attempts to help. As the last one (from Jeff) lit up the screen on her cell, she cried. There would be other jobs, other students, but never would she have this again. Ever.

So, she would see Dr. Portes after classes rather than before. As she scribbled a note and stuck it on her bookbag, a tap on the door took her attention.

"Come on in, Allie. Since when do you knock?" Samantha picked up her coffee and took her place in one of the side chairs. Allie offered an awkward grin and sat in the other. She kept her coat on. Temperatures had dropped these past few weeks.

"I wanted to come in early and tell you I hate this. All of it. That we held a stupid séance. That campus politics is what it is. Most of all that you're leaving." As tears fell, Allie put her hand up as if to avert an interruption. "I know I'm graduating in May anyway. And I understand why it's necessary in terms of tenure. But the unfairness of it." She closed her eyes. "I don't know what to do with that."

Samantha refrained from the no-one-said-life-is-fair spiel. She hated that phrase. As a child, anytime she complained about something not being fair, her parents would say that to her. As if that somehow made the unfairness acceptable. Life *isn't* fair. But when it isn't, somebody needs to fix it. Because it *should* be fair. But what do you do when it can't be fixed? That's where she always struggled. Then and now.

"I don't either." Samantha found relief in admitting it. "I struggle with this too, Allie. As much as we try to do right"—Samantha shook her head—"things like this happen. I wish I had answers, but I don't."

The outside door of Prescott opened, and the clatter of footsteps brought Allie's hands to her face. She wiped tears, cleared her throat. Levi and Chess, Sydnee and Jeff—all came in without comment. Backpacks plopped off at the door; students, in their usual places around the coffee table.

"Thank you, each of you, for telling me you know I'm leaving in December." Furtive smiles slipped from each of their faces. "I dreaded telling you almost as much as leaving. But I did want to acknowledge it face to face." She leaned forward, coffee in her hands.

The room was silent.

Jeff spoke first. "I'm glad you told us. It was awkward. Knowing, I mean, but acting like I didn't."

"For me too." Sydnee's voice was softer than they were accustomed to. "I don't know what to say, other than it sucks."

Mumbles of agreement came from around the circle.

"You won't, like, duck out of our lives, will you?" Chess sat hugging her knees.

"Of course not. I'm here for you as much as you want me to be. In fact"—she shrugged in nonchalance—"I hope to make each of you as sick of me after I leave as you are now. But in the meantime, for the next few weeks, I'll be here for you to come by any time."

Levi said, "You've ghosted us the past week or so.

What was *that* about?"

"I thought it would be easier. To be less available, leave gradually."

"It wasn't," they said in unison.

Samantha's laughter broke what remained of the tension in the room. "I know, right. I'm sorry."

Throughout the next few minutes, as the others chimed in with comments about Samantha's departure, Sydnee glanced at her cell several times. Deliberating over whether or not to speak was not the norm for Sydnee. When Samantha could wait no longer, she demanded, "Out with it, missy."

Sydnee also never waited for a second invitation. She jumped up, went to her backpack, and retrieved a piece of paper. "I didn't want to shut down the so-long-farewell bit, but I did some more digging on Annika's death. Sort of, you know..." She glanced at Levi and mumbled, "To make up for my prank.

"Anyway, I found this article that came out in the Chandler paper. Remember, that was her hometown." Sydnee leaned across the back of Samantha's chair and handed her the sheet of paper. "One of her professors, a Dr. Ethan Livingston, was quoted as saying Annika was an extremely gifted math major but unfortunately had some"—she made air quotes—"insurmountable obstacles so she left without graduating."

"Insurmountable obstacles," Allie repeated. "Wonder if they had anything to do with her suicide."

Samantha chewed on her thumbnail as she scanned the article. *Dated a little over twenty years ago, about a week after Annika's death. Ethan Livingston...I knew him. He taught math.* The hair on the back of her neck stood on end. *What happened to Annika at Hayward?*

Sydnee sat back down. "Made me wonder, too. Plus, the name Ethan Livingston sounded familiar. Remember, Allie, he posted several comments on Laura's blog."

Ethan had information about Annika? Samantha's stomach did a flip. *How weird would it be for me to just call Ethan and ask what he knows? It's been a while...he's probably retired by now, but still...*

"So yesterday I sent a message to this Dr. Livingston fella and asked if he could tell us more about Annika." Sydnee's eyes sparkled as if she held the answer to global warming.

Samantha chuckled softly. She wavered between shocked admiration at Sydnee's boldness and curious dread of what she was about to tell them. "Lay it on us, Ms. Baldwin."

"Unfortunately, that's as far as I got," she replied.

"Then why bring it up?" Levi threw his hands in the air.

"Because," she said, "he's going to call me any minute. He couldn't talk yesterday, but said he'd call me back at—" Sydnee's cell beeped. Her eyes popped. "—right now. I'll put it on speaker."

"Wait," Samantha demanded. "Put him on hold."

"Dr. Livingston? Thank you for calling. Can you hold, please, for just one moment?" Confusion creased Sydnee's forehead.

Samantha reached for Sydnee's cell. "I know Ethan. Let me talk to him."

Of course, anyone else who took her cell, she would have wrestled to the floor, but even Sydnee had a measure of propriety when it came to college professors.

"Ethan? This is Samantha Hayes…Fine, thanks…You?…Retirement, that's wonderful!…Actually, I just this minute found out that one of my students, Sydnee Baldwin, left a message for you to call…That's right. We, Sydnee and several other students of mine, have developed an interest in the Annika Lavelle story. We heard you knew her and might be able to tell us more. They're all here in my office. Is it okay if I put you on speaker?"

Samantha pressed the button and set the phone on the coffee table.

"Hi, Dr. Livingston, this is Sydnee. We hear Annika had problems at Hayward. What was that about?"

"Hello, Sydnee. Yes, Annika wrote a paper which her academic advisor stole. Published it without even putting her name on it."

A math teacher at Hayward stole Annika's work? Len Titus was the reason Annika left Hayward!

Ethan continued, "It seems the professor had agreed to work with Annika to get the administration off his back about being too busy for students. Then while he was busy scuffling with colleagues, Annika did the lion's share of the work. Turns out her work was good—I mean really good. He was up for tenure and his application was somewhat lacking. I guess he thought this publication would tip the scales."

Samantha had mixed feelings. She was intrigued to finally hear Annika's story and to learn that Len was part of it. But she was also uneasy. Would her students connect the dots that their Dr. Titus was the professor they were right now discussing?

Ethan said, "Annika was upset, naturally. Went to

the professor and complained. Evidently," he lowered his voice as if the plagiarism police were within earshot, "he bullied her into silence for a while. Then she came to me, and I got her to file a complaint. Upshot was he got canned."

"Ethan, I'm confused," Samantha said. "If the professor was fired why did Annika leave?"

"Never knew for sure. Talk at the time was that he threatened her."

Samantha's stomach clenched. "When you say *threatened*, you don't mean…"

"Lord, no!" Ethan hooted. "Samantha, you've read too many of your husband's books. No, I mean he threatened her *academically*. Not sure what he could have done since he'd been ousted, but, Samantha, she was a kid—what—about twenty years old? She was scared and we all just assumed she wanted a fresh start somewhere else. But wait," Ethan said. "You remember the professor, don't you? Len Titus? He was the scrawny little—"

"No way!" Sydnee exclaimed.

"—dictator no one liked much."

Allie grabbed Syd by the arm and covered her own mouth with the palm of her other.

Levi muttered, "Bet we weren't supposed to know *that*."

"Yes, Ethan, I remember him." Relief washed over Samantha. Without her crossing a professional line, her students now knew their Dr. Titus was not all he seemed. What Samantha could not say as their teacher and Len's colleague, Ethan could since he was neither.

But her relief ran deeper. Len's *exploitation* of students ran deeper than she could have known.

Whatever the specific reason he had been let go was nothing she knew about or contributed to. The self-blame she had carried for decades vanished—easily and completely. If only her self-blame over Annika's death could do the same.

"Dr. Livingston, this is Allie. We assume Annika's death was a suicide. Do you know for sure?"

"It was suggested as a possibility, along with it being accidental."

Something niggled at the edges of her consciousness. Had Len ever mentioned Annika to her? No, he was too calculating to broach a topic that might expose his own misconduct. His comments were more often intended to disparage *others*. Just look at all he had done since she applied for tenure.

Wait—tenure—that's it! Annika's name *had* come up at the tenure committee meeting in relation to the séance. But who actually brought it up? Samantha grappled with memory fragments. Had Len been the first to mention Annika's name? Yes! Because Samantha had been confused when he asked about "this *America* person." Was that his way of feigning a lack of familiarity with the name and the person?

Samantha stole a glance at her troupe. *Go big or go home, Samantha.* "Ethan, Len knows of our interest in Annika's death and is using my students' attempts to," should she mention the séance? "*learn more* to get me dismissed from Vanderlaan. Would Len have any reason to think he might be blamed for Annika's death?"

"Nah. Remember, the police never bought it as a homicide." He paused. "Unless Annika *did* kill herself as a reaction to Len's monkey business, in which case maybe she's haunting him or something." Ethan snorted. "If so, then good for her."

Chess's eyes lit up. Sydnee shook her head and wagged an index finger in Chess's direction.

Samantha asked her group, "Do we have any more questions for Dr. Livingston?" No one did. After each of them voiced their appreciation for his time, Samantha thanked him and ended the call.

After a few moments, Allie glanced at each of her peers and spoke. "Samantha, we won't say one word about Dr. Titus and his part in Annika's situation or in yours either."

Levi jumped up. "No wonder you were so mad that he told me how to behave around you. He used me, didn't he, to get back at you? And that's why you called him vindictive?"

"And the day you came back to your office, furious," Jeff said, "that was about Dr. Titus?"

Sydnee asked, "Do you ever just want to punch his lights out?"

Samantha nodded throughout and smiled at Sydnee's spot-on assessment. She leaned forward with an energy she hadn't felt in a while. "I wonder if he heard about the séance and thought I was messing with him. Like I knew what he had done to Annika and was putting him on notice."

"And he wanted you out of here," Allie said, "before you made trouble for him."

Samantha didn't know. But what Len Titus thought or wanted no longer mattered. From his career struggles and the demise of his marriage to his unrelenting quest to push her out of Vanderlaan—Len had commanded too much of her energy over the past two decades. No more. And Annika—Samantha would always regret that she had let her down twenty years ago by not intervening in time. However, she could help right that wrong by intervening *now,* on Annika's behalf. And she would. Samantha's misplaced loyalty to Len and guilt over Annika's death gave way to enthusiasm for the task before her.

She leapt from the sofa and paced. "I have carried unnecessary guilt for some of Dr. Titus's circumstances and even—" She waved her hands in front of her. "Never mind. I can't say more than that. But that's over. I'm going to set the record straight as to who drove Annika from Hayward and why. And while I'm at it," she said, more to herself than to her students, "one of my colleagues needs to set the record straight on *this* campus. I can't do it for her, but I will help her if she'll let me." Samantha snapped around to her entourage, hands on hips. "And I'm speaking up for myself."

"About tenure?" Allie's eyes sparkled.

"About tenure and about Titus's vendetta against me. If anyone leaves Vanderlaan, it'll be him, not me."

Chess squealed and clapped. Sydnee whooped and hopped up. A chorus of "We're in!" "What can we do?" rang from the others.

She couldn't predict how this would end. Would Len add another dismissal to his resume? Would Samantha be able to clear Annika's name without backlash? She didn't know. But Samantha was determined to not look back one day with regret over what she failed to say or do today. Right now, that was enough.

"But wait." Samantha quieted the group. "I

resigned. The first thing on my agenda is to retract my letter of resignation." She grabbed her jacket and moved toward the door. "And don't you all go to class anymore? Go on. Get out of here. I'll see you later today."

As they all picked up backpacks and slipped on jackets, Chess stopped Samantha with a hand to her arm. "None of you has said anything about the obvious." She rolled her eyes at their confused stares. "About what Dr. Livingston said? That maybe Annika has been haunting Dr. Titus!"

Everyone chuckled as Sydnee moaned and dropped her head back in distress. "The man was kidding, Chess."

"You don't know that, Syd." Chess shook her head. "Maybe Annika is behind every bit of this."

Chapter 42

Monday, November 19

That night, Len slept like a baby. A baby with colic. He tossed and turned for hours, then fell into a fitful sleep that ended in a nightmare.

He sat at his desk grading homework—each one worse than the last. The knock on his office door only fazed him slightly. A quick glance told him a new student needed his time. "Come in," he barked.

"Dr. Titus," she began tentatively. "I've just transferred in. I'm a math major."

When she paused, he rolled his free hand without looking up, to speed up her request, comment, whatever.

"May I sit down?" She sat without waiting for a response. "I'll be in several of your classes next semester, and I hear you let students assist with your research. If you have a position open, I'd appreciate the opportunity to work with you."

"I do sometimes," he acknowledged. "I'll keep you in mind. Leave your name and contact information with the secretary."

He finished the stack, shoved it into a file folder, and picked up another. She made no move toward the door. "If that's all, Ms.—?"

"Lavelle."

His eyes shot to hers. His heart pounded. He

jumped up. "What do you want?"

"To speak the truth. Dr. Titus, you weren't—"

"Leave."

"Not until I've told you that you didn't—"

"Go! Now!" he said through clenched teeth. How dare she come in with her pleasantries. He didn't want the truth. He stood, hands on hips, head turned away.

She stood. Walked to the door. Whispered, "You can't hear my message until you're ready. I'll be back."

He leapt out of bed. Flailing away at the covers. Will this ever be over?

****

That night Samantha slept better than she had in a while. She finally had a plan for conquering the chaos that had become her life. With any luck this whole situation would be behind her soon. She had barely drifted into slumber when she was visited by a stranger. A determined stranger.

"Dr. Hayes?"

"Hmm? What?" Samantha turned toward the voice to see a woman with blonde bangs that reached to her oversized glasses frames.

"I have something important to tell you, but I don't have much time. You weren't to blame for—"

"Who are you?" Samantha asked. "You look familiar. Have we met?"

She shook her head. "It doesn't matter. But listen to me: You aren't responsible for—"

"I know." Samantha yawned. "Everyone tells me I'm not responsible for things I know I am responsible for. Just go. I need to sleep." She waved a dismissive hand and turned over.

"Go to The Fountain. Look for the scarab necklace to find answers," the visitor said as she disappeared.

Reflexively Samantha reached to her neck, feeling for the familiar pendant. It wasn't there. "Is it lost?" Her head swiveled. "Where is it?"

But the visitor had gone.

Samantha awoke with a start, her hand still at her neck, heart pounding. She slipped out of bed, quietly, so as not to awaken Rob, and opened her jewelry box. Her scarab pendant was there, where she had left it when she got home this evening. She shook her head, yawned, and crawled back into bed. *What was that about?* She snuggled into her pillow and drifted back to sleep.

Chapter 43

Tuesday, November 20

"I acted in haste, Dr. Portes." Samantha sat uncomfortably in an overstuffed, leather chair. The furniture was stately, befitting that of a university president's office. The problem was, it required a choice. One could sit on the seat's slippery edge and hope a shift in body weight didn't send one slithering off. Or one could sit against the unreasonably distant back and dangle one's feet inches above the floor. Neither made for a comfortable discussion between two professionals. "I hope it isn't too late to change my mind," she added while switching from the latter to the former.

Dr. Portes sat across from her in her chair's twin. "I don't understand, Samantha. First thing this morning I was hit with a number of emails asking that you not be let go. Why the concern? Monique told me last week there was a to-do about your tenure, but since I hadn't heard anything from you—"

"Hadn't heard from me?" Samantha asked.

"A resignation."

"But you *did* hear from me."

"Anything *official*, I mean. I know tensions run high when tenure's at stake, but until I get an official—"

Samantha leaned in. "You didn't get my letter of

resignation?"

"No, but I haven't gone through mail this morning—"

She shook her head. "No, Miguel. I delivered it myself almost two weeks ago. You never got it?"

Dr. Portes rose and stepped outside his office and returned with his secretary. Joyce confirmed that he had not received mail from Samantha in the past two weeks. Certainly nothing addressed to the president that she had failed to deliver.

Samantha swiveled in the leather chair to face the door where Joyce stood. She grasped the arm to prevent an inopportune plummet to the hardwood floor. "I didn't leave it with you, Joyce. It was after hours so I was about to slip it into the mail slot. But I didn't have to since—" Samantha still didn't recall the name of the person who received her letter that evening. "—since the other office worker—the young woman—was here. I'm sorry I don't remember her name."

Miguel Portes and Joyce exchanged glances.

"Who worked late that evening? It would've been Wednesday, week before last."

"No one works late," Joyce said. "Not since the vice-president's office down the hall was broken into first of the semester. Unless several of us stay late together, no one does."

"Well, *somebody* stayed late *that* night. I didn't know her—I assumed a former student—but she knew me. Called me Dr. Hayes. I handed her my letter, and she assured me you would get it first thing the next morning." She addressed the last statement to Dr. Portes, who remained silent.

Samantha flapped her hands as if that would

prompt their memories. "You know, the blonde woman, with bangs, wears glasses, very polite."

Joyce answered firmly, "I don't know what to tell you, Samantha. No one in the office fits that description."

****

Samantha left the president's office relieved but confused. How had he not received her letter of resignation? And who had she given it to that evening outside his office? Samantha had hesitated briefly before handing her the envelope but since the woman had come out of Portes's office...But wait. Had she actually come out of his office? Samantha had been startled by the young woman's voice. She had turned then saw her in the darkened doorway. So whoever she was, she *had* come out of the office and *had* been there alone, contrary to what Joyce had said about policy.

Would Joyce lie? Samantha had no reason to think so. But why would Dr. Portes deny receiving her resignation if he had? Samantha shook her head in aggravation. None of it made sense.

At least she still had a job. Granted, maybe not for long—there was still the committee's recommendation that she not get tenure. But she had a little bit of time to right things before she was officially told to pack up her office. And besides, maybe the trustees wouldn't side with the university committee. From what she heard they always did. But if there was one thing she had learned this semester amidst the room connection, the Annika sightings, and Len's mission to oust her—she had to expect the unexpected.

****

Len walked into Shelley Hall and headed toward

his office. Before he made it, however, she appeared in the hall coming out of Barb Skeen's office.

His heart pounded. *Did she see me? What does she want?* He ducked into the faculty lounge. Lights out. Empty. *Good.* He quickly, quietly closed the door. Stood in the dark. Alone.

****

While pondering her wayward resignation letter and her chances for tenure, Samantha had walked across campus. She paused as she reached her destination—Shelley Hall—took a breath and opened the door. Time to fix as much of this as she could.

Samantha walked toward Barb's office with a confidence she wasn't sure was warranted. Had she the right to go against Barb's wishes even if it saved her own neck? Could she protect Barb from the fallout when she applied for tenure herself? She hoped so. Because if someone doesn't stop Len Titus, none of us are safe, tenure or not.

"Samantha!" Barb yelped as she and Samantha almost careened into each other at the door of Barb's office. After they each made noises of apology, Barb caught her breath and motioned for Samantha to have a seat.

"I can't believe you're here. I was headed to your office."

"My office?" Samantha sat down as Barb closed the door.

"Samantha, I don't know how to begin, so I'll just say it. I'm filing a complaint against Dr. Titus."

****

Len remained in the faculty lounge. A few moments had passed. Had she left? A quick peek would tell. Hand to the doorknob. Samantha's voice. He jumped back. *Wait!* What was *she* doing in Shelley? Her voice again. With Barb's now. Laughing. Muffled. Hand back to the doorknob. A quick turn. Tentative peek. Left. Then right. All clear. One cleansing breath and he resumed his dignified amble toward his office.

****

Barb put out her hand as if to stop Samantha from protesting. "I heard he pressured the committee to have you fired. I won't let him do that to you. At least not without speaking up about the stolen work. If I had spoken up sooner, maybe you wouldn't be in this situation."

"Thank you." Samantha breathed a sigh of gratitude and relief. She hadn't had to breach a confidence. Barb's good judgment came through. "But how did you hear about Len and the committee?"

"You know how people talk." Barb settled into her chair. "I hadn't been here long this morning when one of the committee members came by to see Dr. Titus. He wasn't in and she asked for a notepad and pen to leave a message. She said it was important, something about your tenure application, that she was on the committee and—"

Barb turned toward the door, rose, opened it, and peeked out. "That's odd." Barb bit her lip as she reached for the notepad on the edge of her desk and glanced through it. "She didn't leave a message for him. Not on his door at least." She tossed the notepad back on her desk.

"Maybe she changed her mind?"

"Maybe." Barb didn't seem convinced.

"Who was it?"

"Oh, I didn't know her."

"Kathryn Day is on the committee," Samantha offered.

"Wasn't her. I know Kathryn."

"Then it had to be Priscilla. She's the only other woman on the committee."

"I guess. Is Priscilla young? Blonde hair and glasses? Real pretty?"

"Not hardly. She—" *What?*

Barb pointed toward the hall. "You had to have passed her. She left my office maybe two seconds before you came in."

A shiver grazed Samantha's spine. "I didn't pass anyone. The hall was empty." Before Samantha could unravel the impossibility of Barb's last statement, someone unlocked the door across the hall. A glance confirmed he was in. Before she had time to change her mind, Samantha pushed herself out of Barb's office, across the hall, and into Len's office.

Her heated anger from their last meeting had become cool confidence. As Len dropped a briefcase and coat onto his desk, she began. "Len, I'm here to put you on notice. I'm fighting for my job. I'll speak to Monique about it first and then I'll file an appeal with the trustees—"

"What good will that do? They won't overlook our committee's recomm—"

"They will when Barb blows the whistle on your exploitation of new faculty."

"She'll never—"

"She will. And they'll listen when I speak to them about our history and your push to chair my tenure committee."

"You do and I'll tell them how you got me fired from Hayward. You overstepped there and you're—"

"No, you won't." Her voice was cold. "Because one word about your abuse of power with Annika at Hayward and you'll be out on your—"

"Samantha, stop. Wait." Len's face turned white. He trembled. He closed the door, motioned for her to sit. "I had nothing to do with what happened at Hayward." He ran a hand over his head, leaned against his desk, swallowed hard.

Len continued. "I did *appropriate* Annika's work. But I was desperate, Samantha. We had to get out of my parents' house. My wife threatened to leave me. I needed tenure. We…needed stability. Then Annika's paper. It was…More than I…Without something fast, I couldn't—" Len shook his head as if to shake the bits and pieces of his story into a coherent whole. "And yes, I feigned ignorance the other night at the meeting. I didn't—" He swallowed and gulped in air. "I didn't want it to follow me here."

"Follow you? It didn't have to *follow* you. You've behaved as badly here as there. Between stealing colleagues' work and using students to get back at—"

"No, Samantha." He squeezed the back of his neck, closed his eyes. His voice softened. "I'm not talking about that. Her death. I didn't want Annika's death to follow me here."

"Her death? How could it, Len? From what I hear, you weren't responsible—" Her eyes widened. Her voice lowered. "You *weren't* responsible, were you? I mean you didn't—"

"Of course not, Samantha!" He pushed himself off his desk and circled around it to his chair. "What do you take me for?"

Samantha rolled her eyes. "Is that a rhetorical question?"

He peered over the top of his glasses. "I am not a killer." He moved a stack of mail from one side of his computer to the other. Tossed a rogue paperclip into a drawer. He grabbed a pen and lobbed it from one hand to the other. "At least not intentionally. I've always worried that maybe…"

"Maybe what?" Who *was* this man who was concerned about someone else?

He tossed the pen to the desk. "Nothing, Samantha." Whatever glimpse of vulnerability he had allowed himself was gone.

"No, tell me, Len. Do you think Annika killed herself?"

"I didn't say that."

"And that it was because of you?"

"Of course not!"

"Look. Len. You have behaved deplorably to your colleagues and students for as long as I've known you. But did she kill herself and was it because of you?" She shrugged. "I don't know what happened to Annika—why she died or how. But I do know that nothing good comes from carrying around guilt indefinitely, whether it's warranted or not. We just fix what we can, show ourselves some grace, and let go of what we can't control."

Just call me Debra and put the check in the mail.

"Besides," said Samantha, "do you have any reason to believe it was suicide? From what I hear, the cause of death was never determined." Did Len know something about Annika's death? She hadn't considered him a source of information until this moment.

Silence.

He trembled. His face drained of color.

"Len?" Samantha prompted him to continue. "You look like you've seen a—"

"Leave, Samantha." He leapt from his chair and opened the door. He stood there—wordless—no eye contact, jaw muscles working behind a mouth clamped shut.

A few seconds passed. Whatever he had almost said wasn't forthcoming so she left. She walked from Shelley Hall into the cold but sunny day. Len seemed almost spooked. Did he believe he *had* seen a ghost? Oh well. In the words of Ethan Livingston, *If Annika is haunting Len, then good for her.*

She laughed out loud. *Oh, dear. I'm spending too much time with Chess.*

Chapter 44

Tuesday, November 20

By four o'clock that afternoon, Samantha was seated in Nate's Cafe on Chandler's Main Street where she sipped a caramel latte from a table with a clear view of the door. She wanted to know when Laura David, nee Lavelle, entered the coffee house. Last evening, she had gotten Laura's contact information from her website and placed a call. She expressed interest in Annika and asked if they could meet. The sudden fascination from people at Vanderlaan had to spark curiosity in Laura and was likely the reason she agreed. While Samantha would have to play a little loose with the truth, she was ready to learn why Annika had died.

Ready or not, Samantha's stomach did a somersault when a forty-something-year-old woman who looked just like the website photo came through the door and immediately scanned the room. Laura had an athletic build and wore her brunette hair pulled back in a headband. Her teal sneakers were the precise shade that threaded through the jacket of her sweat suit. Upon spotting Samantha's wave, Laura nodded and motioned her intent to order before coming to the table.

After Laura was seated and they exchanged greetings, she stated the obvious. "I'm surprised my cousin's death has generated such an interest this long after the fact." She flipped a packet of low-cal sweetener back and forth. "May I ask why?"

All business, this one. Samantha began the explanation she had rehearsed. "I taught at Hayward about the time of Annika's death. I met her a few times and heard from my students when she quit school." At Laura's nod of acknowledgement, Samantha continued. "I later learned that Annika dropped out because her mentor published her work under his own name."

Laura spoke softly. "That's right."

"Then the professor was fired. Annika left Hayward and died soon after." Samantha hoped Laura would carry it from here. When she didn't, Samantha proceeded cautiously. "Then one of my students found out she lives in the room where Annika died. And, oddly enough, I lived in the same room as a student so…" Samantha leaned in. "The thing is, Laura—and I know it's none of my business—but I've always wondered what happened to Annika. How did she die?"

See, Laura, nothing unusual here. Just a couple of odd ducks morbidly curious about your dead cousin. And, by the by, I may or may not be responsible for her death. And for the love of all that's holy, please don't make me tell you about the séance and that until another one of our merry band confessed we were convinced your dead cousin dropped by to borrow a broom!

Laura was matter-of-fact. "Do you know what anaphylaxis is?"

"It's an allergic reaction, isn't it?"

Laura nodded. "Yes, and it can be quite severe. The throat closes shut. The person can suffocate—sometimes within minutes. That's what happened to Annika."

Anaphylaxis?

Relief.

"Her death was accidental," Samantha said, more to herself than to Laura. Annika's death was tragic but not suicide. And nothing Samantha could have prevented.

"Right." Laura fiddled some more with the still unopened sweetener. "We all knew she was allergic to hazelnuts. A few years before, she had a reaction to a cake Mom made with hazelnuts. After a few bites—" Laura shook her head and closed her eyes for a moment. "Really scared us. The ER doctor told us Annika was lucky and that future reactions could be even more severe—life threatening even. Totally freaked my parents out. They forbade her from ever eating them again. Wouldn't even allow them in the house."

"*Your* parents forbade her? Weren't you and Annika cousins?"

"We were." She nodded. "Our fathers were brothers. But Annika came to live with us when her parents were killed in a car accident right before she started high school."

Ah! "And that's when she moved from Owenton to Chandler," Samantha said. "But Annika ate them the night she died. What happened?"

Laura glanced at Samantha as if she debated whether to answer. She sipped her coffee and continued, "Annika was visiting me at Vanderlaan. She had just left Hayward and was pretty upset about how things ended there. So I suggested she come stay with me over my birthday weekend. She could meet some people and see what she thought about the school.

Maybe transfer there the next semester." Her eyes seemed to ask for Samantha's agreement.

Samantha nodded, offered a sad smile.

"The evening Annika died I had been down the hall with friends. One of them had baked me a hazelnut birthday cake. But Annika didn't go." Laura shrugged. "Said she was tired. I brought some cake back to my room for later. And I was in a hurry. My boyfriend and I were going out, he would be there any minute, and I wasn't even close to ready." Laura opened her mouth and shook her head as if the truth were too incredible to say aloud. "And I didn't think to mention the nuts to Annika." She lifted her shoulders and hands in question. "Why *didn't* I think to mention it? I was in a hurry, but still."

An almost panicked expression crossed Laura's face. How many times in the past twenty years had Laura mentally replayed the events of that evening? The same questions. The same answers that didn't suffice.

"Then I left." She put the still unopened sweetener back in its caddy. "And at some point after, she ate some of the cake and…" Laura sat up straighter, took a breath. "She was my cousin and my best friend. I don't know how to forgive myself."

Samantha reached over, squeezed Laura's hand. Twenty years of self-recrimination. Samantha knew only too well the burden of guilt for not doing enough. The weight. The second-guessing that becomes a way of life. How it creeps into every situation and relationship. She sent up a prayer that Laura would forgive herself in time.

"I'm so sorry, Laura. I understand. I've also held

on to guilt far longer than I should have. I know the burden, the damage it can do."

Laura's expression transformed from intensity into relaxed appreciation. Then, with a glance at her watch she indicated they were done. As they stood to leave, Samantha asked, "Did Annika ever go by another name while at Hayward? I'm asking because some of us knew her as Annika; others, as Grace."

Laura cocked her head to the side. "It was her middle name. I think she did try to go by Grace for a while. But professors kept using her first name. I don't think it ever caught on."

Samantha thanked Laura again for indulging her questions. So little had been reported in the campus and local papers, Samantha added, even as much as a picture of Annika, which, to her anyway, seemed odd.

Laura explained, "That's because my parents asked them not to. You see, at first a few people thought Annika's death was a suicide. It wasn't. But my parents wanted to keep people from talking. And they carried some weight at Vanderlaan, so..." Laura fished for something in her purse. "I snapped a picture of a photo of Annika before I came today. I don't know why." She offered a self-conscious half smile while she pulled out her cell. She tapped and scrolled several times then turned the screen toward Samantha.

Samantha caught her breath. Her heart skipped a beat.

"Is something wrong?" Laura asked.

"This is Annika?" Samantha snapped her head toward Laura.

"Yeah," Laura answered slowly. "Why?"

Samantha pulled out her own cell. "May I snap a

picture of this?"

Although Laura looked confused, she nodded.

How could Samantha begin to explain to her that this was the woman from her dream?

Chapter 45

"This has got to be a dream. No—a nightmare!" Samantha paced the length of Debra's office. "Or maybe I've completely lost my mind." She stopped to chew on a thumbnail and give Debra a chance to contradict that last option. Debra only smiled.

"Don't just sit there smiling. Tell me—am I crazy? I just saw a picture of a woman who was in my dream just a few nights ago."

"Hold on, Samantha," Debra said. "No—I don't think you've lost your mind. And all we know for sure is that you dreamed about someone who turned out to look like a picture you saw after the fact." She shrugged. "That's not crazy material."

Samantha stopped pacing, sat in the chair next to her therapist. She leaned in and, still at lightning speed, whispered, "But that's not all; I saw her. That day I turned in my resignation—she was the one who accepted it. No one from the president's office could tell me who she was, but it was her, Debra. I know it. And in the dream, she looked familiar, but I couldn't place her."

She rose and started pacing again. "I *saw* a *dead* person. Someone who's been dead for"—she flung her arm—"twenty years." She stopped, held her face with both hands. "Although, what difference does that make? Dead for a day, twenty years, a hundred years. Dead is dead."

Debra shook her head. "We don't know you saw a dead person. We only know you saw someone who looks a lot like this Annika who is…"

Samantha waited, arms crossed, face expectant. "Go ahead. Say it. *Dead.*"

Debra chuckled. "Okay, *dead.*" She pushed her chair back, out of her client's path. "What about a prank? Are you sure Levi isn't behind this?"

"A prank." She stopped, mouth open. Shut it again, shook her head, and resumed her pace. "No, the woman I saw came out of Dr. Portes's office. Levi wouldn't have access to the president's office, and he didn't even know I was going over there."

Samantha flopped into her usual chair to catch her breath. "But let's say he somehow knew the person who works evenings in Portes's office and thought it would be funny to get a little Annika-mileage out of it. I know it's a longshot but since Allie found Laura, maybe Levi got Laura to play along." Samantha sat up with renewed energy, pulled out her cell, tapped, and scrolled. "You know, it *is* kind of funny."

"Calling Annika?" Debra peered over her glasses. "Do you have enough bars?"

"Ha ha." Samantha put her cell to her ear. "Hi, Levi. You in class…? Then you shouldn't have answered! Hang up and come see me when it's over." She ended the call and settled into her chair. "That has to be it. Levi's involved."

"Or Sydnee. She pulled that bit with the séance."

Samantha shook her head. "No, she still feels awful about that. She won't do anything for a while."

297

"But wait, tell me more about this dream you had. What happened?"

Samantha waved a dismissive hand. "Oh, just that I'm not to blame for something or other."

"She didn't say *what*?"

"Not really. And then she asked me to go to The Fountain to look for the scarab necklace to get answers."

"The necklace? The one you always wear?"

"I thought so, but mine isn't missing. And answers to what?"

Debra shrugged. "Maybe your unconscious knows more than we do."

Samantha slumped back into her chair. "I don't know, Debra. If I thought a trip to visit Chess's Aunt Ruth would get me anywhere…"

Debra waited. A half-smile on her lips.

"I need to go, don't I?" said Samantha.

"I don't see what harm it would do."

"Okay, but first I need to make sure Levi isn't behind all this."

****

"I hate lying to Sam." Levi stuffed his cell into the pocket of his jeans. He sat with Allie at The Campus Cafe. On this last day of classes before Thanksgiving break, most students were packing if not already gone home for a long weekend. The sparse crowd gave them freedom to talk freely without eavesdroppers.

"I do too, Levi," Allie said, "but you can't tie up your phone." She looked at her watch. "Are you sure he has your number?"

"I'm sure, Al. Chill." But Levi was anxious, too. Dr. Livingston would return their call any minute and they would ask him to speak with Dr. Titus. While Samantha would be livid if she knew they went behind her back, someone needed to act. The sooner the better.

Minutes passed. "I'm supposed to meet Sam in her office after my fake class is over." He glanced at the clock on the wall. "If he doesn't call soon, I need to leave, and you'll have to—"

Allie grabbed Levi's arm and whispered, "Shh! Samantha just walked in."

****

"Hi, you two." Samantha pulled up a chair and sat. "Levi, tell me the truth."

"The truth?" Levi shot a panicked eye toward Allie, then back to Samantha. "How do you *know* these things," he whispered.

"I see all and know all, Mr. Corliss." She tapped her finger on the table between them. "Just make it easy on yourself and fess up. Do you know the woman I gave my letter of resignation to? The one no one can identify?"

His forehead creased. "I don't know what we're talking about."

"Then you got Laura to show me a picture of her and call her Annika." She made air quotes when she said her name. "I'm not mad. It's funny actually." Samantha sought Allie's acknowledgement, then smiled to reassure the student most likely to drive her to an early grave. "Did you do this, Levi?"

Levi chuckled and leaned back in his chair. "No, ma'am. But I sure wish I had've." He asked Allie, "You thinking Sydnee? Dang, that girl's tireless."

Samantha was confused. Levi seemed sincere. And now that she thought about it, it would have been cruel for them to pull Laura in for a joke about her own dead cousin. No, Levi was clean, as were the rest of her crew. She shivered realizing she was back to wondering whether she was seeing dead people.

Levi's cell buzzed.

Allie sprang from her chair. "Sam, will you buy me a donut? I'm starving and I don't have any cash." She then linked arms with a startled Samantha and pulled her toward the near-empty case of pastries.

****

After a brief greeting, Levi described Samantha's tenure situation to Dr. Livingston, all the while stealing furtive glances toward the pastry counter. He sped through his request hoping Allie would stall until he could gain consent, thank the good doctor, and get off the phone.

Dr. Livingston was as cordial as the day before. Yes, he agreed Samantha had been treated unfairly. And yes, he appreciated their concern and desire to help. But no, he would not act without Samantha's knowledge.

Samantha was now trouping back to their table. Allie skipped behind her yammering about being thirsty. Disappointed but hurried, Levi turned away from Samantha to sign off. Levi expressed his appreciation. Sure, he understood. Worth a shot. No problem. "Thanks anyway, Dr. Livings—"

"Is that Ethan?" Samantha wiggled her fingers toward Levi's phone. "Let me have it. I need to talk to him." A resigned Levi dropped his head and handed her his cell. Did Samantha know what they'd done? Probably not. She seemed more excited than mad.

****

"Hello, Ethan. I found out what happened to Annika." She nodded at Allie and Levi as she boasted a smug grin. "You were right. It wasn't suicide. She died of anaphylaxis. She was allergic to hazelnuts. But wait, let me put you on speaker." She handed the cell back to Levi, who tapped and placed the phone on the table between them.

"Yeah, Samantha, I knew that," Ethan said. "But people back then were divided on whether it was accidental or suicide. You know, like maybe she ate the hazelnuts intentionally. But I never bought it."

"And you were right. I spoke with Laura, Annika's cousin, and she said Annika never intended to kill herself. She just didn't know nuts were in the cake. Evidently, Laura forgot to tell her, and Annika never asked."

"Never asked?" Ethan said. "Annika wouldn't eat *any*thing if there was even the slightest chance it contained nuts. She almost had to see a list of ingredients."

"Really?" Samantha squinted at Levi and Allie.

"She came to my house for ice cream once with one of my classes. We had made a couple kinds, hazelnut and some other kind, probably strawberry. Those were our favorites. I remember Annika would only eat the strawberry and wouldn't even eat *that* until she asked which one we made first."

"Which one you made *first*?" Levi asked.

"Yeah, she said if we made the hazelnut first and any traces were left behind, they could have gotten into the strawberry, and she could still get really sick. One of the students joked about Annika being paranoid, but I told them allergies were nothing to joke about. And as it turned out we *had* made the strawberry first, so she ate."

"And you're sure about this, Ethan? It's been twenty years."

"I'm positive. Our son was allergic, too, and it was serious. Samantha, I remember the conversation. And another thing—no way it was suicide. Nobody's going to choose *that* as the way to die."

It didn't add up. Laura said Annika's death was accidental. Ethan claimed it couldn't have been and was equally certain it wasn't a suicide. Could Ethan be mistaken? Could her death have been unrelated to the allergy? Laura was more likely to have the facts straight. But was she lying? If so, what was she hiding?

Chapter 46

Sunday, November 25

The Sunday after Thanksgiving was difficult for Samantha. Their daughter had spent Thanksgiving with friends in California as she had every year since living on the coast. Elyse didn't have much time off so a trip home for Thanksgiving wasn't workable. Lucas had spent the long weekend with his girlfriend and her family. But Samantha and Rob understood the difficulty of holiday travel while juggling jobs and spending time with significant others. They didn't mind and looked forward to seeing everyone at Christmas.

This was also the first time in years she hadn't used Thanksgiving weekend to decorate for Christmas. But with the chaos of her life these past few weeks, she didn't mind waiting to bring up the bins from the basement and cover every shelf, table, and mantel with greenery and nutcrackers.

But in all honesty, it wasn't the absence of her children nor the postponement of decorations that made the day difficult. Her funk had more to do with the undeniable urge she'd felt all weekend to drive to The Fountain. What did she expect to find there? She didn't know. Had her dream about the scarab been a message? Possibly, but from whom? Was Debra right? Did Samantha know at some level that answers awaited her at The Fountain? Maybe. Samantha certainly respected the inner *knowing* which guides us in ways we don't always understand. The unconscious, some called it. Intuition. A higher power. Were they different names for the same life force?

But it was more than that. Samantha was still troubled by the fact that before she had even seen a picture of Annika to know what she looked like, she had seen her twice: once several weeks ago outside the president's office—the woman no one else had seen or knew anything about—and again in a dream earlier this week. *That* was the root of her unrest.

And that was what finally prompted Samantha to drive to The Fountain early Sunday evening. She was hard-pressed to see the purpose, but she had to go. If nothing else, she'd meet Chess's aunt, visit for a few minutes, then head home. Maybe it would help her forget that stupid dream.

After Samantha signed in and collected a visitor's badge, she followed the directions of an attendant to Ruth's room. However, as she reached her destination an aide came out of the room and quietly closed the door. Ruth was napping. Did Samantha wish to wait?

Samantha grumbled to herself. *Well, what does that mean? Was I supposed to come here or not?* She turned to retrace her steps to the front entrance just as a woman in a wheelchair rounded the corner pushed by an aide who was a student of Samantha's.

"Hello, Dr. Hayes. Are you here to see Chess's aunt?"

"Hi, Hannah. I was, but she's napping. I was just debating whether I should go or wait a while." She smiled and nodded to the woman in the wheelchair.

"You should wait, honey," the woman in the

wheelchair chimed in. "She'll be glad to see you. I'm Liv."

Liv. The woman Chess had told them about. The one with Alzheimer's. "Hello, Liv." Samantha took the hand offered. "I'm Samantha, one of Chess's professors." Samantha glanced at her watch. *How long would Ruth nap? Maybe she could stay for a while…*

"Are you going to supper?" Samantha asked. "Can I take you?" At Samantha's questioning glance, Hannah handed over Liv's care, smiled, and nodded her approval. The clatter of dishes and utensils guided them toward the double-wide doors leading to the dining hall. Round tables with plastic, gingham tablecloths awaited them, each with seating for four.

Once Liv was situated at a table, Samantha pulled up a chair and chatted with her as Liv ate. Some of her banter was coherent; some not so much. Memory was fickle for Alzheimer's patients. Lucid moments sometimes sprang unpredictably from clouded confusion. They talked about the food, although Liv believed she had cooked the meal herself. Liv was excited about the Christmas season but hoped she could find a big enough turkey for all the people she would host this year. Samantha rolled gracefully with each statement and didn't argue or correct.

"Miss Liv, you're wearing a lovely wedding ring. How long were you married?"

"Oh, not near long enough. I married when I was thirty and was married for forty years when my husband passed away. He was a dear man. We had a good life together with our girls."

"My husband and I have been married for thirty-two this past May. Do you have any secrets for a long marriage, Miss Liv?"

While Liv had no secrets for wedded bliss, she did seem to shift a bit into the present. She held out her left hand. "My ring *is* pretty, isn't it? He was always generous, my husband. In fact, he's the one who picked out this necklace. I wear it every day." Liv pulled a necklace out from under her collar and held out the charm for display.

Samantha's heart leapt to her throat as Liv held out a gold scarab charm much like her own. Her hand moved to her own necklace, held it out for Liv to see.

Liv smiled. Her eyes met Samantha's. "You have one, too."

Samantha's heart beat faster; her thoughts swirled in astonishment. Although her dream had prompted her to come here, she hadn't really expected anything to come of it. But here she was, nonetheless, sitting with someone who had just shown her the scarab necklace she had been told to find. Any doubts she had about the purpose of this visit evaporated quickly and completely. Did that mean Liv had information to help unravel the mystery surrounding Annika and the mysterious room connection? Samantha couldn't imagine how. But right now, that necklace seemed as good a place as any to begin.

"Miss Liv, will you tell me about your necklace? I assume for you to wear it every day it has special meaning for you. You say your husband gave it to you?"

Liv's face relaxed a little. "Oh no, he gave it to our girl. She had a hard life. He asked her to not be afraid of change. To face it head on. Because that's how we grow. Our girl wore this necklace every day. And when she died, I began wearing it. To keep her close, I guess."

"Your daughter died," Samantha whispered as she relaxed into her chair. No wonder Liv talked so much about the past. To have lost a child...Samantha couldn't even imagine. But to blame herself...now *that* Samantha *could* imagine.

"I'm so sorry, Liv." Samantha squeezed her hand. "Do you mind if I ask what happened? I don't mean to pry, but—"

"Allergies, they said. Our girl ate a piece of cake with hazelnuts in it; she was allergic. But"—Liv shook her head—"she never would have eaten cake or anything else without asking first what was in it."

An allergy to hazelnuts? "Miss Liv, was Annika your daughter?"

"Yes." Liv smiled. "Our niece, actually. We took her in when her parents died. But we loved her as our own. And when she died..." Tears fell again.

"I can't imagine how difficult that must be. I knew Annika—sort of—and I met your other daughter, Laura, just this week. Laura told me about Annika's allergy and how she died."

"Then you know!" Liv grabbed Samantha's hand. "Please don't tell. They said it was an accident, but we always knew better. She planned the whole thing. We always thought she'd adjust eventually. But she didn't." Liv caught her breath. "If I had only done something sooner."

Oh my, Liv still believes Annika died by suicide. Of course, Liv would have known at the time, along with everyone else, that Annika's death was an accident. But with Alzheimer's, what a person remembers comes and goes seemingly at random; what they know one moment, they don't remember at all the next. Samantha couldn't bear Liv believing that Annika's death was suicide when it wasn't. Especially if she blamed herself. Clarifying the facts for Liv now didn't mean she would hold onto that information for any length of time. Still, Samantha had to do what she could in this moment to put Liv's mind at ease.

Samantha held Liv's hand. "Liv, I've spoken with Laura and she told me about Annika's death. She told me about her allergy and the fact that she hadn't known about the hazelnuts when she ate the cake." Samantha held Liv's gaze. "She didn't do it on purpose, Liv. It was an accident. Nothing you could have prevented."

Liv pulled her hand free. "Of course, she didn't do this to *herself*! I never thought for a minute that she did." Liv clutched the wheels on her chair and began moving the chair and herself away from the table. "But don't tell me I couldn't have prevented it. I know I could have!"

Samantha was confused. While she wanted to reassure Liv, she seemed to have only made matters worse. How much could she do for Liv in her present state? Very little, it would seem, as Liv was becoming more agitated by the moment.

"Maybe I should get you back to your room," Samantha said as she took the handles of the wheelchair.

Liv stopped Samantha with a hand to her arm. Leaned in. She looked around as if frightened and whispered, "We always knew, but we didn't tell anyone. And I never will because it won't bring her back. And now Laura is all I have. You understand that." Her eyes pleaded for Samantha to agree.

"I understand," Samantha tried to reassure her. "Just let me get you back to your room. I'll call a nurse who can—"

Tears welled in Liv's eyes. She whispered, "They said it was her allergy—" Liv paused to clarify. "—because they knew about the cake. But it wasn't strong enough to kill her, they said." A fire shone from Liv's eyes. "But our girl was strong enough. Once when they were little, I caught her trying to smother—" Liv shook her head. "I had to pull her off. She said they were just playing. But I knew. The allergies might have started it, but Laura ended it!"

Samantha sat back down.

"Laura was always jealous of the attention we gave Annika." Liv sobbed as she continued. "And we didn't know what to do. Annika needed us. We thought Laura would eventually adjust to Annika being in our home. But she never did." Liv shook her head; her crying subsided. "And then she was gone. Turning Laura in wouldn't bring Annika back. So we had to keep quiet.

"At least for now." Liv made another visual sweep through the dining hall, then whispered, "Before he died, my husband and I wrote it all down and put it in safe keeping with our lawyer." Liv's eyes met Samantha's. "But for now, it'll just be our little secret."

****

As Samantha left The Fountain, she sent a text to Chess, asking her to round up the others to meet at Samantha's house. They now sat together—all but Sydnee who promised to come as soon as her shift ended—around her kitchen table, pulling together pieces of the Annika puzzle.

Samantha concluded her tale. "She's lived with this secret for the last twenty years."

Levi paced. "Laura was jealous of the attention her parents gave Annika and killed her for it. But how? According to everyone who knew Annika, she wouldn't have eaten anything she hadn't checked out first."

"Or when someone she trusted *said* it was safe." Samantha held her mug out to Levi for a refill. "Laura convinced her somehow and, according to Liv, was there to finish the job if necessary. She's played the part of the remorseful cousin to the hilt for the past twenty years. Fooled everyone. Except her parents." Samantha accepted the now full mug from her gracious waiter. "Thanks, Levi."

"But with Mrs. Lavelle's memory, how do we prove any of this?" Jeff asked.

"We don't have to prove it." Samantha waved a dismissive hand. "If Liv is remembering things accurately, she claims that she and her husband put all this down in a document and gave it to their lawyer, for safe keeping, as she put it, to be opened after their deaths." She leaned against the cabinet. "But I will go down to the police station tomorrow and tell them what I know."

At least some of what I know. Samantha didn't plan to include the part about seeing Annika both in a dream and in person before she had even seen a photo of the dearly departed. Some things should be private between a woman and her therapist.

Yet standing in her kitchen with this group weakened her resolve. After the semester they'd shared and the fact that by now Annika felt like an honorary member of this merry band, she found herself reaching for her cell. She pulled up Laura's picture of Annika and, before she could reconsider, said, "I've been hesitant to tell you all this since I don't know what to make of it myself but—"

"Knock. Knock." In walked Sydnee. "I'm here and I want details." She bounced herself up onto the cabinet. As the others brought Sydnee up to speed with the news of Laura and Annika, Samantha put her cell back on the counter and poured Sydnee a coffee.

"Hey!" Chess tapped on the table. "No one's said a word about the obvious." At the blank stares, Chess continued as if they were dullards who simply could not connect the dots. "That Annika really is behind all this!"

Sydnee hopped off the kitchen counter. "Chess, you are hopeless. Dead people don't come back to mess with the living." Samantha's cell phone slid with Sydnee off the cabinet, still open to the picture of Annika that Samantha had gotten from Laura. Sydnee picked it up. "Hey, where'd you find her?"

"Where did I *find* her?" Samantha asked.

"Yeah," Sydnee said. "The girl I got to play Annika at the séance. Last I heard, she had successfully eluded Levi. Where was she?"

Samantha's stomach flipped. "*That's* the Annika from the séance?" As Sydnee placed the cell and picture before the others, each of them nodded.

Samantha pointed at her cell. "*That's* the picture Laura showed me last week. *That's* Annika."

Chapter 47

Sunday, November 25

As Laura signed into the guest registry at The Fountain, the name *Samantha Hayes* occupied the line immediately before her own. She had signed out only a few minutes ago. Laura shot a glance at the space where guests were to identify the resident they had come to see. *Ruth Frost*, it read. And squeezed in, as if an afterthought, *Liv Lavelle*. Laura's gut tightened. Dr. Hayes had visited her mother. Why? And what had they talked about? Laura sped down the hall toward her mother's room. How much did her mother know about Annika's death? And what, in her confusion, might she have let slip?

Laura had long suspected her parents knew more than they were saying, although they had never let on. Not with the police. Not with the people of Vanderlaan. Not even with Laura herself.

Of course, Laura had played the frantic bit pretty well when she found Annika that morning. Her scream. Her rush down the hall to the dorm director's apartment. Her call to 911. *Help!* she cried over and over until no one could doubt Laura's shocked anguish. Her hysteria played well among her friends who rushed in to comfort. In fact, it had taken three friends, the dorm director, and an EMT to calm her enough to give a statement to the police.

Yesterday had been her birthday, she had told them. Friends surprised her with a party and cake. No, Annika missed the party—didn't feel well. Laura brought leftover cake back to the room to eat later. She forgot to tell Annika about the nuts. Yes, her cousin knew she was allergic. No, she couldn't imagine why she would eat it without checking its contents first. Yes, Annika took her allergy seriously. No, she would not have done this to herself. At least she didn't think so.

Laura's hedge at the end left open the possibility of suicide. Not a bad fallback should suspicion for Annika's death ever fall onto Laura.

And everyone believed her.

But why shouldn't they? Laura had kept her growing resentment a secret over the years, even when Annika absorbed more and more of her parents' time. *Annika* was confused. *Annika* was adjusting. *Annika* was sick with grief. Well, Laura was sick too—sick of Annika! Sick of sharing her parents and room and friends. Sick of accommodating Annika's every need. Occasionally, her parents would take Laura aside and remind her how much Annika needed them. Encourage her to make allowances. Emphasize her responsibility. And Laura would comply. She had been raised to comply.

Until that incident with Annika's professor. The one who stole her work. Laura wanted to scream—*Let him* have *your work and give me five minutes of undivided attention from my own parents!* She knew then it would never end. Annika would always have one more dish of fresh hell to serve up as a means of stealing the family spotlight.

That's when she decided.

At Laura's suggestion, Annika visited Vanderlaan over Laura's birthday weekend. She couldn't have been more attentive. She showed Annika the campus. Introduced Annika to all her friends. Halfway talked her into transferring to Vanderlaan herself.

Then Laura's talk of her birthday to the right friends ensured that she would get a party with her favorite cake. No one was even around hours prior when she slipped Annika the over-the-counter sleeping pill, making certain she would sleep through the party. And when she strolled into her room later with leftover cake, no one was there to witness her offer a slice of the supposedly nut-free dessert to a groggy Annika. And when Laura stayed in the room to be certain Annika ate the cake before learning its contents from another resident, no one was the wiser.

Then it happened. Annika began struggling to breathe, a common symptom of anaphylaxis that she recognized immediately. This was the moment Annika had been practicing for her whole life, so Laura wasn't surprised when she grabbed for the purse that held her epipen.

But Laura had been practicing too. She commanded Annika to lie still while she retrieved her purse. With movements slow and methodical, Laura slipped Annika's purse off the desk, removed the epipen, placed it in her own pocket, and lobbed the purse onto Annika's bed. "You won't find it there." Her speech void of any emotion.

Annika frantically spilled her purse's contents on the bed and scrambled to find its life-saving contents. Annika's breathing wasn't as labored as Laura had anticipated. Then with more energy than Laura would have predicted, Annika lunged at her throat, grasping the collar of her blouse and pulling Laura with her as she fell back onto the bed. Her grip was tight. *Could Annika survive this? Maybe.* But Laura couldn't let that happen. Not now that Annika knew what Laura had done.

Laura shoved Annika back down. Annika's grip weakened, her breath coming in gasps. Laura yanked Annika's pillow from beneath her head to the front of her face and pinned her to the bed. Laura waited through Annika's weak attempts to break free, for her body to go limp.

When it did, Laura released a jagged breath along with the pillow. She shifted her weight, pushed herself from the bed. Pausing, panting, a smile played at her lips. She turned toward the door. *Now to dispose of the epipen. Where no one would ever—*

A dull pain hit the middle of Laura's back as hands grasped at her from behind toward the pocket which held the epipen. Laura grabbed Annika's hand and twisted it while pushing back against her cousin who now fell easily onto the bed. The purse, Annika's make-shift weapon, lay on the floor, as limp and lifeless as Annika now appeared to be.

But Laura had to be certain this time. She felt for a pulse and even the slightest breath. Nothing.

And what about the room? She hadn't planned on such a struggle. But maybe that was okay. Wouldn't Annika have turned the place upside down looking for the missing epipen? Sure.

The purse's contents strewn across the bed? That fits. Leave it.

Her bedding in disarray? Someone desperate for

her next breath would flail about. No need to straighten it.

Laura backed toward the door, giving the room one more scrutinizing look. Would it pass as a place where someone died alone without anyone's help? She released the breath she had been holding and nodded. It would.

Now she only needed to toss the epipen. But wait; Annika always kept one with her, and everyone knew it. If it were missing, that would raise suspicion for sure. But what if it were here? Laura scanned the room. Just hidden—misplaced. Laura removed it from her pocket, wiped it clean of fingerprints, and rolled it under the bed. It clicked as it hit the wall. That would be reasonable if some of the other items from Annika's purse had also fallen from the bed. Laura placed several items onto the floor. Definitely a safer choice.

And if Annika hadn't found the pen in her purse, what would she have done? Laura pulled out dresser drawers, scattered their contents as if they had been jumbled in a frantic search. And her suitcase! Annika would have searched there. Laura opened it and left it on the floor.

Laura nodded. That should do it. One last check for a pulse. For a breath. Nothing.

With confidence that Annika would be completely unable to attend the birthday party, Laura slipped out locking the door behind her.

It was easy enough to beg off the party on her cousin's behalf: *Annika wasn't feeling well. Took something to help her sleep. Might come later. Wants us to go ahead with the party. Enjoy ourselves.* And enjoy herself, she did. For the first time since Annika had taken over her family, Laura felt free, happy. Afterward, Laura went out with her boyfriend, not returning to her room until the wee hours of the morning where she went to bed and immediately fell asleep.

It was the next morning, Laura claimed, before she discovered a non-responsive Annika. And when her parents were called in, through tears and inconsolable hysteria, Laura begged their forgiveness for her tragic gaffe. Laura explained that she had brought cake from the party to save for later. And since Annika was always so careful, Laura never dreamed she would eat any. Her parents' stilted reassurance made Laura wonder if, at some level, they knew. While they never once brought it up, occasionally Laura caught them watching her as if she were someone they no longer knew.

Of course, this was before her mother developed Alzheimer's. Laura wasn't as concerned about her mother's fading memories as she was with the associated lapse in judgment. If her dad were still alive, he could cover for any slips her mother might have. But since his death last year, Laura didn't know what her mother might say and to whom she might say it.

No, her mother probably wouldn't remember the conversation with her visitor, but Laura had to try. She sat down and attempted a casual tone. "Mom, did you have a nice visit with that teacher?" She tilted her head. "What was her name?"

"I don't remember. She's a friend of Ruth's niece." Her mother smiled, as if she had a secret she rather enjoyed. "I told her not to worry. Parents will do anything to help their children." She patted Laura's hand. "Just like I've done with you."

Laura's smile faded. "What was she worried about? Did she say?"

"Oh, she's not upset anymore. She's figured it all out."

Laura's voice hardened. "Figured what out?"

Liv fidgeted with the throw on her lap.

"Mom?" Laura lowered her head to catch her mother's eye. "What was she worried about? What was her name?"

"Oh, I don't remember her name. She's from the university."

Laura leapt to her feet. Her heart raced. People from Vanderlaan had tried to get information from her mother. She thought she had successfully quashed the curiosity about Annika last week when she met with that teacher.

She knelt beside her mother. "Please try to remember what she asked. What you told her."

"You'd have to ask her, honey. I don't remember."

This was pointless. Laura pushed herself up. She raked a hand through her hair while her heart pounded. *I thought they were nightmares. Terrifying, sure, but harmless. Those piercing eyes, the fiery stare, that knowing look. And then the words Annika spoke to her night after night: "People need to know the truth," she had said. "I'm here to help them find it."*

Chapter 48

My Death

By now you know that my cousin Laura was less than happy with my intrusion into her family. She tried to hide it, of course. From her parents, our friends, and everyone at school. But I saw it. In the side glances and steely stares. I chalked it up to her being a bit spoiled and assumed she would get used to not being the sole focus of her parents' attention. So I never brought it up. Not to Laura. Not to anybody.

However, I couldn't have asked for better people than my Aunt Liv and Uncle Aaron to offer me a home. They treated me as their own and tried their best to help me adapt. To their credit they didn't shower me with platitudes. I never once heard them say, *Everything happens for a reason* or some such.

They did, however, suggest that when circumstances don't seem to have meaning, we have to create meaning with how we respond. Then they gave me a necklace with a scarab pendant. They told me the scarab represented transformation. They said that tragedy always changes us, but it's up to us to decide how. And that if I was open to it, the tragedy of losing my parents could transform me in positive ways.

So I tried. Developing a new normal wouldn't be easy but I'd give it my best. During my senior year of high school, Hayward offered me a full scholarship. I was thrilled and accepted it right away. Of course, the minute I decided on Hayward, Laura decided on Vanderlaan. And I understood. She needed distance. Maybe if we only saw each other over breaks and the occasional weekend, she'd stop seeing me as a competitor and we could become friends.

At first college was everything I'd hoped for. I loved the academic atmosphere, my classes, and most of my professors. When I heard that one of them, Dr. Titus, was looking for a research assistant, I went to his office and asked him to consider me for the position. He said he would and shuffled me out of there pretty quickly. I'd heard he didn't like students, but I wasn't looking for a friend, only a research opportunity. I told myself it'd be fine. After living with a spoiled cousin, I could certainly handle a cranky professor.

And I could have if *cranky* had been the worst of it. But what did he do? After giving me the data and instructions on what he wanted, he pretty much made me do all the work. He wouldn't answer my emails or calls, was never in his office when he was supposed to be. Other students said his behavior was nothing new and was why his job was on shaky ground. I knew then that I was pretty much on my own.

So I wrote, proofed, and edited that paper within an inch of its double-spaced, one-inch margins of a life and sent it to him ahead of the deadline he'd given me. And it was pretty good if I do say so myself. In fact, it was so good it showed up a few weeks later in an online journal with hardly any of it changed. But why hadn't he told me, I wondered, that our paper—my very first one!—had been published?

Then I saw it. Right under the title where it lists the

authors, it read: *Len Titus, Ph.D. Professor of Mathematics Hayward College.*

And that was it. I wasn't listed as second author. I wasn't given an acknowledgement. I wasn't even mentioned in a footnote as the naive sap he'd conned into doing his work.

I was furious and told him so. But my anger didn't faze him. He had tenure to think about, he said. Not enough research. Not enough publications. Deadlines approaching. Blah blah blah. Dr. Livingston, another one of the math profs, told me I could file a complaint with the Hayward Ethics Committee, which I did. It was a big mess, and when it was over Dr. Titus left Hayward. And so did I. Of course, I could've stayed but by then my desire to study *anything* at that school had died.

So I considered transferring to Vanderlaan. A few of my friends from high school were there. And even though that was Laura's turf, I thought it was big enough to accommodate us both. Plus, why should Laura control where I went to school? I was fed up with hateful people calling the shots for my life.

About that time Laura invited me to visit Vanderlaan over her birthday weekend. I was surprised but pleased. She seemed sincere and I desperately needed a getaway. Maybe being at different schools had softened her feelings toward me. We were both growing up and this would be a good time to see what our relationship might become.

Turns out, I was giving Laura *way* too much credit. What I had always labeled as adolescent animosity was nothing less than adult-size hatred. She had invited me for a visit so she could put an end to me once and for all.

At least that was her plan.

By the time she listened for my breath and checked my pulse that last time, I had already slipped out of my body.

I no longer needed breath or a pulse.

What I needed—was justice.

Chapter 49

Monday, November 26

Monday morning began for Len Titus as did most Mondays after a holiday weekend: a quick glance at a flurry of emails before he answered the most urgent. After he clicked *Send* on the last one requiring an immediate response, he pulled a stack of ungraded papers from his desk tray and got to work. If he hadn't been so wiped out over the weekend, he would've finished them by now. But his sleep hadn't improved any, nor had his demeanor; together they resulted in one assignment after the other deemed unsatisfactory and marked as such.

Knock. Knock.

He sent up a cursory glance. "Come in," he growled.

"Hello, Dr. Titus," said an eager young woman who evidently hadn't heard of his disdain for Monday morning chatter. "I'm sorry to disturb you. Do you have a minute?"

He motioned toward the chair across from his desk as he kept marking papers.

She sat as she continued, "I'm new here and they've assigned you as my advisor. I can't wait to get into my upper-division courses." She barely suppressed a giggle. "You teach two of the classes I'm taking next semester. Oh, and is it true you let students assist with your research?"

Was I ever that young? "I do. Just leave your name and email with Lisa." He tilted his head toward his secretary's office.

When she didn't respond as he had hoped—that is, with a quick farewell and timely exit—a flash of alarm shot through his belly. His stomach tightened. He jumped out of his chair and turned his back toward her as he stuffed the stack of papers into his briefcase. He would hand these back today. Might he need the textbook? Maybe. Into the briefcase it went. *She's still here.* His heart pounded. His breath caught. Next, he tossed in several items of dubious importance to his tutelage of students in Math 101: an unopened three-pack of white-out and a package of padded four-by-six-inch envelopes with new, improved, self-stick adhesive technology.

Stop it! Eyes closed. Jaw clenched.

Her voice came as it had in his nightmares. "I only want to tell you—"

"The truth—I know," he spat the words at her. Len allowed himself a peek in her direction. Despite himself, he clamped his eyes shut again.

"It's not even frightening. The truth, I mean. It'll be free—"

"I want you to leave. Now. Don't come back." His voice was quiet, frigid with self-control.

In a soft rustle, she moved toward the door. "When you're ready for the truth, you'll hear it. From someone."

With jagged breath, he opened his eyes. She was gone.

This is where he was supposed to wake up and

realize he'd been dreaming. But he didn't. And he wasn't.

He knew what he had to do.

****

At precisely six o'clock, Len Titus entered the Shelley Hall conference room. He found the university tenure committee sitting around the table, most of them scrolling on their phones. Charlie fidgeted with an ink pen. Priscilla maintained her trademark expression of boredom. She was entirely too important to be here. They had gathered at his insistence that they meet one more time to complete unfinished business. He promised the meeting wouldn't last long but needed to happen no later than Monday evening. They grumbled and questioned. He ordered and bullied. It's what he did best.

With very few pleasantries, he sat at the head of the table. "Thank you all for being here on such short notice. I'll keep it brief. We all have places we'd rather be, I'm sure."

"What's this about, Len? Do we have a last-minute applicant?" Greg asked.

"No, nothing like that." Len waved a dismissive hand. "Dr. Hayes's application needs further review. We've acted with unwarranted haste, and I suggest we support rather than oppose her request for tenure."

Kathy's head snapped up. Charlie dropped his pen. Priscilla groaned and threw in an eyeroll for good measure.

"Whatever for?" Lancaster demanded. "We've covered this, Len. She was completely uncooperative in curtailing her students' misbehavior. Wouldn't even *pretend* to listen to our suggestions!"

Len read from her application as if he had just today been given access to it. "Her track record speaks for itself. She has the necessary degrees and has served here the requisite number of years. She carries her share of the workload, teaches, publishes, advises." He held out his arm as if to say, *Any fool can see she's qualified.*

"All of this was true three weeks ago, Len," Kathy said. "What happened? You get flak from someone higher up?"

Len's eyes darted to Kathy. "Higher up? I—" He broke eye contact and continued with a voice quiet with self-control. "No, Kathryn. I haven't received flak from the administration. It's just that—" He swallowed. "Personal differences between Dr. Hayes and myself might have clouded my judgment." He stacked the papers neatly in Samantha's file. "I apologize if you find my rationale unclear. I assure you it will become clearer in time."

"Clearer in time?" Priscilla escaped boredom long enough to pose a question. "What is that supposed to mean?"

"Just what I said." Len placed both hands, palms down, on the table. "Now, let's take a vote and get out of here."

And although Lancaster and Priscilla continued to grumble, they were outvoted by the others who recommended Samantha be granted tenure.

****

In a seat with little leg room, Len congratulated himself on the day's accomplishments. He had secured Samantha Hayes's job, at least as far as it was within his power to do so. He had sent the new recommendation as an addendum to the first one he'd sent. The administration would see it first thing in the morning.

Shortly after, news would reach Samantha that he no longer opposed her tenure. That should satisfy Eleanor Waters. She had pestered him long enough about his vendetta against Samantha. *What do you have against Samantha? Why do you not want her here?* Then that night several weeks ago Eleanor cornered him at The Patio demanding to know if he would be fighting Samantha's tenure. Eleanor was like a dog with a bone.

And if that weren't enough, Kathy Day had been there and had seen Eleanor sitting at his table. It would be just like Kathy to misunderstand and start a rumor. *Me and Eleanor*. He shivered. *Perish the thought.*

The university ethics committee and Barb Skeen would also receive a letter expressing his remorse for stealing her work and using it as leverage for his last grant proposal. Two days from now, the Hayward administration would receive his letter of apology for "exploiting student work for professional gain." It would come with a check written for a substantial amount and designated to establish a scholarship fund in Annika Lavelle's name.

And finally, this morning's mail would deliver his letter of resignation to the president's office, effective immediately. This had been the most difficult of the letters to write. To say he enjoyed his students would be a stretch. For the most part, they drained his energy and time while contributing little to his life. Even so, he was too young to retire, and teaching was the only thing he had ever done. But with all former colleagues soon privy to his professional malice, he'd be lucky if they'd recommend him for a job teaching dogs to sit.

Still, he'd be content to teach dogs to sit, roll over, or do calculus if it brought an end to the nightmares and apparitions. Would Annika stay away now? *Please*, he begged the universe's cooperation. *I can't do anymore!*

The flight attendant commanded his attention. "Please place your seats upright and stow all items below the seat in front of you as we prepare for landing."

He would prepare. For the landing. For a new life. He popped his seat upright, folded and latched his tray. Pushed his carry-on with all the belongings he would need for the foreseeable future under the seat ahead of him. Out his window, the skyline of a new life drew near.

It couldn't be any worse than his old one.

Chapter 50

My Journey

My parents taught me that nothing was more important than truth: finding it and speaking it. They were journalists and more than once during my childhood exposed powerful people involved in a range of nefarious activities. As they saw it, with each CEO or senator they exposed, they were helping to create a more just society.

I was proud of them and wanted to follow in their footsteps. Not that I wanted to be a journalist. Numbers were my forte and, the way I saw it, played an important role in the search for truth. After all, without calculus, where would we be in our understanding of the physical world? Even our knowledge of human behavior requires that we know which hypothesis to accept or reject, and for that we need statistics. So yes, I had their passion for truth. What they accomplished through words, however, I would accomplish through numbers.

Little did I know that I would spend more time in the pursuit of truth *after* my death than I had prior to it. This became clear shortly after I slipped out of my physical body right there in Laura's room. That's when she first appeared.

She introduced herself to me as Giah and explained that she was here to help me transition into the next part of my journey. Exactly what that journey would entail she wouldn't say, other than it would give me peace and rest. *That* sounded good. I had just lost a wrestling match while oxygen deprived, so rest and peace seemed my due. And before you ask, no I did not sprout wings or a halo. I know that for a fact because I checked.

Then right away, Giah told me I had two options. (I gather this to be an added perk for those who meet an untimely end at someone else's hand.) Option one, she told me, was to release my murderer to the consequences imposed by the powers-that-be here on earth. This would be the speediest way for me to move on to the next part of my journey. But, she cautioned me, if I chose this path, my murder might never be avenged on earth, meaning Laura might well be free of all consequences until her own death.

I didn't like this option and told Giah as much. To date, Laura had convinced most everyone that she was beyond reproach. She had even taken *me* in, and I had been wise to her hijinks for years. So, letting justice hinge on her narrative of today's events? I didn't think so. "Option two, please," I said to Giah.

Option two, she said, was to hang around in some indeterminate, cosmic limbo where I could try to avenge my death by wielding what influence I now had.

"Ooh!" I said. "I'll have influence?"

"We all have influence." She waved her hand in dismissal. "But I have to warn you. Influencing others isn't much easier after death than it is during life. Oh, you'll have a few advantages you didn't have before. You'll be able to enter their dreams, pose as one of them for brief periods of time, and the usual rules of space won't apply to you anymore." To demonstrate, she disappeared and immediately reappeared atop Laura's desk on the other side of the room. Then just as quickly reappeared directly in front of me which, to be honest, was a little unnerving. I gasped and leaned away from her. An appreciation of personal space was not Giah's strong suit.

She continued, "But your influence is limited by their willingness to *be* influenced. For instance, if they demand you leave, you have to leave. Their own relationship with truth will curtail how much you can even say to them. Remember, Annika, you've transcended mortality; they have not. They're still bound to the very human tendency to refuse truth when it's difficult to hear. And they'll often block what they don't understand and don't want to process. Your actions won't necessarily change any of that."

"They won't listen to me is what you're saying," I concluded.

"I'm saying that some will; some won't. But it hinges on their openness as much as anything you say or do." Giah went on to tell me that I would have a limited amount of time to accomplish my mission. The amount of time I would have depended on quite a few factors, some of which Giah wasn't even privy to. However, she did say I would feel a decline in cosmic energy when I got close to my limit so I should pace myself.

"And, Annika," she said, maintaining my gaze, "holding others' peace hostage isn't without consequences. It will take a toll on your own peace as well."

Giah's warning notwithstanding, this was an easy

choice. I'd never have peace until Laura faced consequences. This much I knew. And with me out of the mix, she'd never face anything. So that's how I came to this land of limbo awaiting her earthly judgment and my heavenly rest.

At first things moved along fairly quickly. I found out right away that Aunt Liv and Uncle Aaron weren't as naive as I had suspected. While they had never let on, they knew she had done it. And not just by failing to mention the hazelnuts either. They knew her actions were premeditated and as full of venom as that cake was of hazelnuts. Yet they simply would not confront Laura, much less tell anyone else. She was all they had, and they needed to keep her out of prison.

I get that, I suppose. But where did that leave me? On my own, that's where. No one had protected me from Laura *then*. And I was the only one who could avenge my death *now*. I was more convinced than ever that I had chosen the better of Giah's options.

Then I learned something that necessitated I switch tactics. I found out Dr. Titus was feeling guilty about my death. Although he'd left Hayward by then, he'd heard about my death along with a rumor that I had died by suicide. He thought he was to blame. Well, if that didn't take the cake—oops, no pun intended. None of this was his fault since I hadn't been the least bit suicidal. Believe me, I'd've paid money to kick *his* epipen, if he had one, all the way to kingdom come. But suicide? Never.

And yet...having him believe he was responsible wasn't without appeal. I mean, he had betrayed me. Some squirming on his part seemed altogether fair.

But that's when I hit a snag. If I let everyone

believe it was suicide, Dr. Titus would continue to feel guilty, but Laura would get away with it. If I outed Laura, Dr. Titus would be off the hook, and I didn't want that either. So I decided the only solution was to keep them *both* worried about being found out as long as I could. And then when I was ready to move on, I'd continue my mission to expose Laura and hope that by then Dr. Titus would have learned a lesson or two.

Okay, okay, I know it wasn't right. But at this point my thirst for honesty was taking a back seat to my hunger for justice. And no, I'm not proud of it. But in my defense I was new at this being dead thing.

But regardless, and however ill-advised it was, it worked for a while. I'd pop into Laura's dreams to remind her that she could be found out at any time. She wouldn't sleep for days as she waited for the other shoe to drop. She'd check in with her folks and without tipping her hand make sure they still had her back. And then she'd relax and go back to business as usual. I also visited Dr. Titus regularly. He saw me in his nightmares too and occasionally I'd be the face in a crowd. I'd make sure he caught me watching him; give him a half smile and a knowing look. Then after questioning his sanity, he'd double down and become more obnoxious than ever.

With my efforts only briefly disturbing my earthly nemeses, I was starting to doubt my ability to settle the score with either of them. To be honest, it wasn't as much fun as I'd expected, and my higher self was pestering me to cut out the shenanigans. The fact is, Giah was right: holding the peace of others hostage was taking a toll on my own. As long as I held Laura and Dr. Titus captive, I would never be free. So I was a bit relieved when circumstance intervened to force my hand.

You see, a few years ago I found out that someone else—a completely innocent person—was blaming herself for my death. Seems she was a supervisor for a counselor I saw briefly during my time at Hayward. She heard something about suicide and was afraid she should have known or done something. Of course, this was totally inaccurate since I hadn't in fact killed myself at all. And while I could justify messing with Laura and even toying with Dr. Titus, this Dr. Hayes person? No. I couldn't let her blame herself when she had absolutely nothing to do with my death.

It was time for the truth.

So I went to work. I did a little digging on Dr. Hayes and found out she had graduated from Vanderlaan herself. Kind of odd, wasn't it, that that's where Dr. Titus was teaching? And you'll never believe this—I didn't either at first—but Dr. Hayes had been a student at Vanderlaan years before and had even lived in the room that I died in! (I've suspected for some time now that I'm not the only one orchestrating things up here. Giah says to look into that first chance I get.)

I knew then that I had to get Dr. Hayes to leave Hayward and sign on at Vanderlaan. She was a bit skeptical at first—you know, because of Dr. Titus—so I got her grandfather to remind her of how important change can be. The idea of that reminder coming in the form of a necklace like my own—don't think I wasn't proud of that one! I have to say, being dead has taken my creativity to a whole new level.

Anyway, since I'd need to bring my untimely death to her attention, the room connection would be the perfect way to do it. I then maneuvered things so a couple of incoming students would also live in rooms that our Dr. Hayes had previously occupied. I selected Allie and Levi because I knew they'd hit it off with her if I could just get them to go by her office a time or two, which of course they did. But neither of them ever mentioned where they lived. So other than some camaraderie and a lot of snacking, nothing happened. I had to make this bigger.

So the next year, I arranged a couple more room assignments. I chose Jeff because his inclination toward the spiritual would move office conversation in that direction. Sydnee I chose because, well, if you must know, I envy her. If I would've had her bravado as a living human, I could've taken on Dr. Titus *and* Laura with both hands tied behind my back.

And that is how it came to be that Dr. Samantha Hayes ended up with an office full of students who lived in her former rooms. And I really thought that would be the hard part. But getting them to make the connection between their rooms was harder. I used up a risky amount of cosmic energy hiding then returning Jeff's computer. Giah tells me that stunts with physical matter are more draining than the everyday folderol, but I wasn't worried. Jeff was academically conscientious, Allie had a sports car, and Levi was dying for a ride. It was energy well-spent. And once that first room connection was discovered, the others fell into place.

Now before you ask, I had nothing to do with Chess finding the office. Believe me—I would love to take credit for that one, but she came in on her own. And even though she doesn't have one of Dr. Hayes's rooms, I let her stay. And what a stroke of luck! At first she was the only one that even *got* it. And the séance idea—nothing short of brilliant! Who else but Chess would've put *that* in motion?

I hadn't planned to drop in that night until Sydnee got the idea of playing that prank on the others. But I showed up several evenings in a row in the breakroom where she works and introduced myself as a new employee. I worked the conversation around to campus life and her friends. Before long we were laughing about this joke she wanted to play on her friends. I offered to play along and got cast in the role of—who do you think? *Myself*! Thank you, Sydnee. I knew you were a good choice.

I do admit that Dr. Hayes's decision to resign caught me off guard. I had to shut that down or my whole plan would have failed. So I made sure to intercept her letter of resignation to ensure that no one ever saw it. I also planted the idea with Sydnee of contacting Dr. Livingston as her penance for what she saw as her séance hoax. I knew Dr. Livingston telling what he knew about Dr. Titus's plagiarism would settle Samantha's guilt over Titus losing his job years ago at Hayward.

Getting Samantha to let go of guilt over my death though, that was tougher. I finally came to Samantha in a dream to nudge her in the right direction. Aunt Liv is The Fountain of Youth's fountain of information if you just know what you're listening to. Telling Samantha to look for the scarab confused her at first since her necklace was still where she had left it. But I knew she'd make the connection once she saw it on Liv. I'd have laid it out more explicitly if I'd have had more time. But I was feeling my energy slip away each time I made an appearance, so I had to be brief.

Now I've accomplished most of what I set out to do. Dr. Hayes is free of guilt over my death and any pangs of conscience related to Dr. Titus. She will also be staying at Vanderlaan where she can work free of any ne'er-do-well colleagues. And Laura is finally facing the consequences of her actions. Dr. Hayes went to the police with all she had learned about my death, including the fact that Aunt Liv and Uncle Aaron had given their attorney a document laying it all out. Evidently it wasn't to be opened until after their deaths, but the police got a search warrant and sure enough— everything Laura's parents had witnessed over the years was spelled out, including what they had pieced together about the night I died. It was a long time coming, and it took more out of me than I could have imagined at the onset, but the truth finally came out. Laura has now been arrested for my murder and I'm ready to move on to whatever is next in my journey. Things have worked out for everyone.

Everyone, that is, except Dr. Titus. When I switched strategies, I continued visiting him in dreams, this time with a different purpose: I wanted to tell him he played no part in my death. I regretted tormenting him and was ready to free him and thereby free myself. But each time I tried, he shut me out. And, as Giah had told me, we cannot stay once they demand we leave. Sadly, he seems no closer to listening now than he was when I started.

The last opportunity I could offer him was the day he saw me in Shelley when I dropped in on Barb Skeen. I was there posing as a tenure committee member to let Barb know how bad things were for Dr. Hayes. I knew once she realized, she'd do her part and blow the whistle on Dr. Titus. But when he ducked into the faculty lounge to avoid me, I knew I was out of chances with him. At that point, my energy was all but depleted. I could no longer initiate an interaction. I hoped he would do so himself.

But he didn't.

And one thing I've learned: while the truth does set us free, we must be willing to hear it.

I hadn't been ready to hear it from Giah. Dr. Titus wasn't ready to hear it from me.

I hope one day he will hear it from someone.

Chapter 51

Wednesday, November 28

Samantha struggled to open her office door. Her key scratched the lock several times as it repeatedly missed its target. Her view was obstructed by a box of donuts and her purse, both of which scuffled against grocery bags holding fresh supplies of candy and drinks. She was about to drop everything to make for an easier connection when the key caught, slipped in, and turned in the tumbler. Samantha flipped the light switch and dropped everything on the first chair she came to.

Last evening, she had asked the five to come by her office first thing this morning. They would be here any minute. She made coffee but left the candy and drinks for them to unpack. Samantha squirted caramel goop into her mug as her coffee maker gurgled and hissed itself to life. She had just flopped into a chair and put her feet on the table when her entourage arrived.

"And *what* do you think you're doing?" Levi asked as he came to a stop just inside the door. His eyes shifted from Samantha's face to her feet perched on the table, then back again.

"The table's mine, Levi. I bought it." Samantha smiled.

"Forget the table, Levi." Chess scrambled to the pile of groceries, still sitting where Samantha had deposited them. "She's restocking her supply!" Chess exclaimed as she lifted items from each bag.

Sydnee added, "Ooh, and she bought donuts! Nice addition to the office, Dr. H. Are they for us? Jeff, don't grab. I get first dibs on the ones with icing."

"Who's grabbing?" Jeff argued. "Just gimme a scone."

"Play nice," Samantha said. "Everybody, get what you want and sit." Her feet came down as she giggled. "I've got news."

"Bet I know what it is." Levi stepped over the table. "Dr. Titus was out the past couple days and rumor is," he lowered his voice, "he isn't coming back. Is that it, Sam? You planning a party? Can we come?"

"Wait." Allie grabbed Levi's arm. "Dr. Titus left Vanderlaan? Levi, this is big." She climbed onto the sofa. "Does that change things for you Samantha? It does, doesn't it? With Dr. Titus out of the way, will you get tenure?" Allie's voice accelerated with each question.

Samantha held up a hand as if to slow Allie's train of thought. "Others at the administrative level still need to—"

"And *that's* why you restocked the supplies," Chess said. "I *knew* it! You aren't leaving!"

"What a relief!" Sydnee scooted in next to Chess.

Samantha laughed. "Just once, I'd like to tell my own good news."

Amid congratulations and hugs from Allie and Chess, they all settled in for their mini celebration. Within minutes the donuts were gone, candy stashed away, juices and sodas packed in the fridge.

"Gotta say, I'll be glad for things to get back to normal." Sydnee licked icing off her fingers.

"Do you mind?" Levi made a face and handed her a napkin. "Besides, when has this office ever been normal?"

"At least not since we found out about the room connection," Chess said. "If I had known when I picked a college that I'd be placed in the middle of this office and all its drama, I'd—"

"What?" asked Sydnee. "Take a class in forensics first?"

"No, Syd. I would have watched more of those documentaries on supernatural phenomena."

Sydnee pulled her ball cap over her eyes and groaned.

"Now why do you do that? After everything that happened, how are you *not* convinced that Annika did every bit of this?" Then she switched focus. "Dr. Hayes you're convinced, aren't you?"

Samantha swayed her head from side to side. "I never want to rule anything out." She sipped her caramelly concoction. "The room connection led us to Annika's death, and ultimately to how she died, and—" She chose her words carefully. "That helped me settle some things personally and professionally that I hadn't been able to settle otherwise."

Sydnee squinted. "You always get weird when someone mentions Annika. There's more to this than what you've told us."

Silence.

Sydnee asked, "And you won't tell us, will you?"

"Nope," Samantha said. "But I do admit, the takeaway for me was pretty significant. And Laura's been charged with her cousin's murder. Dr. Titus's escapades were brought to light. None of it would have happened without the room connection." Samantha shrugged. "Supernatural? That's a loaded word, Chess. But yeah, something happened here that went beyond natural."

Sydnee said, "But you don't honestly believe that Annika, from twenty years ago—"

"Who else, Syd?" argued Chess.

"Who else?" Jeff said. "Anybody hear of God?"

"Why does it have to be a *who*? Maybe it's a *what*," Allie said. "This was Samantha's scarab beetle experience." She pointed to Sydnee. "And it would be yours too if you'd just be open to the idea." She nodded. "Synchronicity. A meaningful coincidence with no evidence of cause and effect."

Samantha got up, tossed her cup into the waste basket, and moved to her desk to gather class material. "I can't argue with that. It was definitely the most meaningful coincidence I've ever encountered."

Allie asked Sydnee, "Then what *do* you think happened? I can't believe you don't have an opinion."

"I *do* have an opinion. This whole room coincidence. The picture of Annika. Synchronicity. All of it." Sydnee bounced off the sofa, slung her backpack over her shoulder. "It's science that we just haven't discovered yet."

"C'mon, Syd." Levi flopped his head back. "*That's* convenient."

"No more convenient than synchronicity, ghosts, or God."

Levi turned to face her. "So you're saying this whole room connection can be explained by science even though science can't explain it." He offered his most sarcastic smile.

"I'm saying—" She offered the sigh of one who has suffered much. "—that science can only answer questions someone has thought to ask. And at some point, my doubting friend, someone will ask the right question in the right way and science will explain it."

Jeff jumped in. "That actually makes sense, Levi. And that argument doesn't preclude the possibility of a God who is in control of science as well as all information we've yet to discover." He shot a questioning glance at Samantha.

"True," Samantha said. "I don't think belief in God is at all contradictory to science. Nor is it inconsistent with synchronicity as I understand it."

She opened the door as each of her crew grabbed coats and book bags. "I don't have an answer, but I hope you won't close yourself off from things you don't understand. And in the meantime"—she waved her arm toward the hall several times—"if I want to keep this job—and I do—I have a class to teach."

****

Sydnee buttoned her coat and stuffed her hands into her pockets as she left Samantha's office. She called out good-byes to Allie and Chess as they headed in opposite directions outside Prescott. She told Jeff to let her know if he wanted her help with any girls. He shook his head but smiled. Levi told her to be the scientist today who asked the right questions in forensics class. She stuck her tongue out at him. Made him laugh.

If she could only find a way to ask the right question, she would. Like, *Who was the chick I got to play Annika at that stupid séance?*

She pulled her coat tighter against the cold air and

tried a rephrase. *Did she play into my plan? Or did I play into hers?*

Chapter 52

Wednesday, November 28

That evening, Samantha sat in Debra's waiting room, flipping through a magazine and shaking her leg to the beat of an oldie-but-goodie. Occasionally she would whistle along. When the receptionist picked up humming at the chorus, Samantha smiled. Today she had a lot to sing about and began telling Debra about it before she hit the proverbial couch. Debra made tea as Samantha quickly recapped the high points of this past week. She stopped herself in the middle of stirring to ask, "You retracted your resignation and got tenure?"

Samantha giggled and clapped. "I did! Retract it, I mean. Whether I'll get tenure or not depends on the trustees, but without Len to block it..." Samantha shrugged. "Monique told me his letter said he was moving as far away as he could get from Vanderlaan and 'reminders of his regrettable past.' " Samantha provided air quotes.

"Regrettable past," Debra repeated. "It's certainly that. But wonder what convinced him."

"Don't know. He behaved oddly the last time we spoke. I even felt a little sorry for him. Evidently, he's been troubled by guilt all these years—"

"I should think so." Debra sipped her tea.

"No, I mean he *should* feel guilty about stealing her work. But more than that." Samantha lowered her voice as if Len might be hiding in the closet listening in. "Debra, *I* think he felt unwarranted guilt all these years over Annika's death and—"

Debra squirted tea as she choked out a laugh. "You don't say."

Samantha plucked several tissues from the box, handed them to Debra who dabbed at her sweater.

"And what's your takeaway from *that*?" Debra asked.

Samantha sat back, let herself relax. Here, she could say what she couldn't to her students. "That I did the same. I held on to unnecessary guilt for Annika's death." She shook her head in disbelief at what had been outside of her reach but was now hers for the taking. "I was entirely without blame for Annika's death." She closed her eyes and released a cleansing breath. "Letting go of this is a game changer for me."

"How so?"

"Ha! Seriously?"

"*I* know *how so;* I'm checking to see if *you* know *how so*."

Sam nodded and smiled. "Fair enough. How so..." Her gaze wandered to the window. "I did my best, then assumed the outcome resulted from what I *didn't* do." She bit her lip. "I had no way of knowing everything going on in her life—her cousin's malice and complete lack of compassion." She cast her glance back to Debra. "And Rochelle."

"Rochelle?"

"I assumed I pushed *too* much with her. Missed that she was sick."

Debra smiled. "And..."

"And"—Samantha returned the smile—"I had

simply demanded her respect. I didn't cause her death."

"Let's do Len next." Debra leaned back and offered a singsong beginning: "You felt guilty about Len losing his job at Hayward, but…"

"But," Samantha completed the statement, "his exploitation of students ended his career at Hayward. Not my encouragement for anyone to speak up."

"And—"

Samantha laughed. "*And t*he resulting demise of his marriage and trouble finding another job had much more to do with his lack of character than anything I did."

"And his leaving Vanderlaan so suddenly…"

Samantha threw up her hands. "I can't even take credit or blame for *that*. That came entirely from—" She shrugged. "I have *no idea* where that came from." She laughed and sped along, "But I didn't do it!"

Debra laughed. "You didn't."

"But that isn't the only part of the game it changed. No more feeling overly responsible for my students. I intervene for some, not for others. Sometimes they want more; sometimes they want less. I *hope* I'm getting it right." She pursed her lips. "But regardless, I'm doing the best I can. And to be honest, it's the same for Len. I hope his change of heart is sincere and I wish him well. But I can't fix it. No one can take someone else's journey. And if they don't want our help—" She shrugged.

Debra said, "So many things we simply have no control over. Their decisions, their past histories. All we *can* control is ourselves and our own intentions."

A smile tugged at Samantha's lips. "And we can't control room assignments."

"What was that about?" Debra lowered her voice. "Any insights there?"

Samantha bit her lip. "Without the room connection, we wouldn't have discovered Annika's story. I wouldn't have learned how she died. Len would still be exploiting colleagues and students." She shook her head. "Something or someone intended for my students to live in my former rooms—for our paths to cross in *this* way at *this* time."

"Who or what was it?"

"I see God's work in a lot of things. Is synchronicity a part of that?" She sucked in a breath. "Or even—"

"Annika?"

Samantha met Debra's gaze. "I saw her, Debra. Before I had seen her picture, I *saw* her in my dream and *in person* coming out of the president's office."

Debra nodded. "I remember."

"And the other night at my house, Sydnee saw my picture of Annika." Samantha lowered her voice. "She said that was the person she got to play Annika at the séance." Samantha's hands went to her mouth.

Debra's lips parted, mirroring Samantha's awe.

"Remember all the anxiety I had when I first came to Vanderlaan? Could that have been tied in with being at the place where Annika Grace died?" Samantha leaned forward. "This room connection seems to be one more example of what I've learned with Annika and my students and Len and Rochelle."

The breadth of this transformation was extensive, touching so many burdens she had carried for too long. She released a breath she seemed to have been holding for decades.

"What's going on behind the scenes of our lives is more complex than any of us know." Samantha sank back into the sofa. "And I'm *so* relieved."

"Relieved?" Debra asked.

"It's not all on me."

Chapter 53

Friday, December 7

The remainder of the semester at Vanderlaan was relatively uneventful for Samantha. Her application for tenure continued up the academic chain without any additional snags. Final exams began amid the usual pleas for extra credit opportunities. Samantha held firm to her no-extra-credit policy, however, and reminded them that studying for finals would be a more productive use of their time.

While she typically hosted a get-together for her students during finals week, the stress of the semester had convinced her to ditch it this year. But with the resolution of the Annika mystery and without the need to pack up her office, Samantha now enjoyed an abundance of holiday spirit. She and Rob put up a tree and decorated the house. She made Christmas cookies and candy while he hung lights and set up their nativity scene on the front lawn.

And on Friday afternoon, after her five turned in their last papers and sat for their last exams, they would stop by Samantha's to celebrate the season. Chess initially begged off as she had promised to spend time with her aunt before leaving for home. But when Samantha insisted that she bring Aunt Ruth along, Chess agreed with enthusiasm.

When the doorbell rang, Millie yapped while Levi

barked from the front porch. Samantha scooped her up and opened the door to four of her five. She led them back to the kitchen as she passed Millie off to Levi. While the others exclaimed over the tree and assortment of holiday treats that lined her countertops, Levi and Millie scrambled on the floor for the squeaky rope.

"Where's Chess? Thought you talked her into coming," Sydnee said.

"She'll be here shortly. She's picking up Aunt Ruth."

Allie helped herself to a wreath-shaped cookie. "I'm glad we get to meet her. It's okay for her to leave The Fountain?"

Samantha nodded as she took more cookies from the oven. "She can leave occasionally for a few hours. She visits the Seeleys a few times a year but rarely goes anywhere else." She placed the hot pan on the stove top. "Chess said she's excited to meet all of us."

Rob came in, turned on some holiday jazz, and offered to serve up the eggnog he had made for the occasion. As he served cups of his signature drink, he bantered with Allie about the color of the walls and with Jeff about his next book.

"Levi," Samantha called out over the music and canine repartee arising from the floor. "Take Millie into the den, please. I don't want her underfoot when Aunt Ruth arrives."

Sydnee munched a chocolate covered peanut butter ball. "You shouldn't be underfoot either, Levi. Either get off the floor or stay in the den with Millie."

"They just drove up." Samantha scurried to the front door and returned a few moments later with Chess and her Aunt Ruth. Chess bounced with excitement as she helped her aunt to a chair and began to introduce her friends. "This is Dr. Hayes's husband Mr. Donovan. And this is Levi—"

"Oh, I know that's Levi." Ruth laughed and patted the chair next to her. "You come sit by me, young man. I hear you have all the spunk that Chess hopes to acquire. Good for you. Teach her well. And you"—she turned to the next one—"must be Allie. You have helped her more than anyone to feel included in this group. I thank you for that." She held Allie's hand for a moment before moving on. "And...Jeff, is it? Chess tells me you are the most thoughtful, intelligent person she knows. And unless I miss my guess, you"—Ruth sized up the last of the troop—"are Sydnee Baldwin, the bossiest and most outspoken student on the Vanderlaan campus."

Amid laughter and exclamations of agreement, Ruth continued. "And you are Dr. Hayes, whose office has given my girl a home away from home. I appreciate your hospitality to her and to me." She turned to Chess. "And aren't you the sneaky one? You brought me here without telling me where we were going."

"What do you mean, Aunt Ruth?" Chess's forehead wrinkled. "I told you we were going to Dr. Hayes's house."

"But you didn't say—" She shook her head. "Of course, you couldn't have known. You were so young." She took Chess's hand, held it. "This is the house your grandparents lived in. They died when you were so young. In fact," she added, "you and your mother lived here with them when your father was in the service."

Silence.

Ruth chuckled as she continued, "You used to

practice writing your name right over there by the door. Of course, you couldn't get any farther than your first initial. But you were so proud. Your mom never could break you of that." Ruth chuckled at the memory as Rob's and Samantha's eyes met.

Chess's eyes darted to Samantha. Her squeal broke the silence. Her hooped earrings danced as she leapt across the room and all but tackled her mentor. "I *lived* in *your house!*"

"Of course, you did!" Samantha whooped as she wobbled to keep her balance. "Why did we ever doubt it?"

Chapter 54

"Okay, thanks, Dr. Hayes. I'll add this class right away."

"You're welcome, Nikki. Let me know if you have any problems. And send the next one in, please." Samantha's first class of the new semester wouldn't meet until noon, but she had been working for hours. The student who just left was one of several who needed to make last minute schedule changes. Meanwhile, others waited their turn outside her office door. Even with their words muffled, Samantha recognized the rhythm of easy banter that suggested friendship and familiarity.

Within the next thirty minutes, she helped seven students adjust schedules and gave four of them directions to their first classes. She encouraged two students to audition for the spring musical and convinced another to give it at least until classes *started* before deciding college wouldn't work.

Was there anything more exciting than the first day of a new term? Samantha's heart sang in gratitude that she was surrounded by youthful energy and was a part of these students' lives. Even more exciting was that any minute now her crew would trail in to regale her with stories of winter break, ask a million questions about their research projects, and begin a litany of

354

chatter about their new classes.

"Dr. H., we're back!" Sydnee's voice rang out as she careened into the office, Jeff close behind.

"Hey, you two! How was your break?" Samantha rose and hugged each. She made some coffee for herself while they each fell into chairs.

"Visited Braylon U. and loved it," Jeff said. "Talked with a couple of their faculty. They've got everything I want. It's such a good fit for me, Dr. H. I've decided to apply for their Master of Arts in English."

"Good for you! And when the time comes just let me know where to send a letter of recommendation."

"Will do." Jeff nodded. "Did Lucas and Elyse come home for Christmas?"

"They did." She smiled at his thoughtfulness. "They each brought a significant other," Samantha said as she provided air quotes. "Both lovely people. We had a wonderful time."

"And what about you, Ms. Baldwin?" Samantha pulled her legs underneath her and sipped her coffee. "How was your holiday?"

"Pretty good. I was able to help a lot at the store over break. My brother Joey was sick almost the whole time, but we finally found out what's wrong." Sydnee flopped her head back. "Allergies, Dr. H. To *everything*." Raised her head. "Including hazelnuts."

"No," Samantha whispered.

"Yes!"

Jeff said, "Maybe it's synchronicity, Syd. How does the little guy feel about séances?" He ducked to avoid the pillow Sydnee lobbed in his direction, then tossed it back. "Does it *ever* occur to you to play nice?"

"It *occurs* to me, but I try not to dwell on it. Hey," Syd switched gears, "Jeff, you haven't mentioned Maddie. You all still a thing?"

Jeff let out a breath. "Syd, I don't want to talk about—"

"It's true then." Sydnee slapped her hand on the chair cushion. "I heard you two broke up." Sydnee waved a hand. "But no problem. We got this. I have a friend that'd be perfect for you. She's—"

"No, Syd!" Jeff covered his ears. "I'm not listening."

"Enough, Sydnee." Samantha held up both hands. "Let Jeff handle this however he wants. He'll figure it out. And, Jeff, I'm sorry. Are you okay?"

"I am, Dr. H. It was mutual."

Sydnee huffed.

"Well, it *was*!"

"Yeah, it was, Sydnee." Levi and Chess came in and plopped book bags inside the door. Levi continued, "I just saw Maddie at The Café. She said mutual. But, still—" He gave Jeff a fist bump. "Sorry, man."

Jeff nodded as he made room for them. "Allie isn't with you all?"

"She's on her way," Chess said. "Just got to campus. Her flight was delayed, and she needs to unpack before her first class. Plus, they gave her a roommate, so she needs to clear some space."

"And what happened over break for you two?" Samantha grinned. *Life is good.*

Chess began. "I had the best time! My parents—"

"Hey, I've got seniority in here!"

"Learn to deal, Levi." Chess continued as Levi feigned offense. "My parents took the twins and me on a skiing trip! I'd never skied, and well, my brothers hadn't either, so we did more falling than anything, but Mom and Dad were like *really* good."

After Chess prattled on a few minutes longer, Samantha asked if she and her parents talked at some point between the sliding and the tumbling.

Chess giggled. "We did. And it's all cool. I told them everything I've been worried about. They had no idea! Can you imagine, Dr. Hayes?"

"I'm so glad. And yes," Samantha said, "I can imagine."

"If anyone cares," Levi said as he held up his arms in V-like pose. "I was accepted into two of the three graduate programs I applied for."

"Congratulations, Levi!" Samantha laughed. "And you thought you wouldn't get accepted *any*where!"

Amid the others' cheers, Levi continued, "I'm still not sure though which one I'll accept, and I have to decide soon. One's a counseling program, the other's a research program. What do you think, Sam?"

"I think you go with your gut, then change programs if it doesn't work." She smiled. "You'll figure it out."

At a tap on the door, Chess leapt from her chair. "And you have a new advisee, Dr. Hayes. Everybody, I want you to meet Arianna. She's a psychology major who's just transferred from Malaysia. Arianna, this is Levi, Sydnee, Jeff, and Dr. Hayes." She pointed to each person as she called their name. They offered warm smiles and greetings as Chess motioned her to a chair.

"Hi, everyone. I don't want to interrupt if your talk is important."

Samantha said, "Our talk is *always* important,

Arianna, so we're glad you're here to contribute. But if you want to meet privately—"

"No, I'm fine. My schedule is completed, and I only have a class in one hour with Chess."

"Yeah, we're both in stats with Dr. Simpson. We are totally prepared for the worst, Syd, so you might have to save us if we need help. Arianna and I just met yesterday but already figured out we both hate numbers."

"What's wrong with you people? And where's that open mind you're always bragging about, Chess?" Sydnee teased. "But yeah, I'll help if you need it."

"Hey, I'm not too bad in stats either," Levi said. "Arianna, I'm a math minor and just got accepted into a graduate program in research." He offered a smug smile to Sydnee who hit him with a pillow. "I'm at your service if you get stuck."

"Hey, everybody!" Allie came in.

"Al!" Levi offered an exaggerated welcome with open arms.

She hugged him. "It's only been a few weeks."

"I'm so glad you're back," Samantha said. "Sit down and tell us about your break. Oh, but first"—she motioned—"this is Arianna. She's a new psych major."

"Hey, glad to meet you." Allie gave her a welcoming smile as she sat on the sofa's arm. "I've been clearing my stuff out of the way so my new roommate can spread out a little bit. But," she took a breath, "I had the most amazing Christmas with my family. We talked about school and my plans for after graduation. Then we decided last minute to fly to New York and visit NYU because"—Allie stamped her feet as a makeshift drumroll—"I got accepted into their clinical program!"

"Yes!" Samantha squealed as the others cheered their congratulations.

"I'm so happy for you, Allie." Chess's voice was tinged with sadness. "But it just hit me. You and Levi will leave at the end of this semester. I'll miss you so much!" She punched the sofa cushion and took a breath. "But I will not be sad! I'm going to enjoy this semester and, Dr. Hayes, we'll let them come back to visit anytime they want."

"*Let* us?" Levi waxed indignant. "Allie and I started this little consortium, Chess. You are merely the heir apparent to the fine leadership I've established in this—"

"Oh, hush." Allie swatted Levi. "Chess, we'll come back to visit, and you'll visit me, too. In the meantime, just enjoy your time here. And you too, Arianna. It really does go by fast. Just relax and enjoy the journey."

"No, bad idea." Levi held up an index finger. "I relaxed way too much those first couple of years and almost didn't get into grad school."

"Almost didn't get in?" Jeff exclaimed. "You got into *two*."

"But they allowed Levi in, so how good could they be?" Sydnee added sotto voce.

Oh, that this moment would last. For them to never leave. The friendships and bickering and fears and laughter and tears and coincidences that were anything but. All of it—if it could just last.

"Okay, stop it all of you." Samantha's voice rose over the din. "You'll scare Arianna and have her running back to Malaysia. Arianna?"

"Yes, ma'am?"

"Ma'am," Levi whispered to Chess. "That used to be you."

Samantha continued, "Allie's right. It does go by quickly. Levi's right, studies should come first. You just have to find a way to balance everything. Make sure you—"

Samantha leaned in and squinted, her gaze fixed on a necklace Arianna was wearing.

"You noticed my necklace." She leaned forward and held the charm out for Samantha to see more clearly. "My mother gave this to me before I left home. She said the scarab is a symbol of transformation. She said that my studying in the States would be a time of transformation. So I wear it every day."

Samantha's eyes darted to each of her five. Allie caught her breath. Levi squinted. Jeff chuckled and slowly shook his head. Sydnee pointed to the necklace, her head atilt. Chess said, "Holy—"

Samantha stopped Chess with a hand to her arm. With her attention back to Arianna, she said, "It's beautiful. In fact, I have one that's very similar." She held hers out to show her. "And, yes, your mother is right. We've all been transformed while at Vanderlaan. Haven't we?" She glanced at her entourage for confirmation. A rush of agreement came from each.

Arianna smiled. "You people are so nice. I hope my roommate is as friendly as you are."

"You don't have a roommate yet?" Allie asked.

"I do. But I haven't met her." She rose and picked up her coat. "I should go back to my room to see if she's in yet."

"Hey," Sydnee said. "Do you realize we haven't asked Arianna the most important question for anybody hanging out in this office?"

Chess squealed and grabbed Arianna's arm. "What room are you in? It's so weird. You'll never believe it, but every person in this—"

"Chess." Sydnee threw back her head. "Let the girl speak."

Arianna said, "I'm in Stratton Hall, room 377."

"You're my roommate!" Allie's hand flew to her mouth. "That means—" She shot a look at Samantha and whispered, "She's one of us."

Samantha's laughter sprang up freely. From a place of peace. From the certainty that the inexplicable coincidences that had transpired were bigger than anything she could have orchestrated herself.

And they led to answers she couldn't have predicted.

Was she surprised? Not anymore. And from the sounds of her merry band as they welcomed this newest member of the entourage, neither were they.

What's more, she knew that these coincidences— these synchronistic mysteries—would continue.

They would continue in the students who streamed through this office and in the community they found here.

They would continue through the inevitable goodbyes this semester would bring and in the new faces who would continue to wander in, needing what this space offered.

The mystery—and the answers—would continue.

A word about the author...

Susan Harris Howell is a psychologist on faculty at a small university in Kentucky where she has taught and mentored young adults for over thirty years. The Spirit of Vanderlaan draws on that career to capture the camaraderie and warmth between a professor and the assortment of personalities which inhabit her office.

While The Spirit of Vanderlaan is her first work of fiction, she has published extensively on equality between men and women. Her first book, Buried Talents, explores gendered socialization and was published in 2022.

Susan is married to Dwayne and has two grown children, a daughter-in-law, one adorable grandson, and an incorrigible beagle, named Doc.

susanharrishowell.com